CELTIC KNOT

An Orphan's Tale of Survival, Family, and Love in Chicago

——— Based on a True Story ———

ECKHARTZ
PRESS

By Robert Patrick Conlon

Celtic Knot is a historical fiction novel based on the life of the author's grandfather, Tim Conlon. The author spoke to every relative who is still alive that knew Tim and heard the countless stories from them and Tim himself before he perished about his full and rich life. Additionally, the author read all of Tim's wonderful poetry and correspondence to friends and family. The author also thoroughly researched the historical events discussed in the novel. This novel reflects the author's present recollections of Tim's life. Some of the characters and institutions are purely fictional. Any resemblance of these fictional institutions and characters to institutions or persons, living or dead, is entirely coincidental.

Copyright © 2025 Robert Patrick Conlon

Published in the United States by
Eckhartz Press
Chicago, Illinois

All rights reserved

No part of this book may be used or reproduced in any manner whatsoever without written permission except in the case of brief quotations embodied in critical articles and reviews.

ISBN: 979-8-9929389-2-0

I. BIRTH

Their chests were heaving from running nonstop for several miles. Tim and Billy were drenched in sweat in the warm August sun, their throats so dry they could barely speak. With heads spinning and hearts racing from adrenaline and fear, they were covered in dirt from crawling under fences and running through creeks and fields until they found the railroad tracks. The plan was to locate the newly built tracks, which had been laid a couple of years earlier in 1883. They guessed based on hearing train whistles at night that the tracks were a couple miles south of the orphanage. Coming upon a fork in the line, the escaped orphans at last stopped to suck in some air. One of the tracks looked like it continued to head southeast toward Chicago; the other veered to the west.

"Billy, I think we ought to split up, or they are gonna catch us." Tim was always thinking several steps ahead, even at the age of eight. He had heard one of the older kids tell the story of another runaway getting tracked down by the local sheriff's bloodhound following the scent. Tim figured that if he and Billy split up, the sheriff and his mongrel could only follow one or the other, maximizing the odds of at least one of them making it free.

Billy, who was a year younger, started to cry. "I don't want to be by myself again - I don't know where to go."

They were best friends and Tim looked out for Billy at the orphanage. It was Tim's plan that successfully had gotten them this far. Muffled barking had been following their trail for the last hour, and it seemed to be getting a little louder as time passed. Tim knew he was right about splitting up. "Billy, I'm sorry, there is no time to talk about it. The coppers will be catching up soon. This way maybe one of us will make it." Tim directed with authority, "I'll head down this track to Chicago - you head down the other way. And don't stop running no matter how tired you get."

They shook hands and looked into each other's eyes. Billy asked if they would see one another again. Tim nodded his head yes but knew otherwise. They began to jog down their separate paths, not knowing what lay ahead. A different sense and level of fear creeps in when you are running for your life in solitude. Tim found himself alone once more, heading back to Chicago, the only town he had known until his parents tragically died a year earlier. He turned back to look toward Billy, who was walking backwards as he stared at Tim. They gave one another a last goodbye with a silent wave, both wearing half-hopeful smiles. Tim and Billy would never meet again.

Tim had been planning the escape from Queen of Heaven Orphanage of Arlington Heights, Illinois for months, soon after he was escorted inside the large iron gates of the prison-like fifteen-foot concrete walls surrounding the grounds. Tim walked alone into the main entrance and was greeted by Brother DuValle, a 40-something, large, muscular man with thinning hair and round glasses, decked out in his immaculate brown Franciscan habit. He glared at Tim with the darkest of eyes. DuValle was someone who Tim later described as the most evil person he had ever met. Tim unfortunately would soon learn why the other boys secretly called him Brother Devil.

Chapter 1
QUEEN OF HEAVEN ORPHANAGE (1882-1886)

In 1882, Archbishop Patrick A. Feehan was quick to recognize that the streets of Chicago had multitudes of children living in the streets and committing petty crimes like pickpocketing and purse snatching, and seemingly constantly evading the police. Father Feehan was concerned that these children had nowhere to go when the cold weather descended in the winter. They were constantly begging for food and were destined for a life of crime with no formal education or adult supervision to make a positive impact on their lives. As one of his first formal decisions as the new Archbishop of Chicago, Feehan made it his mission to build a first-class orphanage to house, educate, and guide these young, otherwise hopeless children.

After some preliminary research, Father Feehan learned of a group of Franciscan Brothers, including Brother DuValle, and thirty boys from Chicago's Bridgeport neighborhood that had moved into Mulcahy Farm north of Arlington Heights, Illinois in the spring of 1882. They lived in temporary housing in a farm building. The orphans worked 200 acres of crops and cared for recently purchased livestock – on the job training for thirty orphans from the city. This appeared to be an ideal location for the new orphanage.

While the Brothers managed the boys' work, Archbishop Feehan and his Board of Managers were busy drawing up plans to build a training school at the Mulcahy Farm site for orphans and troubled young men. In October 1882, ground was broken for Queen of Heaven Academy on a nearly 1,000-acre stretch of land adjacent to Mulcahy Farm. As the facility was built, more orphans arrived. Father Feehan's mission became a reality.

By the time of the official dedication of Queen of Heaven in July

1883, more than 150 boys were in residence. Several thousand people, including many dignitaries, were in attendance at the dedication ceremonies.

The large iron entrance gate and daunting concrete walls surrounding Queen of Heaven were erected at the strong encouragement of Brother DuValle. "It may take time for the boys to embrace Queen of Heaven as their new home. We need to ensure we keep them safe inside until they do." Tim would ultimately decipher DuValle's ulterior motive for being involved with effectively building a prison disguised as an orphanage.

By 1886, the year Tim arrived at the orphanage, there were 325 residents at Queen of Heaven. In addition to orphans, many of the other residents were runaways and troubled juveniles "assigned" to Queen of Heaven by the courts. For each ward, the state provided $47 per year for "education and maintenance." Brother DuValle and the Brothers educated the boys, supervised the farm work, and looked after the residents' spiritual needs.

In the summer of 1886, Timothy Joseph Conlon became a resident of Queen of Heaven shortly before his eighth birthday. Tim laid on his cot in the orphanage at night wondering how his life's journey ended up here. Tim thought about what events could have happened differently that would have changed this course. "How in the world did I get here?"

Chapter 2
DARK IRISH (1588-1878)

Tim was born on July 7, 1878, in the Conlon home in Chicago. He was the son of Irish immigrants John Conlon from Spanish Point and Mary Gillen from Donegal. John was "Dark Irish," as were many from Spanish Point, which derived its name from Spaniards who were shipwrecked off the southwest coast of Ireland in the 16th century. The Spanish armada was caught in a violent storm just off the coast of Galway in 1588. Many of the more than 150 vessels that comprised the armada sank, and sadly, thousands went down with their ships or drowned in the Atlantic. Thousands of the more fortunate Spanish sailors, however, were able to make it safely to shore. The Spaniards who survived quickly assimilated into the beautiful countryside of the west coast of Ireland, and there they remained. The Spaniards appreciated the friendly and welcoming locals, and many fell in love with the Irish women. Their offspring typically had dark hair and blue eyes - "the Dark Irish," a lovely combination of the endearing genes of the Spanish and the Irish. This trait was passed down through many generations to John, and to his third child Tim, both having coal black hair and piercing blue eyes.

The Gillens lived near the town of Ballyshannon, which is located at the mouth of the River Erne in northern County Donegal. In the early 19th century, Donegal was among the poorest counties in Ireland. Donegal is mountainous, and the land largely infertile.

By 1800, most landowners and landlords in Donegal and throughout Ireland were Anglo-Irish Protestants or English. An overwhelming majority of the tenants and peasants were Catholics. "The poorer Irish Catholics often had to pay burdensome rents and live in difficult and sometimes squalid conditions. By the 1830s, circumstances in Ireland worsened as tremendous population growth in previous decades forced a majority of citizens to eke out a living on minuscule plots of land."[1]

In Donegal, wealthy English and Scottish landowners were granted most of the good land in the valleys, leaving the Irish with very challenging farming tracts. The Gillens tried their hand at farming their own land to no avail and resorted to working the land occupied by English landowners for a pittance. Other of the Gillens had some success fishing the nearby rivers and coastlines for herring and salmon. The lack of decent boats and fishing equipment, coupled with extreme cold and typically rough seas in this northern region of Ireland, also made fishing a difficult and dangerous occupation.

As the economic conditions of the early 1800s worsened, a secret society known as the Molly Maguires emerged in County Donegal. The members would meet and conspire against the wealthy English landowners. This resulted in multiple incidents of violence, which caused further divisiveness and tension between the landowners and the Irish workers. One of the Gillen relatives attended a sub rosa meeting of the Molly Maguires at a local pub. When learning of this, Tim's great grandfather Old Man Michael Gillen admonished the relative that the Maguires only made matters worse, and warned of possible arrest. The relative in response gritted his teeth and yelled, "How in God's name could things get worse around here?"

In the 1830s through the run-up to the Irish Potato Famine in 1845, the landowners treated the Irish workers even more poorly, partially in response to the violence of the Molly Maguires, making the lives of economically strapped denizens of Donegal even more horrific.

The English-dominated land system in Donegal and across Ireland prompted a significant increase in immigration to America in the 1830s. Immigrant numbers continued to grow through the 1840s and ultimately peaked at the onset of the Great Famine from 1845 to 1849.[2]

"The Famine, which involved successive and widespread failures of the potato crop on which most Irish depended for their food, resulted in more than one million deaths and more than one million emigrating to the States. Ireland's greatest assets, its people, left in droves. The Famine greatly increased Irish bitterness toward England, since the Irish believed that the British government could have done far more than it did to save the starving masses."[3]

Donegal was the county worst hit by the Great Potato Famine, which resulted in a large number of the citizens emigrating to the New World. Among the displaced were the Gillens, who were devastated to leave their lovely hamlet in 1843 near Ballyshannon, their friends, and relatives. Being nearly penniless with no hope to improve their lot in life by remaining in Donegal, they felt they had no choice but to leave for the land of opportunity. Out of desperation, the Gillens packed up their modest belongings and children, including newborn Mary, and walked for two days pulling a hand cart to the port in Londonderry.

The Conlon clan independently emigrated to the United States in 1843, just before the onset to the Great Famine of 1845. Having several relatives in the newly incorporated town of Chicago, the Conlons were told opportunities were flush there and Irish immigrants seemed more welcome in Chicago than in New York and other East Coast American cities. The Conlons left everything they owned and everyone they knew and loved, searching for new lives, and set sail to America.

The Conlons and the Gillens left their homeland teeming with a myriad of political, social, and economic problems. They, of course, were not alone. "Controlled by England in one fashion or another since the twelfth century, Ireland became intricately tied to its more powerful neighbor with the creation of the United Kingdom of Great Britain and Ireland in 1801. Although that union worked out to the beneficial satisfaction of most Irish Protestants, a vast majority of Irish Catholics, who made up over three-quarters of the Irish population, detested it. Not only did the new political system deny Irish Catholics the chance to control their own affairs, but for some time it also actively discriminated against their religion."[4]

Tim's parents were part of this initial immigration wave to America. The destination for the Conlons and the Gillens was Chicago.

The early years of Chicago were marked by the significant rise in Irish immigration in the 1830s. Some Irish already lived in Chicago when it was incorporated as a city in 1837. John's and Mary's families simultaneously arrived in Chicago in the fall of 1843. In the next several years, Irish numbers grew rapidly, particularly after the arrival of refugees from the Great Famine. By 1850, Irish immigrants accounted for about one-fifth of the city's population. Although the number of Irish immigrants in Chicago continued to increase until the end of the 19th century, their percentage of the city's population was never again as high as it was in 1850, after which extraordinarily large numbers of Germans, Italian, Polish, and later other immigrant groups began to settle in the city, making Chicago one of the most multi-ethnic urban areas in the United States.[5]

Most of the early Irish immigrants in Chicago took on low-skilled, poorly paying jobs at places such as meatpacking plants and the railroad. Being impoverished, the early Irish immigrants settled in poorer neighborhoods, like Bridgeporton (later know as Bridgeport, where the future mayor Richard M. Daley's family settled) on the city's South Side.[6]

John Conlon and Mary Gillen quickly fell in love after they met at a Catholic parish dance in downtown Chicago. They were married after a whirlwind courtship in 1865. John Conlon found work through a relative's connection at the railroad, like many of the Irish immigrants at that time. John had a solid work ethic and earned the respect of his coworkers. His diligence paid off, and John was quickly promoted to foreman.

In the fall of 1871, severe drought conditions lasting 14 weeks, coupled with mostly wooden buildings and sidewalks, made Chicago a serious fire hazard. Legend has it that The Great Chicago Fire started on the evening of October 8 in a barn owned by Patrick and Catherine O'Leary at 137 DeKoven Street on the city's southwest side when the family's cow knocked over a lighted lantern. The O'Learys, however, vehemently denied this accusation. The actual point of origin of the fire has never been conclusively determined.[7]

"The fire burned wildly throughout the following day, finally coming under control on October 10, when rain gave a needed boost to firefighting efforts. The Great Chicago Fire left an estimated 300 people dead and 100,000 others homeless. More than 17,000 structures were destroyed and damages were estimated at $200 million or the equivalent of $6.6 billion today."[8] The fire left a massive swath of devastation approximately four miles long and almost a mile wide, including Chicago's important business district, later known as the Loop, completely razed.[9]

An outbreak of looting ensued shortly after the fire subsided. "Companies of soldiers were summoned to Chicago, and martial law was declared on October 11, ending three days of chaos."[10] It took three weeks of martial law to bring about and maintain order. Following the blaze, reconstruction efforts began quickly, spurring economic development and population growth. Chicago, with its broad shoulders, turned a disaster into an opportunity to rebuild itself to become one of the country's largest, most important, and wonderful cities.

Following the Great Chicago Fire in 1871, the relatively new rail system into and near Chicago was heavily relied upon to facilitate the rebuilding of devastation left by the horrific conflagration. John made a decent wage at the railroad working as a crew foreman. His skills and experience were in huge demand, and it was common for John and his crews to work 16-hour days, seven days a week, month-in and month-out. This exhausting and dangerous line of work enabled newlywed John to save up enough money to buy a proper but modest home in an area just north of the business district at LaSalle and Elm, making John the first Conlon and his wife, Mary, the first Gillen property owners. This made the Conlons beam with pride. They had three children, first Michael in 1872, then Mary, who went by Molly, in 1875, and the caboose Timothy three years later. The Conlons were living the American dream.

Tim became known as "the smart one" early on. He learned to read at a very young age and developed a passion for reading. Tim read anything he could get his hands on: *The Adventures of Huckleberry Finn, Treasure Island, Oliver Twist*. The nuns at St. Mary's Church at Madison and Wabash were excellent educators and started the first Catholic School for Boys in Chicago. The wonderful courses at St. Mary's included not only the three Rs, but also History, Literature, Art, Music, French, Geography, Latin, and Social Studies – quite the curriculum for second grade. The Sisters opened up a whole new world for Tim. He was one of the few lads among his friends who actually liked going to school as his voracious appetite for reading and learning was nourished by the Sisters. Tim's father always had preached, "If you learn how to love to read, you will never be alone." Sadly, as Tim came to discover all too well, there is no other soul more alone than an orphan living on the street.

Chapter 3
THE WILY BOYS (1884-1885)

At eight years old, Tim was a natural leader among his friends. Tim's gang was known as the Wily Boys, after Sister Elizabeth broke up a fight on the playground between Tim and his friends and a group of Italian kids. She yelled, with her attention focused on the leader of the Irish lads, "Tim, you and your group of hooligans are always looking for trouble. Trouble you wily boys shall have!" Sister handed out detentions to all and administered to each of the boys a crack on the knuckles with a ruler. "You wily lads better be on your best behavior the rest of the year, or you can expect to spend more time after school with me." Tim and the newly coined Wily Boys were regular visitors to the detention room and seemed to walk around with permanent red marks on the backs of their hands. None complained as they ultimately believed they deserved their punishment. They also were sure not to advise their parents so as to avoid a second round of punishment at home.

The Wily Boys mostly hung out at the intersection of Clark and Elm. If anyone close to their age frequented "their" intersection, Tim and his friends would be sure to stop them and give them a hard time. This usually resulted in the unfortunate harassed boy hailing his group of friends and returning to confront the Wily Boys. The fights consisted mostly of a lot of yelling and an exchange of name calling, until Tim and his friend Patrick, who was the largest boy in the second grade, would go nose-to-nose with the would-be leaders of the rival gang. Tim would do most of the talking, "You better be on your way if you know what's good for ya!" The plan was for Patrick to be ready to swing as hard as he could at the biggest boy of the other gang if he didn't immediately back down.

Tim instructed Patrick, "We will always give them a final warning, but Patrick, if they don't walk away you have to get the first punch in on their biggest kid. That way the others will be afraid that we were too tough or too crazy by going after their heavy. As long as you can handle their big guy, the rest of us will take care of the others."

Tim had a signal for Patrick on when to take a swing. If Tim felt there were too many of them, or if he didn't think the Wilys could handle the other group of boys, Tim would keep talking and try to come to some sort of resolution, such as, "Ok, you guys seem okay, go ahead and pass." Sometimes, however, the talking didn't work and a scrum would ensue. When the boys showed up at school the next day with black eyes, cuts, or missing teeth, Sister Elizabeth would announce at the beginning of class, "It looks as though the Wily Boys again took on a bit more than they could chew. And I see a few of you may have a hard time chewing anything without all of your teeth, so I'll be seeing you after class this afternoon – all of you!"

Although a bit shorter than his peers, Tim had a confidence that kept the other schoolkids in check. He was also quick-witted and fast on his feet when confronting stressful situations. These characteristics continued on through his life and were what drove Tim to plan and execute the escape from the Queen of Heaven orphanage.

After school, Tim would lead the Wily Boys on adventures, exploring the city that was bustling with activity as it was being rebuilt following the Great Chicago Fire. One such outing included sneaking into the Water Tower on Michigan Avenue. The Water Tower was built in 1869 and was one of the few structures in the Gold Coast that survived the Great Fire. It remains a glorious monument on Michigan Avenue today. Tim swiped his mother's largest umbrella as he left the house. The Wily Boys managed to enter the Water Tower through an unlocked back door, as the front entrance was bolted shut. The lads ascended the rickety stairs to the top of the 182-foot structure. The brilliant idea that Tim had was to test whether a person could jump out of the top window with the umbrella slowing the descent and hopefully breaking the fall. After reaching the top and locating the highest window, the Wily Boys congregated on the top landing. Tim looked over to one of his friends, "Okay Patrick, you have the honor of being the first human to ever try this." Tim, after all, was the smart one. Patrick looked out the window and said, "That's ok, Tim, I'm fine being the second person."

Chicago Water Tower, 800 North Michigan Avenue, Chicago, IL; Compiled after 1933; Unknown photographer; Public Domain.

The rest of the Wily Boys who made the climb at Tim's brazen suggestion also shared Patrick's sentiment. "Yeah, Conlon, this is all your idea – you should have the honor of going first." Tim, who was not one to turn down a challenge, and who had researched in the school library extensively about physics and birds leading up to this adventure, decided he would give it a go. "Okay, you all will be reading about me in the papers as being the first person to successfully jump off the Water Tower." Tim grabbed the umbrella, popped it open, and jumped out of the window. The Wily Boys, with their eyes and jaws wide open, all screamed, "Noooo!" as Tim disappeared.

Tim floated gracefully to a gentle soft landing – um, actually it was whatever the opposite of that would be. For the first nanosecond, the umbrella did its job. Then it quickly inverted, and Tim was in a free fall with his eyes bulging, screaming at the tops of his lungs, "Bloody hell!!!" Fortunately for Tim, the fleeting aerodynamics of the umbrella careened his body into the side of the tower, which was built with a slight pitch widening from top to bottom. This fortuitous design created an ever-so-slight slide for Tim's body to scrape his way down, slowing his rate of descent until he hit the first exterior balcony of the tower, about 35 feet below the top window from which he leapt. He lay in a heap until the Wily Boys ran hollering at the tops of their lungs down the stairs to the rescue. By the time they opened the door to the landing where Tim was lying in a slump, Tim began to awaken from his brief loss of consciousness, with his entire right leg, left arm, buttocks, and head in excruciating pain.

Patrick, hyperventilating, managed to utter, "That was the most amazing thing ever! You did it – you jumped off the top of the Water Tower – and you didn't die!" The boys all yelled out, cheering for Tim as they helped him to his feet and helped him hobble down the rest of the stairs.

This death-defying feat was the talk of the school for the balance of the second-grade school year. Tim's pain continued, and he walked with a limp for a month. He didn't dare tell his parents what happened. Every time he thought about his leap of faith, he laughed but then frowned, thinking he could have done better if only he had a stronger umbrella.

As Tim lay in his cot at night in the orphanage a year later, he committed to jumping off another cliff. Tim knew he had to escape Queen of Heaven even though the risks were too many to count. Tim heard the door to his room slowly open, and he saw Brother DuValle's large gnarly hand on the knob. Tim didn't care about anything else – he had to flee the horror. Tim closed his eyes and envisioned himself again leaping from the Water Tower window ledge – this time with a bigger and reinforced umbrella.

Chapter 4
D'ILLEACHTA[1] (1885-1886)

We are all one phone call, one moment in time, away from our lives changing forever. One such moment arrived when Tim came home for dinner following another after-school Wily Boys' adventure. Expecting the regular family in attendance at their respective spots at the table sharing tales of the day, something was different. The house was atypically dark at that time, and a muffled weeping was coming from the kitchen. "Mom?" Tim's sister Molly came running out of the kitchen and into the parlor to immediately hug Tim. Visibly shaken and teary, Molly spoke the haunting words that Tim could hear with clarity any time he thought of that dreadful day, "Father is dead."

Then Tim's older brother Michael slowly walked into the room, shoulders slumped, and in a zombie-like state he explained what happened. John Conlon and his crew had been working insane hours for months due to the massive rebuilding of Chicago that continued for years following the Great Fire. The crew was mentally and physically exhausted, and mistakes were made. This time a worker's tired mind momentarily lapsed, and an unfortunate error resulted in a construction train car being overloaded. When the car was picked up by an engine to move down the tracks, multiple improperly loaded steel I-beams fell from the car and onto several of John's crew members standing below. Three workers, including John, died instantly. The course of Tim's life's trajectory altered forever.

Tim's mother, Mary Gillen Conlon, was diminutive in size, just over five feet tall so she claimed, and just under 100 pounds. She was, however, freakishly strong – any time a stubborn jar couldn't be opened even by John the railyard worker with Popeye forearms, Mary could twist open the jar with a flick of the wrist. More impressively, she was

---
1   Orphan in Gaelic.

a remarkably strong person mentally and spiritually.

Mary gathered her brood the day John died and preached, "We will all cry privately over the loss of your wonderful father, but at the wake and funeral we will look all of our friends and relatives in their eyes, shake their hands, and hug them without one tear. We are a strong family, and we will always be so. This is our lot in life, and we must carry on. There will be no crying in public." And crying they did that night until the sun rose the following day.

Mary Gillen Conlon taken a year before her death in 1885.

John and the Conlons were well-known throughout the neighborhood, church, and among the railroad workers. As was typical in that time, the three-day wake was conducted in the home and was attended by thousands. Drinks were served and food and money were provided by all. The Irish Catholic community showed up with support and an outpouring of love and respect for John and his family. Such loving gestures were something that was expected of and willingly provided by this tight-knit community then and now.

Tim, Molly, and Michael all followed their mother's dictate, keeping a stiff upper lip and not shedding one tear during their father's wake and funeral. Young Tim kept saying to himself, "Every time you feel sad, just put those feelings aside and be strong for Mother. I'll cry in my bed at night."

Life thereafter instantly became challenging and hard for the Conlons. The one small grace was that the children grew a bit closer and spent more time with one another. Mary and John had a nice nest egg built up over the past few years due to the significant hours he had worked at the railroad. Nonetheless, Mary was determined to find a way to earn money as the new breadwinner of her family of four. She heard through the gossip mill that the Finnertys' neighborhood general store was closing because Finnerty was retiring. Mary promptly set up a meeting with the Finnertys. Mary wore her Sunday best, donned her lucky hat, and marched down the street with her chin up, to the store in her highest heels to make herself look a little taller. Not surprising to anyone who knew Mary, she left the meeting with a handshake deal to take over operation of the business, to split the profits going forward, and agreeing to buy the Finnertys out over the next five years. It was unusual in the late 19th century for married women with children to work outside of the home, let alone own a business. Mary was determined and worked round the clock to learn the nuances of the business and keep the store thriving. The kids were often recruited to assist at the store and were happy to help out their fearless mother.

In the following months, life moved on for the Conlons, and all returned to their regular patterns and rhythms. Tim finished the second grade and continued with the Wily Boys' daily explorations of the many neighborhoods of Chicago. Those long, hot summer days included a swim at Oak Street Beach, looking for the other gangs of boys for a donnybrook, building a fort in Lincoln Park, and playing the new game called baseball with a rock and a stick. Tim loved the freedom of running the streets of Chicago at the age of eight, entirely unsupervised. Unwittingly, Tim and his friends got to know the town and the diversity of its people and cultures. Tim subconsciously kept himself busy that summer exploring to help forget his pain. Many times Tim couldn't forget, and he dwelled on the day he had come home to learn his father had died. Sadly, Tim would try to deaden the pain of his grief by telling himself, "Well, at least things can't get worse." Unfortunately, Tim soon learned that thought is always wholly untrue.

One night, after working a 12-hour day without a break, Mary was closing up at Finnerty's Corner Store. She was about to lock up, then remembered several items needed to be stored on the top shelf. Mary, exhausted, grabbed a nearby chair as opposed to getting the shop ladder to reach the upper shelves. As she stepped up onto the chair, one of the legs of the chair gave way, causing Mary to fall violently to the floor, hitting her head with great force. Mary died instantly. When she didn't return home by 9:00 that evening, Tim's brother Mike decided to walk down to the store to check on his mom. After an excruciatingly long hour, a policeman knocked on the Conlons' front door. Molly and Tim, who were already scared and frightened, answered the door together. The officer was as gentle and kind as he could muster breaking the tragic news to the children. Everything went into slow motion for Tim, Molly screamed and fell to her knees, the room began to spin, and things went black. Lightning struck the Conlons twice in six months – too much for anyone to handle.

Tim was in a fog the following days, with the ritual of the wake and funeral keeping Tim and his siblings able to robotically put one foot in front of the other. Adults, friends, and family would try to engage Tim, but he couldn't or wouldn't give more than one- or two-word answers and turn away.

Tim's uncle, Shelton Conlon, affectionately known as Shelby, was a bachelor who lived on the North Side of Chicago, and the closest relative who lived nearby. Shelton was a successful tradesman who made a decent buck for an Irish immigrant. He was also well-known in most of the pubs in the neighborhood just north of the Chicago River, later called River North, and beyond.

The parish nuns set up a meeting to discuss the Conlon children with Shelton, whose life was immediately turned upside down by the recent events. When Shelton didn't show up for the meeting at the designated time and place, Sister Patricia knew just where to find him. She marched down to Barefoot Jack O'Keefe's, found Shelby bellied up at the bar sipping his whiskey, grabbed him by the ear, and off they went. Barefoot Jack, who tended bar in his bare feet for unknown reasons, yelled out with his Irish brogue, "Hey Shelby, that's the first time I saw a penguin drag someone out of here." This prompted Sister to stop in her tracks, turn around, and glare back toward the loud-mouthed bartender. Barefoot Jack broke up multiple fights and threw out unruly patrons on a nightly basis, but the nun's stare made Barefoot Jack petrified for the first time in his life. The patrons immediately stopped laughing, and you could hear a pin drop in the bar. Barefoot Jack whispered sheepishly, "Sorry, Sister, not funny."

At the meeting with Sister Patricia and the other penguins, Shelton announced that he would agree to take in either his niece or one of his nephews. After some tough negotiations with Sister Patricia lethally staring daggers deep into Shelton's eyes, the nuns "encouraged" him to take the two older children, Mike and Molly, who required less adult supervision. The nuns felt they could place the smart young Tim at the relatively new Queen of Heaven orphanage, where he could continue his schooling with the excellent Franciscan Brother educators.

The nuns' meeting with the Conlon children went about as well as expected – not good at all. Tim, who was still numb from mental stress and fatigue, could not believe what he was hearing. Molly, as she was so prone to do, had Tim's back. Michael, who was the least emotional of the Conlons, understood the reasoning of the deal struck with Uncle Shelton and, of course, went along with the plan. Many tears were shed, accusations made, cussings exchanged. But the end result was Michael and Molly were to live with Shelton and Tim would move to Queen of Heaven.

After that night, things happened fairly quickly. Multiple friends, relatives, and members of the parish helped pack things up and arrange the affairs of the Conlon children, and the parish council structured a sale of the home with the proceeds going into a trust benefiting the children. Sadly, early tragic deaths leaving children orphaned was relatively commonplace in Chicago in the 1880s, with typhoid, yellow fever, the flu, and the general dangerous and unsanitary conditions post-Great Fire. The average life expectancy of a Chicagoan in 1886 was a shockingly young mid-40s. The nuns took on the burden of dealing with and placing the parishioner children, unfortunately knowing precisely which steps to take. Of course, there were more orphans than locations to accommodate them, so it was equally gut-wrenching to see the number of waifs living in the rough and tumble streets of Chicago in the 1880s.

Tim's ever-growing rage at his brother, the nuns, Uncle Shelton, and even his parents for abandoning him at last awakened him from the solace of his brain fog. This sharpness of mind enabled Tim to absorb everything that had happened and all that was planned for his future. His thoughts were now racing and filled with so many emotions: fear about what life at the orphanage would be like; missing his sister Molly, the Wily Boys gang, and yes, even Michael; wondering if he would ever be adopted, and if so by whom; grief over the loss of both parents; moving away from the only city he had known and loved; and anxiety over what would become of him. But mostly Tim felt so alone.

Tim could not sleep the last night he spent in his bed, the only one he had ever slept in, the night before someone from the church was to drive him out to Queen of Heaven in Arlington Heights, wherever in God's name that was. In the middle of the night, Tim walked out onto the porch in his pajamas, looked out at the quiet dark street, and screamed, "Enough! Come and get me! I'm ready!"

Molly found Tim asleep on the floor of the porch at sunrise. They hugged, and Molly promised to write every week, to visit, and importantly, to keep working on Shelton to take Tim in. Tim wasn't able to eat breakfast. When Mike went in for a goodbye hug, Tim punched him in the face and screamed, "Fuck off, ya traitor." Normally this would have evoked an equally aggressive response from the much bigger older brother, but when Mike saw the rage in Tim's eyes, Mike turned and sheepishly ambled away.

The parish horse-drawn carriage arrived at the soon-to-be-sold Conlon home at 8:00 a.m. sharp. Tim recognized the carriage as the one used for both of his parents' funerals. Tim wondered if this was the beginning of his own funeral. A few of the Wily Boys came by to see Tim off. Tim put on his best act for them, with his signature half smile, "Hopefully I'll see you guys soon. Patrick, remember to always find the biggest guy and throw the first punch." With hands in their pockets, heads down, eloquent farewell words didn't come for the lads. Instead, they simply mumbled "Bye Tim," "See ya." And off he went.

It took a good six hours for the two-horse carriage to travel the 23 miles northwest to Queen of Heaven, with a couple of rest stops for the horses along the way. Tim had never been north of what is now called Addison Avenue, where one of his friends from school lived, a block away from where Wrigley Field was later built in 1914. Once they left the main dirt roadway to the North Side of Chicago, the carriage proceeded further northwest toward Arlington Heights on a much narrower and more rustic dirt road. Tim thought of his mom singing in the kitchen making dinner, taking a walk along the lakefront with his father on the weekend, laughing with Molly on the front porch. It is not the momentous occasions, but rather life's simple moments that are so fleeting and that are missed the most about the loved ones you have lost. Tim was in a trance with these simple memories as the horses plodded on.

Finally arriving, Tim was roused by the driver's "Whoa" bringing the carriage to a stop. The huge Gothic iron gate was slowly opened by two straining young boys, and the driver escorted Tim through the gate toward the building's main entrance with a couple of bags of clothes, pictures, his mother's rosary beads, and several of Tim's favorite books. The nameless carriage driver said, "May God bless you, son." Tim walked in solitude toward the orphanage front door. The high frightening concrete walls were bare and colorless. Tim's pace slowed as he approached the main entrance with trepidation. He heard the voice of his dad say to him, as he had done often, "You got this, Timmy, my boy." Tim climbed the steps to the front entrance of the orphanage as the main door was opened simultaneously by Brother DuValle. Tim stood frozen in front of the massive Brother who remained silent and stared into Tim's eyes. Finally, Tim broke the silence, which seemed like an eternity, with a false confidence, "Hiya Father, I'm Timothy Joseph Conlon of Chicago." A booming response came from above, "It's Brother DuValle…and you shall not speak until you are spoken to by me or the other Brothers." Tim looked him in the eye with his half grin and nodded.

One of the other Brothers, with a much kinder, gentler demeanor, showed Tim around the grounds and provided a tour of the main area. Tim was excited to see a decent-sized library near the classrooms, a spot in which he would spend most of his free time. The mess hall had rows of tables with seating for maybe 100, which meant the 300 plus boys were packed in like sardines. The recreation area was a courtyard surrounded by an extension of the ominous concrete walls, with patches of grass amidst the sand and dirt.

Tim noticed a barren tree stump that was about the same height as the walls, which he estimated was about 15 feet high. One of the boys later informed Tim it was called "The Stack." Brother DuValle served, among other titles, as the Academy Disciplinarian. He had the builders cut a large oak tree down, leaving an intentionally high stump. Residents who got in trouble for fighting, stealing, or "being incorrigible" were sentenced to stand upon The Stack all day. One of the Brothers would make the disciplined boy ascend a ladder to the top and stand upon the stump that was roughly two feet in diameter. The other boys' advice to Tim from experience was to never look down because it would make you dizzy and to never lock your knees or risk cramping up or maybe even fainting from being too rigid for so long. And critically, one must be sure to take a pee before heading up The Stack. Even so, most boys would urinate in their pants at least once during the sun-up to sundown 12-hour sentence. Half of the boys would fall at some point due to dizziness, fatigue, or lack of food and water, and many of those suffered serious injuries including broken legs, ankles, wrists, and concussions. If a boy fell and wasn't badly injured, he would be sent back up The Stack straight away to carry out the remainder of his sentence the rest of the day. Tim thought, "Tip of the day – try not to be incorrigible."

Tim was assigned a bunk room with eight cots and 16 'residents,' with two boys to a cot. He was also given a small cardboard box to store his scant possessions. The boys in his room were as young as five and as old as twelve. They were mostly decent kids – all shared a common sadness in their eyes. Tim was surprised how nice the majority were to him and how they looked out for one another, especially the younger lads. Fighting was a serious violation of the Code of Conduct that would certainly get you on The Stack for a day, whether you started the fight or not. Billy McGregor, a seven-year-old from Bridgeport, was Tim's cot mate. Billy tried to act tougher than he was but had an entertaining sense of humor, often imitating the other kids or the Brothers. Tim and Billy quickly became best friends. One colder night, one of the older boys in the bunk room took Billy's blanket. Tim said, "Hey fuck face, give it back now or I will punch you in your throat when you fall asleep."

The much larger boy walked up chest to chest and stared down at Tim, "What did you say?"

"You and everyone here heard me – none of us wants anyone to steal their stuff. We won't stand for your bullshit anymore." Tim knew how to build consensus from his de facto leadership of the Wily Boys – speak in the name of the group, whether they agree or not. It is critical to have strength in numbers, especially when you are small. Knowing that he would be beaten badly in a fist fight, Tim's announced plan to sneak up on the bully at night and crush the thief's windpipe sounded fairly terrifying. The older boy looked around and saw all the boys staring right back at him, showing they were aligned with Tim on the issue. So the older lad reluctantly capitulated and sheepishly returned the blanket, and mumbled, "It smelled like crap anyways." The other boys patted Tim on the back – he was a natural leader. Billy found the big brother he never had.

The first week at Queen of Heaven was a blur. Billy showed Tim the ropes, which food to eat and what to avoid, which boys to make friends with and which ones to avoid, what time to hit the latrine and when to avoid, and which chores to sign up for and which ones to avoid.

It took Tim several nights to get used to the noisy, odiferous room conditions and the ridiculously crowded cot. He thought he had finally hit a groove when, about a month after he arrived, Tim heard the door to his dorm slowly creak open in the stillness of the middle of the night. Tim was about to shoot up in bed to see who it was when Billy held him down by the shoulder and covered his mouth, whispering in his ear, "Don't move, don't make a sound." Tim was frozen with fear as the lumbering silhouette passed by their cot, which was nearest to the door.

What happened after that was hard for Tim to discern, but he detected a deep whispered voice mumble something to one of the boys in a cot a couple of rows down. The boy, Tim speculated, was Anthony, a handsome, tough 10-year-old Italian immigrant from the West Side of Chicago. Anthony started to scream only to be muffled by the larger body. Then a struggle ensued for the several excruciatingly long minutes. Finally, the episode ended with Anthony crying into his pillow in complete darkness as the large silhouette patted Anthony on his head and vanished from the room.

No one dared to get out of bed and check on poor Anthony. Instead, the room was filled with whispers and Anthony's cot mate consoling him. Tim was completely shaken. He looked over at Billy in horror – "What the heck just happened?!" Billy explained to Tim the unimaginable, and how Brother DuValle, the Devil, would pay an unwelcome visit to the bunk room every few nights and seemed to randomly select his next prey. Billy noted that oddly the victims all seemed to have dark hair – not comforting news for a "Dark Irish" lad. Billy, a redhead who had been spared so far, relayed that the best thing to do was keep quiet and keep your mouth shut. Others who had spoken out, resisted, or tattled to the other Brothers were severely punished with DuValle's belt and then sent up The Stack. Worse, the nighttime visits seemed to come more regularly to those who objected or squealed to the Brothers.

Tim had a hard time sleeping after witnessing that living nightmare, and any little noise was an alarm bell that jarred him awake from even the deepest REM sleep. During the next two weeks, The Devil made four unholy visits to other bunkmates. Tim could barely eat or sleep. Billy, who had been at Queen of Heaven for a couple of years, somehow adjusted so that he could function during the days after the assaults. Tim, however, was nowhere close to adjusting, petrified that his number would be coming up soon.

At breakfast, Billy and a few others were wolfing down their gruel and talking about nonsense, but Tim was sitting quietly, staring at his bowl. DuValle, in his flowing, spotless, wrinkle-free robe, strolled by their table. "Mr. Conlon, how are you adjusting to your new home at Queen of Heaven?"

Tim sprang up to his feet and stood at attention, lying through his teeth, "Just fine, Brother DuValle."

"Glad to hear, my fine lad." DuValle stared down with his dark, dead eyes at Tim and smiled before sauntering away. Billy and the others all agreed with Tim that this was not a positive encounter and warned Tim that he should be on high alert.

Tim never did fall asleep that night, his heart pounding. After several hours of Tim staring at the door while lying in his cot, the dreadful happened, as he fearfully anticipated. The doorknob slowly turned and the door creaked open by the large, hairy but manicured hand of the Devil. This time DuValle stopped in front of Tim and Billy's cot – Tim's number came up. Tim was frozen in fear as the dark shadow sat on the cot. Tim closed his eyes but could still see and feel the Devil's ice-cold stare through the darkness. DuValle lifted up his robe and pulled Tim's blanket sheets down. Just as his giant hand touched below Tim's stomach, a bloodcurdling scream echoed across the room. But it didn't come from Tim, it was Billy. Realizing he was risking a severe punishment, Billy threw caution to the wind to save his friend by yelping as loud and as long as he could. Several of the boys jumped up and someone turned on a lantern. DuValle pointed at Billy and through gritted teeth snarled, "I will see you in my office at 8:00 a.m." He then looked down at Tim and just smiled and nodded before leaving.

Tim laid awake the rest of the night doing what he did best, thinking…and rethinking. He needed to survive, and the only way was to escape the orphanage. Finally, just as the sun was rising, the first phase of Tim's well-thought-out and meticulous plan was intact. Now it was time to execute.

Chapter 5
THE ESCAPE (1886)

As the sun started to rise, Tim woke Billy and laid out his plan in a whisper so the others in the bunk room were none the wiser. An important initial step was for Tim to be held responsible for last night's ruckus and be the one up on The Stack so he could surveil the grounds and find a chink in the fortress's armor. Tim needed the vantage point provided by The Stack to view the other side of the wall. This would enable him to observe the comings and goings of visitors, workers, and vendors, and their ins and outs through the various gates and doors during the day. Convincing DuValle to substitute Tim for Billy as the penitent would be a huge challenge. The best Tim came up with was for him to accompany Billy to DuValle's office first thing as ordered and explain that the reason Billy screamed bloody murder in the middle of the night and caused such a racket was because Tim had been so startled and frightened by DuValle entering their bunk room "to check on the boys" that Tim had squeezed Billy's arm so hard his nails broke the skin on Billy's forearm. And therefore, the planned ruse was to explain it was Tim who caused such a stir and should be punished, not Billy. Billy at first refused because he didn't want Tim to take the inevitable whoopin' that preceded the ascent up The Stack in his stead. After much persistence, Tim finally prevailed upon Billy to go along with the plan as they got dressed before heading to the Devil's office.

Both boys took a deep breath before knocking on the door. A deep and sinister "Enter" came from within the office. Once they slowly walked in, DuValle glared at Tim, wondering why he was present, and bellowed, "There better be a good reason why you decided to show up, Mr. Conlon." DuValle grabbed his daunting paddle lying next to a Bible on his large dark oak desk and began to slap it in his hand. Tim again heard his father's voice whisper, "You got this, Timmy, my boy."

Tim looked directly into DuValle's lifeless eyes and relayed the pretext with conviction. Tim then sold it with how he had learned in the Academy's religion class last week that people must take responsibility for their actions, no matter how dire the consequences.

DuValle flashed his sinister grin, turning his attention to Billy. "Is this true, William? I know you would never lie to a Brother as that would be a mortal sin, and if I find out you are lying, the punishment will be even more severe than you can imagine."

Billy was tongue-tied with fear but nodded yes.

"Come here, if that is true, let me see the so-called marks on your arm supposedly inflicted by Mr. Conlon's fingernails that allegedly caused you to scream out like a banshee." While staring at Tim, DuValle grabbed Billy by the arm and rolled up his sleeve. Tim didn't flinch, and his demeanor remained cool and collected.

There were five deep cuts embedded in Billy's forearm with blood still oozing from some of the wounds. Tim anticipated that DuValle was clever enough to check for the purported wounds to confirm the veracity of their story. So just before they left the bunk room earlier that morning, Tim substantiated the fingernail marks in Billy's forearm part of the tale. "Sorry Billy, this is gonna hurt, but we have to do it to put one over on DuValle."

DuValle, though still skeptical, bought into the boys' story and announced his decision – Tim had to spend the day on The Stack and Billy would get the paddle "for acting like a baby and screaming out in such an undignified manner." Billy getting paddled was a slight twist to what Tim planned, but the important part of Tim being the one to perch on top of The Stack was successful. Poor Billy took his five whacks with not so much as a tear – so determined because he was enraged that the Brother called him a baby.

Tim had a quick breakfast, used the bathroom, and ascended up the ladder to The Stack. One of the other Brothers who had a kinder heart counseled Tim on some last-minute advice about surviving

The Stack, which was similar to the advice he had taken in from the other boys of what to do and what not to do. "Don't lock your knees. Don't look down. If you feel dizzy, take some deep breaths. Keep your gaze on the horizon. Keep your mind active by singing to yourself or doing math problems in your head, so as to not fall asleep. Alternate standing on one foot to rest the other foot and leg." And so on…

Tim made it to the top, steadied his balance, and studied his surroundings. As Tim accurately estimated, he was indeed able to see over the walls and into the yard where people arrived, parked their carriages, and left throughout the day. Vendors, visitors, suppliers, potential adoptive parents, and representatives from the Archdiocese would arrive randomly, park their carriages, and proceed to the front door. The food suppliers entered Queen of Heaven through a secondary side door in the West Wall, which was locked from the inside and located near the kitchen and mess hall. Tim searched and searched for any sort of a pattern, but none was found.

Shortly after the morning recess concluded and following the second school bell, which rang five minutes before classes commenced, Tim noticed the arrival of a wagon drawn by one horse with a brown tarp draped over the back of the wagon. The driver dismounted, walked to the rear of the wagon, and pulled the tarp back to reveal the contents – fresh bread. Tim recalled one of the kitchen workers boasting "we have the freshest of bread every day." This likely meant the routine he was about to witness by the bread wagon driver occurred on a daily basis. Tim studied every detail meticulously – he paid close attention to how the bread man loaded up a couple of baskets with loaves of bread, pulled the tarp back over the wagon, walked twenty steps to the side door, and rang the bell. One of the kitchen workers came out almost immediately, so Tim deduced this was the time the bread man regularly arrived at the door as the kitchen worker clearly was expecting him. The kitchen worker unlocked the door with a large church key, let the bread man inside, grabbed one of the two baskets, and escorted the bread man into the kitchen. Shortly thereafter, the bread man was escorted back through the side door in the West Wall, and the worker relocked the door and headed back to the kitchen. Tim counted to 68 from the time the bread man walked inside the side West Wall door until the time he exited back out of the door. So the side door was unlocked for just over a minute. Standing on his toes, Tim could see just over the wall to the other side and observed that the bread man returned to his wagon, double-checked that the tarp was fastened, and drove off out of the Queen of Heaven parking area.

"That's it!" Tim smiled to himself. "It's gonna work." Then he returned to reciting "A Song of the Fairies," which was Tim's favorite poem by the newly published Irish poet William Butler Yeats, singing Irish rebel songs his father used to sing, and doing math in his head in an attempt to try to make it through the excruciating day. Tim was lightheaded multiple times, felt starving later in the day, and was so mad when he eventually had to relieve himself. "Darn it, I almost made it." And then he let it go, not in his pants, but off the top of The Stack like a waterfall – "no sense getting me pants wet." The boys down below who were on their pre-dinner recreation break were roaring with laughter. Tim was laughing too, until one of the Brothers ran over and screamed, "Mr. Conlon, there will be no more urinating off the Stack!"

"Sorry Brother, there isn't a toilet up here. It won't happen again."

Tim made it through the 12 hours on The Stack and was let down. Billy was waiting at the bottom. "You ok, Tim?"

"We got what we needed, Billy – yeah, I'm doing ok."

That night Tim debriefed Billy on the orphanage weak link that he discovered from the vantage of The Stack. They conspired all night and discussed every detail. Each time they heard a noise, the boys immediately shut up and looked at the door to see if DuValle was returning for one of his dreaded nightly visits. The sun eventually rose without the Devil darkening their door.

Billy and Tim tried to act as nonchalant as possible at breakfast. The only items Tim grabbed from his belongings box were his mother's rosary beads and a couple of photographs of his family. Billy grabbed a slingshot his deceased father made him for one of his birthdays. Otherwise, their pockets were empty – not a penny to their name. At breakfast, Tim encouraged Billy and himself to eat something in spite of the very active butterflies in their stomachs, as they would need the energy and were clueless about when they would eat again.

Tim and Billy proceeded outside to morning recess, which lasted a half hour before the morning school bell. Those 30 minutes seemed like an eternity – what if the bread driver rang the bell during recess, what if Tim was wrong about the everyday delivery? So many doubts and worries crept into Tim's head.

The bell finally rang and the boys started to file inside their classrooms. It took the 300 boys several minutes to file inside, and they had to be seated by the second bell which came five minutes later. Billy and Tim held back toward the end of the line, and once inside, instead of turning right to head to their classroom they went left to the lavatory. No one seemed to notice or care – so far so good. Inside the bathroom, which was expectedly empty, they didn't speak and waited for the second final bell to ring, which was the time by which the residents were to be seated in the classroom. The second bell rang right on cue. The boys opened the bathroom door and quickly but quietly walked down the hallway and proceeded back outside, where they sprinted toward The Stack. Hiding behind the large stump, the lads were standing where they couldn't be seen from the side door in the West Wall. Another eternity – "Where is the bread guy?" "When is he coming?" "How long has it been?" Minds raced.

While awaiting the bread man's arrival, Tim looked up at The Stack and said, "You big old ugly excuse for a tree used to scare the pants off of me. I sure hope you end up saving us. Thanks, Old Man Stack."

Just when Tim thought they should scrap the escape and sneak back into the school, the bell at the side door rang. "That's him! The bread man's here just like I told ya." Their eyes turned to the kitchen door, and seconds later the worker came out, fumbling for the key in his coat pocket as he rushed to answer the side door. The worker unlocked the door, and in walked the bread man with two large baskets. Greetings were exchanged, and they walked toward the kitchen, each with a basket of bread in their arms.

Tim whispered, "Okay Billy, this is it – we have 68 seconds to run as fast as we can out the door and jump in the wagon. Ready… go!" Once the worker and the bread man walked through the kitchen door the boys sprinted full speed to the side door. Tim was counting seconds in his head and was at 23 seconds when they opened the unlocked door and slowly shut it exactly as it was, slightly ajar. Now at 36 seconds – they spotted the wagon. Other than the horse turning his head to watch, there was no one in the courtyard, which was a risk Tim was worried about. 48 seconds – the boys untied the tarp and crawled into the wagon. 56 seconds – Tim reached his hand under the tarp and tried to retie the rope fastener back as it was, but was having a tough time accomplishing the task. 63 seconds – Tim still could not fasten the tarp rope. 65 seconds! Tim pulled his hands back inside the wagon under the tarp. "Damn it! I couldn't get it tied." As he counted to 68 seconds, the side door opened, and they could hear the key jiggle as the kitchen worker relocked the side door. They now listened to the bread man's feet shuffle across the gravel, which grew louder as he approached the wagon. The horse snorted as if to signal "we have a couple of stowaways." Tim was convinced the bread man, being a creature of habit, would check the tarp to ensure it was tied down. But when the bread man discovered that the rope was untied, would he pull the tarp up to refasten the tarp back into place? Would he think something was wrong and look under the tarp?

The bread man walked alongside the wagon, checked the tarp

rope, and uttered a curious "hmmmm." He pulled the tarp taut, gave it a shake, and pulled it flush again over the wagon. The whole time both boys had their eyes closed, fingers crossed, and prayed the "Hail Mary" fast over and over again.

The bread man tied up the tarp rope, his hands inches from Tim's head underneath the tarp. They heard him stroll toward the front of the carriage and mount the driver's seat, give a click through the side of his cheek and a "Giddy up, Blue," and the wagon started to move. The boys remained frozen, although they were exploding inside with emotion. They at last made it outside Queen of Heaven. This was the first time in three months for Tim and two years for Billy that they were free of their walled-off nightmare world. It would be just a matter of time before someone noticed their absence, and the Devil would surely be right behind them.

The plan was to stay in the wagon for about a mile, which took a walking horse pulling a loaded wagon about 15 minutes. It was time. Tim gave Billy a nudge and slid his arms under the tarp to stealthily untie the hold rope. He pulled the tarp up ever so slightly to peek out. All Tim could see was prairie as the wagon headed due south on the dusty gravel road. First Tim jumped out, then Billy. They both hit the deck running in case the driver spotted them and immediately darted into the prairie where the grass was up to their waists. Through research in the orphanage library and word of mouth, along with hearing train whistles at night, the boys calculated the railroad tracks running from Chicago to Arlington Heights were a few miles south of Queen of Heaven. By looking at the sun, Tim tried his best to head south, hoping to eventually intersect the tracks. "Come on, Billy, keep runnin'!"

Chapter 6
THE CHASE

The Brother teaching Tim and Billy's first period Elocution class noticed their two empty chairs shortly after the second bell rang. "Maybe Conlon and McGregor are lollygagging again, or in the bathroom," he thought. So the Brother gave it another ten minutes. When the boys were still missing, the Brother excused himself from class and walked to inspect the bathroom, which was empty. Then he jogged to the outside door, but the yard too was empty. Now he raced in a full-out sprint to DuValle's office to report the missing lads.

DuValle leapt to his feet with eyes bulging and his face red. "I'll alert the staff. You enlist all the boys in your class to search everywhere – promise ice cream to the child who finds them. Be certain to interrogate their bunkmates – they may know something."

DuValle summoned the other Brothers and workers to search the grounds inside and out. When the truants were nowhere to be found after about a half hour mad search, DuValle panicked, thinking to himself, "Would they run to the police and report me about the other night? I must stop them!"

A couple of boys recalled seeing Tim and Billy at breakfast and also in the yard before the first bell. There was a ten-minute lapse from the time the bell rang until they vanished. "Who came in through the side door during that time?!" DuValle barked out.

"The bread delivery man, as he does every day," the kitchen worker sheepishly answered.

"Please tell me the side door was not left open and unattended…"

"Only for a minute, Brother, I swear."

DuValle's heart sank. "Oh my God, those little rats concocted the whole scheme for Conlon to get on The Stack and find the way out!" Panicking, DuValle ordered one of the Brothers to contact the local sheriff, who had successfully tracked and retrieved a couple of orphans who fled a year earlier with the assistance of his bloodhound, Bo. DuValle directed another Brother to go the bakery and interview the bread man.

The sheriff's office/house was less than a mile from Queen of Heaven – the sheriff and Bo were quickly enlisted. One of the Brothers handed over to the sheriff the boys' pajamas from their cot to provide the scent for the bloodhound. The sheriff and his bloodhound immediately went into action, retracing the bread wagon's path exiting the orphanage. About 3/4 of a mile down the road, Old Bo began howling and barking – the scent was detected. The sheriff estimated that the boys had about an hour head start. However, the boys had only a general idea of their route, meandering back and forth, running into obstacles such as barbed wire cow fences and creeks, forcing the escapees to reroute multiple times. The hound had a direct route along the scent, and the sheriff was able to bypass several of the detours and double-backs. Consequently, the sheriff and old Bo were confident that they would be able to close the gap fairly quickly.

As the boys at last found the railroad tracks, they could hear barking. Now running down the tracks, the howling grew louder with each passing minute. Tim guessed they were now maybe a half mile ahead of their pursuers. That's when Tim devised his plan on the fly to split up at the fork in the railroad lines just ahead. Tim was choked up after waving his last goodbye to the little brother he never had. "I hope they follow my path instead of Billy's."

The sheriff arrived at the track split about ten minutes after the boys went their separate ways. The sheriff was at first perplexed by Bo pacing back and forth and running in circles, alternating down both of the tracks at the fork. The sheriff spoke to his dog, "Bo, they either split up or doubled back to try to confuse us." This wasn't the sheriff's or Bo's first rodeo. Certain the escapees headed down the rail toward

Chicago as opposed to toward the unknown, they followed the scent after Tim. "We'll know shortly if they doubled back, Bo."

After several hundred yards, the sheriff concluded the boys had split up. They were now hot on the trail after Tim. "We'll at least catch one of these rascals and get information on the other's whereabouts." Once Tim heard barking closing in on him, he was partially relieved they were for whatever reason coming after him, thus sparing his best friend Billy. The other part of Tim's thought was, "Crap, they are coming after me." Tim was becoming fatigued, running slower, and walking more than he was running. The barking grew even louder. "I have to throw them off somehow or I'm sunk."

A creek ran parallel to the tracks about eight feet below the level of the rail line. Tim had read in *The Adventures of Huckleberry Finn* how Huck's friend who was a runaway slave evaded a posse with bloodhounds by running through the creek – seems that running through water shielded the scent from the dog's snout. Without hesitation, Tim jumped off the tracks down the slope and into the creek, which was a couple of feet deep. He waded and walked, splashing through the creek. The barking was now deafening. Trees lining the creek prevented Tim from seeing his pursuers, and the sheriff, who was now only a hundred yards away, from seeing Tim. Tim exited the creek on the side opposite the tracks and ran about 25 yards perpendicular into the field. He then doubled back and jumped down the ledge and landed directly in the water before he plodded on down the creek. The howling grew even closer. Tim looked back and caught a glimpse of the sheriff about fifty yards away holding the jumping and thrashing Bo tightly as they entered the creek. Tim quickly diverted back up the incline to the tracks with his view again blocked by the trees. "God, please, I hope they didn't spot me…" Tim forced himself to keep going. Adrenaline helped, but he was entirely exhausted and could barely keep one leg in front of the other, fearing he would fall to his knees with each next step.

The barking suddenly became markedly different with more whining than howling. It also was slightly quieter. It seemed Bo had a harder time picking up the scent in the water – every few seconds, he would catch a whiff, then it would vanish. This frustrated the poor hound and slowed the sheriff down. It cost the sheriff valuable time to locate where Tim left the creek and ran into the field – followed by even more delay with the double back and forth into the field. By the time the sheriff retraced the steps to the side of the creek where Tim jumped down into the water, the scent seemed to have evaporated. Bo and the sheriff were also tired and thirsty. A person running for his life has more endurance than his or her pursuers. The sheriff yelled out, with his words echoing, "You got lucky today, boy! I'll find you, God damn it – I'll be coming for you!"

Tim was now a half mile away from the stalled search party. The barking went silent. It was now early evening, maybe a couple of hours from sunset. Tim saw an oasis up ahead, an old round barn. He hydrated from a water pump on the side of the barn. There were no signs of anyone. He settled in on a pile of hay in an empty stall inside. Tim was terrified. "I have to stay awake." "I'll just rest my eyes for a moment." Although he successfully fought it off multiple times, Tim eventually fell into slumber for the night.

The sheriff and his dog returned to the orphanage. Poor Bo had to be carried over the sheriff's shoulder the last mile back. The sheriff recounted the chase to Brother DuValle. The Devil was gutted by the bad news. The plan was for the sheriff to contact the Chicago authorities and for DuValle to contact the Archdiocese. "I will find out everything about Timothy Conlon, where he lived, where his siblings now live, who his school friends were, where they played. I will use the power and resources of the Church to get the word out to the schools, priests, nuns, teachers, and parishioners, to be on the lookout for our poor, helpless, and vulnerable lost children," DuValle said with a sarcastic fake cry. Then, screaming, "They must be found at once and returned to Queen of Heaven – I swear to my Maker I will not rest for one moment until those two ne'er-do-wells are back where they belong…in our loving care." DuValle's eyes gleamed as he cast an evil smile.

II. LIFE

Chapter 7
FREE AGAIN

Tim was awakened by the sound of a rooster crowing in the distance as the sun rose. Initially, Tim was a bit startled as he processed where he was and how he had gotten there. As his mind began to get bombarded with thoughts of yesterday's escape, Tim's heart thumped, and he knew he had to get going right away. He stood up, dusted himself off, and returned to the tracks heading to the city. Tim's thoughts were again racing, this time between two main themes: what DuValle and the sheriff are cooking up next, and finding a piece of bacon.

Tim made it about five more miles down the tracks, which gobbled up the entire morning. As his journey grew closer to Chicago, there were fewer open prairies and fields and more farms and houses. Weak from lack of nutrition, Tim diverted from the tracks to the nearby small village of Norwood, which is located halfway between Arlington Heights and the business center of Chicago. Norwood Park would later become annexed into Chicago as one of its northwest neighborhoods. Tim at this point almost didn't care if he got caught – he needed food, and he needed it fast. He wandered into town onto what appeared to be the main street and spotted a fruit store. Tim thought about lifting a couple of apples and hightailing it. Not that he was above that move in such a time of desperation, but Tim figured he already had enough people after him. Some old man donning an apron screaming "Stop that little thief" would not be a good look. Instead, Tim went up to the owner and mentioned he was hungry, had no money, but would be happy to sweep up or help at the store as payback.

Tim caught a break; the owner smiled and said, "That's a nice gesture, young man – take a couple apples and a couple of bananas. Pay me back when you are rich and famous." This reminded Tim that not all adults are evil, and that kindness does exist, something that had left Tim's life after his parents were taken from him. Tim sat behind the store eating the best tasting fruit he had ever consumed. He also guzzled some water from the store's water pump in the back.

When Tim returned to the street, a priest presumably from the nearby church was strolling down Main Street when he locked eyes on Tim. In an Irish brogue the priest greeted Tim, "Lad, are you lost now? Can we have a nice chat?"

Tim wondered if the fruit store owner tipped the priest off about the young waif begging for food. Or did DuValle already get the word out to surrounding parishes? Tim, backing away, said, "That's ok, Father, my mom asked me to pick up some food and return home right away. I have to go". The priest reached out to grab Tim's shoulder. Tim ducked and dashed away like a flash. Now energized with some calories, he picked up the pace, bolted out of Norwood and continued his journey down the tracks to Chicago.

DuValle didn't sleep after the two ragamuffins fled the orphanage. Terrified that his midnight visits to the bunk rooms would be brought to the attention of the police, a relative, or a nun, Brother DuValle personally traveled to Chicago a couple of days after the boys escaped and met with the Archdiocese council. DuValle also visited a near North Side parish where the Conlons were members with the urgent request that the two wayward little boys must be found, taken off the dangerous streets of Chicago, and returned to DuValle's nurturing care. He also met with the Mother Superior of St. Mary's where Tim had attended second grade. She in turn arranged for DuValle to have a meeting with a couple of Tim's friends and esteemed members of the Wily Boys.

DuValle first interrogated Big Patrick, looking for any inkling that Patrick already had contact with Tim, who may be in the company of another runaway, Billy McGregor. Patrick truthfully revealed that he had no contact with Tim, and this was the first he had heard the news. Even if Patrick had seen Tim, there was zero chance he would have ratted out his friend. The Wily Boys had a blood oath to never tattle on a fellow member to a parent, a copper, a nun, or a priest, or run the risk of a beating and an immediate ouster from the Wilys with a lifetime ban.

"Patrick, you will tell Mother Superior immediately if you spot Tim, won't you?"

"Of course, I will, Brother," Patrick, with his hand in his pocket and his fingers crossed, lied convincingly. Patrick ran down the hallway and outside to rejoin recess. He located the Wily Boys and yelled, "Conlon escaped! He's on the lam and this giant scary Brother is after him!"

DuValle made one more stop before heading back to Queen of Heaven. He paid a visit to the home of Uncle Shelton Conlon. Molly answered the door and was fearful the Franciscan was the bearer of bad news about Tim. She escorted DuValle to the parlor where Shelton was sitting, and the men discussed what had happened. As Molly eavesdropped, she smiled broadly after thanking God Tim was okay. "That little imp! He made it out of there. Way to go, Timmy." Molly and Mike were then called into the parlor and received the same admonishment from DuValle as Patrick had earlier in the day. Both siblings truthfully advised they had no contact with Tim. Molly, however, lied with her innocent blue eyes and rosy cheeks, "I will let Uncle Shelton know immediately." It was harder to tell if Mike, who gave the identical answer, was telling the truth. Molly was so overcome by guilt that no one visited Tim during his three-month stay at Queen of Heaven, something that Tim certainly had noticed and would never forget.

The sheriff felt his reputation was on the line, having been outsmarted by two little rapscallions. The sheriff awoke early the next day and traveled to the closest police headquarters in a northwest neighborhood of Chicago to spread the news to be on the lookout for two runaway orphans. The sheriff stressed that it was of great importance to the Catholic muckety mucks to recover them.

The Chicago Police Department was one of the first in the country to use a "Call Booth," a newly invented technology by Alexander Graham Bell in 1876. Chicago updated its signal lines in 1880 with Call Booths. Only an officer or "reputable citizen" would be issued a key that would grant them access to the Call Booth.[11] Inside was a telegraph that was set up with a device that looked like a clock with a bell on top. The officer would move the pointer on the telegraph to one of eleven specific choices (arson, thieves, forgers, riot, drunkard, murder, accident, violation of city ordinances, fighting, test line, fire) and pull a handle. This would send a message to police headquarters alerting them of the officer's activity. They eventually added telephones to the Call Booths that linked the officer with the police department. A telegram with the specifics would follow to all the precincts.[12]

The sheriff effectively initiated a citywide order, (something that would later be known as an All Points Bulletin or APB) for the two boys, with the telegram, along with their photographs. This prompted all the Call Booths to be set off, alerting the police to read as soon as possible the inbound telegram concerning the details of the alert at their respective precincts. While the beat cops would receive a copy and read the information, the city was unfortunately rife with orphans and street waifs. And the police had much bigger fish to fry than two stray minnows lost in the lake. Still, most officers would study the photos closely in hopes it would trigger a synapse in their brains to recognize the missing boys if they ever crossed paths. Otherwise, the Chicago Police Department was busy with keeping peace in the streets of 1885 Chicago.

At long last, after making his way for five days down the railroad tracks, Tim made it to the business center of Chicago, which later became known as "The Loop" in the late 1890s.

In 1803, the United States Army had constructed Fort Dearborn along the Chicago River at the intersection of today's Michigan Avenue and Wacker Drive, becoming the first significant settlement in the area. Fort Dearborn became the location of the Cook County seat in 1831, and the offices of the City of Chicago in 1837 when it became incorporated. The original site of Fort Dearborn and the surrounding area became mainly commercial starting in the late 1860s.[13]

Following the destruction of Chicago's business center and beyond by the Great Chicago Fire of 1871, the ensuing Great Rebuild of Chicago commenced with deliberate speed. Some of the world's earliest skyscrapers, which were built in the downtown area and designed by legendary architects, changed the face of the Chicago skyline. In 1885, the ten-story Home Insurance Building, generally considered the world's first skyscraper, was constructed. Shortly thereafter, other iconic buildings were constructed, such as the Rookery Building in 1888, the Monadnock Building in 1891, and the Sullivan Center in 1899. Just prior to the turn of the century, cable car turnarounds and an elevated railway line encircled the central business center, giving the Loop its name.

Tim knew it was prudent to initially stay away from his neighborhood, his parish, his school, his friends, and his family – the places and people his heart ever so ached to see the most. But that's where the Devil surely would be stalking in the shadows.

"I have it all wrong…that little rat is too smart to go to his friends or family; he'll hide in the crowds of downtown. That's where I will look for him." DuValle was becoming obsessed and thought of little else during most of his waking hours. He developed terrible insomnia, and DuValle's appearance grew more disheveled and haggard each day the boys continued to be at large.

The Brothers noticed that DuValle would sit in his office behind closed doors for hours at a time and randomly scream out profanity-laced gibberish. He also began to miss morning prayers and daily Masses. DuValle, who used to preach "cleanliness was godliness" and whose habit was eternally immaculate, now donned a badly stained and wrinkled frock. The Brothers became very worried about DuValle. "He's not acting right – why can't he move on and let the authorities handle it?" They tried talking with DuValle, but all he would do was recite another rant about how the boys needed to be recovered and returned to their care at Queen of Heaven. Realizing that the police probably would not be much help with all the other monumental crime in the city, the Devil packed his bags and informed the other Brothers that he was moving downtown until he returned with Conlon and McGregor.

The business area of Chicago was booming in 1886. Tim was in awe of the large buildings being constructed in every direction. There were hundreds of horse-drawn carriages lining the streets of dirt and gravel. Men in suits and derbies seemed to be constantly rushing back and forth along the wooden sidewalks. New buildings were being constructed on each of the 35 square blocks of the business district. New "skyscrapers" were replacing the old structures destroyed in the Great Fire. Policemen were present on every corner.

Tim felt he stood out like a sore thumb. He thought it was only a matter of time before a beat cop or someone connected to the church would spot and confiscate him. Tim knew he had to find an area where runaways were more commonplace and where coppers and clergy would not go near. Instead of heading north to his old neighborhood, Tim wandered south of the center of town. In a few blocks, Tim came upon an area known as Little Cheyenne, a terrifying and lawless red light district area – a perfect hiding place for a runaway orphan.

Chapter 8
LITTLE CHEYENNE

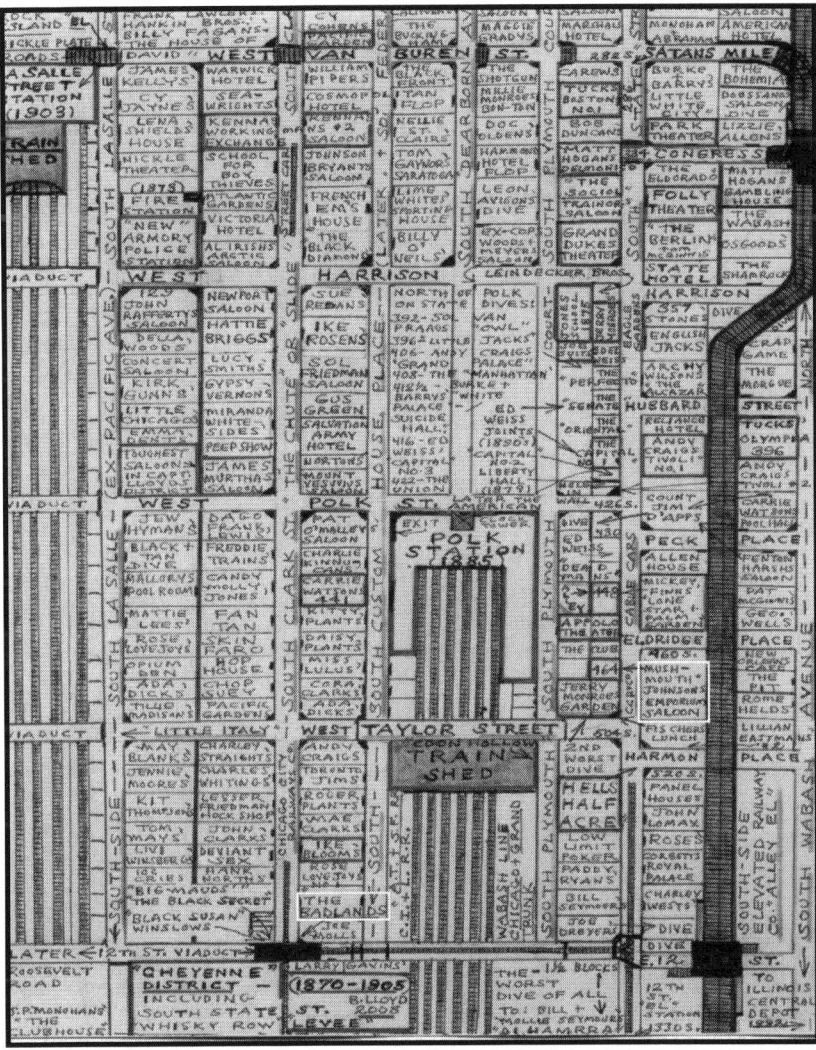

Map of Little Cheyenne – Cheyenne District Brothel Map (1870-1905);
Creator Unknown; Permissions to use granted by Digital Research Library of Illinois History;
Public Domain (Mush Mouth Johnsons and The Badlands are highlighted with white squares).

In the aftermath of the Great Chicago Fire in 1871, the near South Side of Chicago became known for its congregation of criminal elements. The area known as "Little Cheyenne" ran several blocks along Clark Street south of Van Buren. This red light district was described as being as wild and dangerous as the lawless Western states. Hence, it was nicknamed after Cheyenne, Wyoming. A Chicago detective described it as

> "about as tough and vicious a place as there was on the face of the earth. Around the doors of these places could be seen gaudily-bedecked females, half-clad in flashy finery, dresses which never came below their knees, with many colored stockings and fancy shoes. Many of them wore bodices cut so low that they did not amount to much more than a belt." (Digital Research Library of Illinois History Journal, "The History of Chicago's 'Red-Light' Vice Districts; January 2, 2017).

There were 46 saloons, 37 "houses of ill-repute," and 11 pawnbrokers in Little Cheyenne in 1886 when Tim strolled down Clark Street that day. Its streets, alleys, and dives swarmed with harlots, sluggers, degenerates, dope fiends, thieves, and hundreds of pimps for the thousands of resident prostitutes.[14] It was also a place where street waifs could mill about without constantly being bothered by police, church representatives, or do-gooders trying to provide assistance, alleviating the growing epidemic of unhoused children in Chicago.[15]

Tim became the newest resident of Little Cheyenne. In less than three months, Tim lived in three extraordinarily incongruous residences – the Conlon home, Queen of Heaven Orphanage, and now Little Cheyenne. Random thoughts transfixed Tim's mind. "How am I going to make it? I miss Molly. Hope Billy didn't get nabbed. At least DuValle's not here." Not yet, anyway. "Where will I be when I'm 20 years old – if I make it that far…"

Chapter 9
THE INTERVIEW (1897)

Tim looked in the mirror the morning of his big interview with Western Electric in 1897. The 20-year-old had his coal black hair slicked back, dressed in his only suit, a shabby gray pinstripe he had purchased from a resale shop. Tim joked with his friends, "When I found a used suit without any bullet holes, I bought it right away." Tim started working at the Western Electric Chicago plant two years earlier in 1895 as a telephone line troubleshooter. Word got out that a position in the sister company Illinois Bell Patent and Research department was open, something Tim was striving for ever since he started with Western Electric shortly after he turned 18. Tim prepared a resume that was long in life lessons but thin on pedigree.

Ever since he saw the telephone display at the Columbia Exposition World's Fair, also known as the Chicago World's Fair, in 1893, Tim had been reading everything he could get his hands on at the Chicago Public Library about Western Electric, the manufacturing arm of the Bell Telephone Company, and all its innovations, new technology development, and patents. At the age of 15, Tim showed up to the Columbian Exposition, nicknamed The White City due to the ivory-colored buildings that made up a majority of the Fair's structures, early enough to enter inside the Electric Pavilion exhibit and observe one of the first long distance phone calls made from Chicago to New York.

An Egyptian temple from 1800 B.C. was the highlight of the Western Electric Company display in the Chicago World's Fair's Electric Pavilion. The Western Electric display was intentionally provocative, with its intended juxtaposition of the new and the old. Egyptian graphics were made to look modern with glowing electric lights, and ancient Egyptians were depicted making telephone calls.[16] As the Electric Pavilion Guidebook explained:

The next most prominent exhibit in the [Electrical] building is that of the Western Electric Company, of Chicago, immediately to the east of the main south entrance. This company has three pavilions, one as an Egyptian temple paneled on the outside most uniquely with Egyptian figures and groups associated with electricity. For instance, there is a group of Egyptian maidens, of the time of Rameses the Second, operating a telephone board, and another group is of men of the same period laying telegraph lines. The concept is very popular. (Worldfairs; en.worldfair.info.; Electricity – Expo Chicago 1893; Quoting Original Fair Brochure).

Bell Telephone Exhibit – Electricity Building; 1893; The Project Gutenberg EBook of Official Views Of The World's Columbian Exposition; C.D. Arnold (1844-1927); HD Higinbotham; Public Domain.

Tim was fascinated by the newly invented telephone and its possibilities, thinking it would be the future of how people would communicate. Western Electric was a company he targeted for employment. Tim kept looking for job openings. However, it was a modern company for its time and was fairly strict about not employing any workers until they reached the age of 18. Tim read about the company history and followed its growth until he met their hiring minimum age requirement.

Western Electric expanded during the 1870s from a workforce of 20 people in 1870 to 105 men and 25 women by 1880. In 1881, when annual sales had already grown to nearly $1 million, the firm was purchased by the American Bell Telephone Co. (the company that would become AT&T); it was renamed the Western Electric Company and became Bell's manufacturing arm. From 1886 until the late 1890s, Western Electric was prospering at its new Chicago plant just west of downtown at Clinton and Van Buren Streets.

Tim applied for a technical worker position at the Clinton Plant shortly after his 18th birthday. Tim was naturally handy and well-read on the various products manufactured by Western Electric. He impressed with his enthusiasm over and knowledge of Western Electric's history and products related to the new cutting-edge technology. The position involved mostly on-the-job training and learning the plant's operations for Tim, really a perfect entry-level position for someone aspiring to someday work in the Patent and Research Department.

Opportunity for Tim knocked two years later in 1897 at the age of 20 when a Research and Development Department position opened. Tim was fairly nervous before the big interview. He practiced his answers to anticipated questions as he continued to stare in the mirror. Tim whispered to himself, "This old suit is way too big on me. And, by the way, my highest level of education is the second grade…I'm screwed. Hope this will be a little easier than my first interview." This thought drifted Tim's mind back to his first "job interview" at the age of eight, the day he first strolled down the streets of Little Cheyenne.

(1886)

Tim again was starving as he entered Little Cheyenne for the first time. Tim needed a job immediately so he could buy something to eat. He tried to gather information on how to get food from a couple of the other street kids he noticed in Little Cheyenne, but the waifs scattered away when he approached. "Why are all these kids so darn twitchy?" As he later learned, there was an "every person for him or herself" environment among the children living on the streets of Little Cheyenne, and no one was to be trusted.

Tim wandered over to the first building in front of him, a dilapidated three-story brick building near the corner of State Street and Taylor, not unlike other buildings in the row of structures that made up the block. Dust blew everywhere when the horse-drawn wagons and carriages rumbled down the dirt streets of Little Cheyenne. The building's lower level housed Mush Mouth Johnson's Emporium Saloon, a fairly large but dingy shot and a beer joint with a boxing ring in the center of the room adjacent to the long bar. The ring was surrounded by three or four rows of seats to watch nightly bare-knuckle fights.

Tim read the name of the bar above the front door, chuckled to himself at the name Mush Mouth and said "I have to check this joint out." Tim pushed open the swinging doors, just like in the Old West. The light from outside made the older man in a bar apron who was sweeping the barroom floor squint and shade his eyes with his free forearm, which had a tattoo from the Civil War. "Get outta here, kid!"

"I'm looking for work, sir – please, I'll sweep for money or food." The man paused a moment and stared at the diminutive boy. "Go talk to Mush Mouth behind the bar, but it's Mr. Johnson to you."

Tim approached the bar where several faceless, burly men sat quietly drinking their whiskeys. The bar was higher than Tim's head. Old Mush Mouth was chomping on a thick cigar and cleaning a tumbler with a dirty gray towel. He sported a sleeveless tee shirt underneath his bartender apron, exposing the same Civil War tattoo as the sweeper. Tim later learned that Johnson was a sergeant for an Illinois platoon, and he ran his bar in a similar militant fashion – "You have a job to do, do it well, or there's the door."

"Mr. Mush Mouth..." Everyone stopped and turned their attention toward the young high-pitched voice of Tim.

"What did you call me?!"

Shaking, Tim managed to utter, "Sorry sir, I meant to say Mush Johnson...I mean Mr. Johnson."

After glaring at Tim for a few more seconds, Johnson and all the patrons burst out laughing. "That's ok, son, everyone calls me Mush Mouth – Mr. Johnson is me dad's name." The men chuckled. "What is it you want, boy?"

"I'm looking for work, sir."

"Hmmm. I could use someone to clean up after hours and do some odds and ends. But what I really need is a kid to sing in between rounds of the fights. See, the lad who used to sing for me stopped showing up. Shame – he was pretty good. Do ya sing, boy?"

"Yes sir, I was in the choir at school."

"Well, let's hear it!"

All the patrons swirled around in their barstools to watch the impromptu audition. Tim took a deep breath and sang at the top of his lungs a couple of Irish rebel songs his dad had taught him, "Wild Colonial Boy" and "The Rose of Tralee."

"Who would have thought those nuns forcing me to sing in the choir everyday would have paid off?" Tim whispered to himself.

Mushy, as the regulars called him, took the cigar out of his mouth. "What do ya think, lads? His voice ain't much, but he is loud. And he seems to know the right songs."

The men shrugged, and muttered, "Yeah Mushy, he carried the tune okay – he has heart – hire the poor kid."

Mush said he would compensate Tim with whatever food was left over in the kitchen after they closed for a late dinner, and breakfast in the morning before opening. As was the tradition, Tim could also keep the pennies thrown by the patrons into the ring after Tim sang in between boxing rounds. "Deal?" Johnson extended his hand to Tim to shake.

Tim shook his hand. "Deal – thanks so much, sir."

"I ain't no sir, call me Mush Mouth. What do I call you?"

"Tim," but no last name was given, always being mindful of DuValle. Tim's first interview successfully concluded, and he landed a job.

(1897)

"Hopefully, I won't have to sing for the President of Western Electric this time." Tim smiled to himself as he headed to the interview. That detour down memory lane to Mush Mouth's gave Tim's confidence a boost. When you are able to survive everything Tim went through, sitting down to convince someone that you are the best man for the job doesn't sound that scary or challenging. In 1888, Tim read a new book, *Twilight of the Idols* by German philosopher Friedrich Nietzsche, translated to English, who wrote, "Out of life's school of war—what doesn't kill me makes me stronger." It seemed a fitting motto for Tim.

Tim waited for what seemed like a week for his interview with six other twenty-somethings with much nicer and better-fitting suits without any bullet holes, until his name was called. The interviewer was a balding 45-year-old with wire-framed glasses and a shirt pocket filled with pencils and a slide rule. Tim noticed all the diplomas on the wall. Of course, the first question after some awkward preliminary chit chat was, "Tell me about your schooling."

Tim was ready for that one. "I attended the St Mary's Catholic School until the second grade. The Sisters there taught me how to love to read and so much more. Then my parents died, so I ended up in Queen of Heaven Orphanage in Arlington Heights. I ran away from there and lived on the streets of Chicago where my real-life lessons began. I have never stopped reading, learning, and trying to improve."

The interviewer's jaw dropped, and he didn't know what to say next…"You come highly recommended by your supervisor, who informed me that there was never a technical issue you couldn't successfully tackle. How in the heck did you learn so much about our products and how to fix them with such efficiency?"

"I read about things that interest me, and I read every chance I have." Tim then explained how he had been amazed at the Western Electric display at the Columbian Exposition and how that cutting edge technology had fascinated him ever since.

Impressed and intrigued, the interviewer tried to dig deeper. "Tell me about your most challenging experience, and how you resolved it…"

Tim had too many such examples to count. Whichever one he selected to discuss with the interviewer, Tim knew he would blow away the competition. Tim then recalled when the Devil finally caught up with him in Little Cheyenne.

Chapter 10
THE DEVIL IS CLOSE BEHIND (1886)

DuValle continued to obsess about the runaways, constantly replaying a well-scripted drama in his head with the police knocking on the door of the orphanage looking for Brother DuValle to question him about salacious accusations levied against him by two orphans. As much as he tried to block that dark inner dialogue from his thoughts, it replayed over and over. DuValle rarely slept. He was now spending his time at a rectory a few blocks north of the Chicago River, the northern border of the Loop. Brother DuValle requested a room there as a basecamp from which he conducted his daily search operations for the orphans.

DuValle arranged a meeting with the nun in charge of the Catholic Outreach Program, which focused on unhoused children. "May I inquire of you, Sister, if you were a smart-witted runaway orphan, where would you flee to stay out of harm's way from an angry Brother with the church on his side and the police in pursuit?"

The Sister explained, "Dear Brother, the lost children are sadly plentiful throughout our menacing city, but mostly they congregate in areas where they are left alone by the police and the church. They seem to flock to neighborhoods that are incapable of change and seem utterly hopeless."

"Are there any such decrepit zones near the business center, Sister?"

"Oh yes, there is a horrible and wicked place just south of downtown, where the few police that occasionally frequent there are paid off to look the other way, and church representatives are fearful of muggings or worse. This hell on Earth is called Little Cheyenne. But, my Brother, please tell me you aren't planning to wander down there alone?"

The Sister continued, "I will pray hard that your missing boy is truly smart-witted. As I mentioned before, there are no honest police, clergy, or nuns present there to bring him back, and there unfortunately is no one to protect him from the many evils that are rampant in that wretched place. So many souls go to Little Cheyenne and are lost there forever."

DuValle strangely laughed in response. "If that little street rat can survive in Little Cheyenne, I most certainly can. So don't you worry about me, Sister." DuValle's eyes gleamed as he flashed a wicked smile.

The nun was taken aback by DuValle's laugh and response. "Brother, I would never refer to a homeless, orphaned child as a street rat. Are you sure you are well, Brother?"

DuValle did not answer. He just weirdly giggled and stared at the Sister.

"I will pray hard for you too, Brother."

Brother DuValle jumped into the parish carriage waiting outside and directed the driver to proceed to Little Cheyenne straight away. "Are you sure you want to head down there, Father?"

"Did I stutter? Little Cheyenne now!"

The driver said, "Okay Padre, your funeral." The driver found it very odd that DuValle was talking and laughing to himself during the entire route. Once the driver reached Little Cheyenne, he yelled, "This is as far as I go. Right across the street, Father, are the gates of hell."

(1886-1887)

Routines help people forget, and Tim found a rhythm to survive in Little Cheyenne. Tim slept on the floor in the bar. His alarm clock was Old Man Mush Mouth opening the front door at 9:00 a.m. Tim's routine was to wake up and grab whatever morsels of food he could find in the kitchen from the patrons' used plates from the night before. Mush would bark out a few orders and send Tim on various errands. Tim swept up and cleaned the bar, kitchen, and outhouse in the back alley. Then Tim typically would take a break and leave the saloon midday. During these breaks, Tim would explore Little Cheyenne, checking in with a few fellow street kids he had met, to talk and play made up games.

Late afternoons, Tim would head over to sweep the floors of The Badlands, one of the scores of brothels in Little Cheyenne. Maisey O'Shaughnessy ran the house of twenty or so working women. Maisey prided herself as running one of the few woman-owned brothels that was known as a "decently clean spot." Maisey always tried to treat her workers fairly.

Having grown up on the streets herself, Maisey had a soft spot in her heart for orphans. She came across Tim when she frequented Mush Mouth's one evening. Maisey mentioned to Mushy that she could use a hand around The Badlands. Mush Mouth pointed his cigar at Tim, saying "There's your man – he's a really good kid and smart too."

Tim would sweep up The Badlands' parlor before the evening rush and take out the garbage. In exchange, Tim could use the changing room to wash up every few days. Occasionally, during inclement weather, Maisey would serve Tim some tea and a meal, and if it was a quiet night she allowed Tim to sleep in one of the beds, a much more comfortable option than sleeping under the bar at Mush Mouth's or in the dirt alley.

Every evening just before the sun went down, Tim made sure he was back at the saloon. A lot of dangerous ghouls wandered the streets of Little Cheyenne after nightfall. Tim moved cases of beer up and down the stairs and cleaned whiskey glasses and dirty plates. When the bare-knuckle fights started at 8:00 p.m., Tim ran drinks back and forth to the seated patrons. Boxing was mostly illegal in the United States in the 1887 but flourished in places like Little Cheyenne where the coppers were bought and paid for. Marquis of Queensbury rules were not followed until John L. Sullivan defeated Gentleman Jim Corbett in 1892 in the first non-bare-knuckle heavyweight championship in America. Prior to that, fights were bare-knuckle prize fights where the boxers matched up based on general girth, height, and weight. Rounds were around five minutes, and the fight would continue until someone was knocked out or simply too exhausted or too bloodied to carry on, sometimes well into the 20th round.

Between rounds, Tim would climb into the ring and belt out an Irish standard at the top of his lungs given the lack of a microphone. The crowd, made up mostly of Irish immigrants who were already half a dozen drinks into the night, would sometimes sing along. At the end of the song, just before the next round was about to start, as tradition would have it, pennies were thrown into the ring and Tim would frantically scamper around to snatch them up. This was Tim's only paycheck.

Although the official closing time for saloons in Chicago was at or before midnight, at Mush Mouth Johnson's Emporium Saloon last call was when the last customer left the bar. Usually, the final drinks were served around 2:00 a.m. to a few stragglers, as a good many would depart for Maisey's Badlands and the like after the last fight at midnight.

Tim would forage in the kitchen for his dinner after he sang his last round. He'd then sweep up, clear the remaining dishes, and wash the tumblers. Exhausted, Tim would at long last find a spot at the quiet end of the bar or near the boxing ring, grab his blanket replete with moth holes that was hidden in a kitchen cabinet, and curl up to sleep.

If Tim was fortunate and allowed to crash at Maisey's, he would make a mad dash as fast as he could down the three blocks from Mush Mouth's to The Badlands, as it was the middle of the night. He remembered his father told him, "Never trust anyone you meet after midnight." This was so true, especially in Little Cheyenne. Other sayings from his dad that Tim often quoted included "Never play cards with a guy named Doc," "Never eat at a place called Ma's," "Look for the man the world calls wise, and hold on to him with a grip of steel," and "Mankind is seldom true." Sadly, Tim only recently understood what the last saying meant.

That was Tim's routine, day in and day out, night in and night out. Keeping busy kept Tim alive and kept the memories of his family, friends, happiness, and sadness mostly tucked away. His main focus was staying undercover and fed, which Tim managed to do for the next year in Little Cheyenne.

Tim's routine was disrupted one night while he was running the gauntlet down his regular route from Mush Mouth's to Maisey's at 2:00 a.m. Tim turned the corner, a half block from the Badlands, when he stopped dead in his tracks. He couldn't believe what his eyes discerned in the darkness one block away…the Devil!

A year earlier, after the parish carriage dropped DuValle off at the north end of Little Cheyenne for the first time, he took up residence in a nameless flop house above a nameless saloon. The room was dark, smelled of urine, and the mattress was bug-infested, none of which bothered DuValle to the extent it even registered with him. All he thought of was those two "street rats" mouthing off to a police officer. "I never did anything wrong. I provided comfort to lonely children. They are liars, liars." He used to pray for forgiveness and for the urges, as he called them, to go away. Now, all he prayed for was to find Conlon and McGregor.

Brother DuValle's lack of sleep was making it hard for him to concentrate during the day. What started out as quiet murmuring of words and giggling to himself had evolved into constant aloud self-dialogue and laughter. Initially he tried unsuccessfully to stifle this new insane tic, but ultimately the Brother wasn't even cognizant that he was talking to himself audibly. It was as if DuValle could not distinguish his inner voice from his speaking out loud. His internal dialogue was now for the world to hear.

DuValle's formerly immaculate Franciscan frock became even more wrinkled and filthy from the blowing dust of Little Cheyenne. His daily ritual over the next year was to walk up and down the streets looking for homeless children, then grabbing them and looking into their faces to see if it was Tim or Billy and, if not, showing the frightened children a picture while interrogating them whether they had seen either boy. The terrified boy or girl would scream and try to break free from the Brother's grasp. They, of course, would also disavow ever laying eyes on Tim before, even if they had. Street kids had a serious unwritten rule of not ratting anyone out. Any such violation resulted in immediate ostracizing with a beating before they were thrown out of the neighborhood. Many of these street waifs would have fit right in with the Wily Boys.

DuValle's insomnia became so severe that he resorted to taking "sleeping pills" purchased from one of the many Little Cheyenne drug peddlers. Only heaven knows what the drugs' ingredients were, but they did little to help him sleep and indeed made his psychosis worse. The Brother began to have a wild look in his eye. The mix of whatever pills he was popping and lack of sleep was creating hallucinations. The face of every boy or girl he accosted looked exactly like Tim, until the child screamed. DuValle would shake his head and rub his eyes until he saw the poor child's real face and then toss the frightened kid aside. He would carry on his search, yelling out nonsensical gibberish. "I know they are here! I've seen them!" He wandered the streets night and day and became known by the locals as the Mad Monk.

At 2:00 a.m. that night, on his way to Maisey's, Tim gasped when he saw the dark lumbering figure emerge into the light of a gas streetlamp a block away. He instantly recognized the Brother's

frock, albeit filthy and disgusting, with his unmistakable large frame, round glasses, and thinning hair. DuValle stopped swerving, waving his arms, and screaming and stood up straight in the middle of the dark and eerily quiet street. It seemed as though time stopped. The Devil then slowly turned his head in owl-like fashion toward Tim, as if he felt Tim's presence. Tim and the Devil at long last met again. The Devil laughed and pointed his long, crooked finger in Tim's direction. DuValle then hissed melodically, "I found you!"

DuValle started to run toward Tim, who was frozen with fear. Tim wanted to turn and flee, but like a nightmare we all have experienced he could not move his legs. The Devil's pace grew faster as he closed in on Tim. He was close enough that Tim could again see those dark lifeless eyes that had haunted him ever since that midnight visit in the orphanage a year earlier. That memory instantly transposed his fear to anger that coursed through Tim's body. In that split second, rage jumpstarted Tim's adrenal glands. Just as DuValle's outreached long, hairy fingers were inches from Tim's neck, Tim spun around and ducked under the Devil's lurching arms. DuValle grabbed nothing but air and fell awkwardly to the ground, his glasses flying several feet away. Tim, in a burst of speed at a velocity he never before attained, headed back toward Mush Mouth's and flew through the swinging doors just as Mr. Johnson was ready to close up. Mush Mouth could see Tim was sweating and had a look of terror in his eyes. "What in Sam Hill happened, kid, you okay?" Tim rushed through his explanation with as few words as possible, knowing time was of the essence. Mush Mouth's time in the Civil War taught him to think fast under pressure. At Mush Mouth's suggestion, Tim darted behind the bar and hid.

One minute later, the Devil darkened the saloon and threw the swinging doors open. Mush Mouth stood with his massive forearms crossed and his back leaned up against the bar chomping on his ever-present cigar. "We're closed, Padre."

DuValle strained to keep his composure. "I'm looking for a runaway boy from my orphanage. I saw him scamper in here."

"No one has come in since last call an hour ago."

With his uncontrollable giggle, DuValle grinned and asked, "May I look around to confirm the veracity of that statement?"

"Have at it, Father, but I'm locking up in a couple of minutes." Diverting DuValle away from the bar, Mush Mouth walked over to the boxing ring, turned up a lantern, and beckoned him to follow.

DuValle scanned the boxing room and slowly stalked around, looking behind the rows of seats and lifting the apron to look under the ring. DuValle then realized he was purposely being escorted to the boxing area, which meant Tim must be hiding in the bar. Rushing past Mush Mouth, DuValle jumped behind the bar and screamed, "Got ya!"

The bar was empty. Old Mush Mouth knew the diversion to the boxing room would give Tim enough time to sneak into the kitchen and run out the back door to the alley.

"Uh, Padre, there ain't no one back there. Are you feeling okay, pal? You don't look well."

Stunned, with eyes darting back and forth, DuValle confessed he wasn't sure how he felt, or whether he actually saw Conlon run into the saloon. He collapsed on a stool at the bar, removed his glasses, and rubbed his eyes, softly uttering, "I'm unsure about everything."

Mush Mouth took this opportunity to pour a whiskey for the Brother. DuValle at first was offended, pushing the glass away. "I confine my drinking to the Lord's blood at Mass."

Mush Mouth looked around the bar. "Ain't no one here, Father, and I sure as heck won't tell no one. Here, it will calm you down."

DuValle's body felt warm and comforted as the whiskey traveled down his gullet. "May I have another?" Mush Mouth grimaced when DuValle downed a few pills he grabbed from his cassock pocket with his fourth whiskey.

"Time to call it a night, Brother." Mush helped a wobbly DuValle to the door and watched the deteriorating man stumble down the street into darkness.

By the time DuValle finished his first drink, Tim had made it to Maisey's. She saw the fear and sadness in his face. Maisey held him and rubbed his back as he cried himself to sleep. This was the first time Tim had been hugged by anyone in over a year since his mother passed away. Tim thought about his mother's warm smile and felt comforted for the first time since she died.

(1897)

While choosing to relate this story as an example of a challenging situation, Tim answered the interview question with a more circumspect and sanitized version. Even so, the wide-eyed interviewer's mouth was agape. "That is amazing, at the age of eight you lived on the mean streets of Little Cheyenne? Why did you run away in the first place?"

Tim had never told anyone except Maisey about the assaults by DuValle until much later in life. Tim answered, "I missed my friends and siblings."

"Whatever happened to DuValle? Did you ever see him again? Did he ever get caught? Where did you run to next? How did you survive?" He almost forgot he was conducting an interview.

As the rapid-fire questions were posed, Tim was transported back to the morning after the terrifying encounter with DuValle, and how he planned to evade the Devil once and for all. Tim also recalled learning the meaning of the Yiddish saying, "Man plans, God laughs" the hard way.

(1887)

The next morning Maisey knocked on Tim's door with a breakfast of tea and a biscuit.

"Tim, I thought about your situation all night. I would like to go speak with Mr. Johnson about having you take a leave of absence from the saloon for a few weeks. Hopefully, this Mad Monk character will give up trying to find you and move on by then. In the meantime, you can work here full-time cleaning up and serving drinks."

"Thanks so much for everything, Mrs. O'Shaughnessy. May I go with you to speak with Mush Mouth, eh, Mr. Johnson? I want to thank him for getting me out of such a jam last night."

The two strolled down to Mush Mouth's, which was just opening up for the day. The whole way down Tim's head was on a swivel, his eyes darting back and forth on the lookout for the Devil. Maisey sported a hair pin that doubled as a lethal knife to use as needed in Little Cheyenne. Tim heard a story of how Maisey once jammed her hair pin in the eye of a mugger so deep that it pierced his frontal lobe. He knew Maisey was ready if the Devil approached.

Arriving at the bar, Tim ran over to shake Mr. Johnson's hand and thank him for his help. "No worries, kid, I'm sure you'd do the same for me – us working stiffs in Little Cheyenne have to stick together."

Maisey and Mush Mouth had known one another for many years, as he was a regular customer of hers when he was a younger man. They spoke quietly at the bar outside of Tim's earshot. Tim picked up a broom and began sweeping. Mush Mouth looked over. "That's why I like that kid. Always taking the bull by the horns." The plan was for Tim to stay away from the bar for a few weeks until the smoke cleared. Both Mush Mouth and Maisey agreed to get feelers out on the erratic and insane Brother the locals called the "Mad Monk" to learn where he was staying, what he did during the day, and where he bought those pills.

Maisey remarked, "I've seen it before. At the rate the Mad Monk is going, it's just a matter of time before he is swallowed up by Little Cheyenne."

Mushy noted, "He sure liked the whiskey I served him – not seen a man of the cloth down it with such vigor. I'll have one of my guys find out where he is staying and see what he's up to. I'll let you know. Take care of the boy. Make sure he keeps practicing his singing and working on hitting those high notes without screaming."

DuValle got out of his cot, hungover from the cheap whiskey he threw down at Mush Mouth's the night before. That was his first drink besides wine at Mass since being a teenager. His insomnia grew even worse, with his mind racing about capturing the runaways and replaying that dreaded scenario that haunted him of being arrested and defrocked for sexually assaulting the orphans. However, for the first time in over a year a new obsession entered his thoughts – whiskey. He dreamt of how it had provided such a warm and soothing, albeit temporary, comfort to his tortured soul. DuValle's new routine was to have an eye-opener in the bar on the first floor of the flop house. He seldom bathed of late or even washed up, and his cassock was almost unrecognizable as it was beyond wrinkled and disgustingly filthy with street dust. While the "sleeping pills" didn't cure his insomnia, he craved them if he didn't dose a couple times a day.

When he thought of it, DuValle would finish his drink in whatever bar he was visiting and wander outside to continue his search for Conlon and McGregor. DuValle focused his search efforts in the two or three blocks surrounding Mush Mouth's, where he had laid eyes on "that little street rat." The Mad Monk would grab every kid he came across and could get his large filthy hands onto, convinced at first it was Tim, then angrily toss them aside when he realized his mistake. "Curses! Conlon's throat was within inches of my hands!"

For the job of shadowing DuValle, Mush Mouth asked his friend

Ira Shapiro, a Jewish immigrant from Austria, who had served as an intelligence officer in Sergeant Johnson's (Mushy's) platoon in the Civil War. Ira was the smartest man in the troop and an easy pick for Johnson. Post-war, Shapiro was a frequent and skilled bare-knuckle boxer at Mush Mouth's, which was how he earned most of his money. Being fiercely loyal to Mush Mouth, who saved Shapiro's life during a battle toward the end of the war, he quickly accepted the new mission to surveil DuValle. "You mean that crazy priest who yells at everyone and talks to ghosts in the street? All I'll have to do is listen for him."

Ira located the Mad Monk after a couple of hours of asking people in the street when they last saw him. Shapiro tailed him for the rest of the afternoon, following the Devil from tavern to tavern, with his bizarre intermittent strolls on the streets where he'd harass little children, grab them, stare into their faces, and then shove them aside. In the evening Ira followed DuValle down an alley to where a known drug dealer conducted business. Then the Mad Monk returned to the bars and hassled innocent kids along the way in between belts and popping pills. This pattern continued well into the night until DuValle returned to his room at the flop house in the wee hours of the morning.

Ira followed DuValle for three days. Although the Mad Monk was volatile and erratic, Ira felt he now knew the Mad Monk's general routine, which itself was fairly predictable. Ira later reported to Mush Mouth that DuValle was an "alcoholic drug addict with psychotic hallucinations – a tortured man who seldom slept, was entirely unkempt, and was mean-spirited to everyone he encountered, especially the homeless children." Ira was seriously concerned that if the Mad Monk got his hands on Tim it would be a very dangerous and likely violent encounter. From a few brief conversations Ira had with DuValle at one of the bars, Ira thought with a high degree of probability that "DuValle is not conducting a locate and retrieval operation – he is on a seek and destroy mission." Indeed, Shapiro was concerned that the Mad Monk was going to kill the boy.

Mushy asked Ira to follow the Mad Monk one more night and to try to engage him to determine how long DuValle planned to be in Little Cheyenne. Ira agreed and set out to find the Mad Monk at 7:00 p.m. Knowing DuValle's usual haunts at that particular time, Ira happened upon DuValle stumbling in the street a few blocks away. Passersby tried to get out of his way or pushed DuValle aside and swore at him if he got too close. But suddenly, DuValle deviated from his regular routine by proceeding down a dark walkway between two buildings leading to an alley, one that he had not frequented during the previous three days of surveillance. Ira tailed DuValle down the alley while staying out of view. The alley was full of garbage cans and rats. There were also several street children hunkered down for the evening, covered with rags and cardboard as their makeshift beds. Ira observed that while this was a new detour from his usual antics, DuValle appeared to know where he was going. This was not the Devil's first visit to this out-of-the-way nook where a dozen or so kids were huddled as they prepared to go to sleep.

Ira was in the shadows twenty feet behind and had a terrible feeling of dread come over him as he watched DuValle approach the sleeping children. One of the boys heard the Devil near and screamed, "He's here again, scram!" All scampered away except for one slight little boy who was not quick enough to his feet. DuValle grabbed the boy by the neck and slapped him. When the Devil began to remove the boy's belt and stick his hand down the boy's trousers, Ira had seen enough. Without a word, Shapiro ran over to DuValle and coldcocked him with one of his famous right crosses. DuValle dropped like a rock.

Stunned but still conscious, DuValle looked up at Ira, who said, "If you ever touch another kid, I'll fucking kill you." The Devil started to laugh hysterically. Shocked by this reaction, Ira stared back into his dark, lifeless eyes and said, "You really are mad."

When DuValle got back to his knees, he spit at Ira. Not a wise move – this prompted Ira, mostly out of instinct, to beat the ever-living crap out of DuValle. Ira threw a dozen vicious right and left bare-knuckle punches to the Devil's face. Even after he lay in the mud unconscious, Ira drilled three more whacks to his bloodied face. DuValle's glasses were smashed, with pieces of the broken lens embedded in his swollen, blood-soaked cheeks and eyes, making his face unrecognizable. Ira stood up, breathing heavily from adrenaline, and returned the favor by spitting on the motionless bloodied body. "Fuck you, you piece of shit."

Ira turned and walked away. The children were huddled around the corner watching what had transpired and collectively breathed a sigh of relief. They then ran over to DuValle and grabbed anything of value – his ring, pearl rosary beads, and wallet. The little lad who was accosted gave DuValle a swift boot to the face before they all scrambled off to find a new location to sleep that night.

Ira returned to Sergeant Mush Mouth with a full report of what transpired that evening. Ira's knuckles on both hands were swollen and covered in blood, with glass shards from DuValle's spectacles embedded in his fist. "My God, Ira, this Mad Monk was truly a monster. I say good riddance to him, and God bless you for ridding us of that wretched soul." Mushy sent Ira over to Maisey's to share the news of the Mad Monk's demise and stuffed twenty dollars in his pocket for the effort.

The next morning, one of the kids returned to the alley to retrieve some of his chattels left behind before they fled. The boy slowly approached the bloodied heap of a body to look to see if he could snatch any other valuables they may have missed. As the child grabbed the gold cross from the necklace, the Devil's right index finger jerked and he gasped in a breath.

The boy screamed and ran away. "The Devil is alive!"

No one saw the Mad Monk for months, although Tim heard the other street kids tell stories of having seen him, badly injured and crawling on his belly out of the alley in the middle of the night. As DuValle learned, however, for some tortured souls, staying alive is a worse fate than death.

(1888-1891)

Tim's usual routine resumed, spending half his time at Mush Mouth's and the other at Maisey's Badlands. Tim began to actually save a few pennies, that turned into quarters, that turned into dollars. When Tim turned ten in 1888, nearly two years since fleeing the orphanage, he began tending bar a few shifts at The Emporium when Mushy needed a break, although he had to utilize the assistance of a stepstool to reach across the bar. Tim also made time to resume his weekly trips to the Chicago Public Library, which he had done before his parents died.

The Chicago Public Library opened to the public on January 1, 1873. Before the Great Fire in 1871, there were a few privately operated libraries within the city, which could only be accessed by members for an annual fee. A majority of books in these private libraries, and those belonging to the Chicago Library, were destroyed in the blaze.[17]

"Responding to the disaster of the Great Chicago Fire, Thomas Hughes, British Member of Parliament and author of *Tom Brown's School Days*, led a drive in Great Britain to 'present a Free Library to Chicago, to remain there as a mark of sympathy now, and a keepsake and a token of true brotherly kindness forever.' The result of this endeavor was approximately 7,000 volumes being donated to the new library from universities, publishers, and individuals, including Queen Victoria and Alfred Lord Tennyson."[18]

The impending British book donation created an issue for Chicago's municipal leaders. There was no provision in either city or state law which allowed cities to raise funds to maintain free public libraries. A petition was quickly organized by leading Chicagoans that asked then Mayor Medill to call a public meeting to establish a free public library for Chicago. The result was the Illinois Library Act of 1872, which was soon followed by a city ordinance proclaiming the establishment of the Chicago Public Library.[19]

Donations flowed in, not just from Great Britain, but from many other European countries, including a significant donation of books written in German for the many German-speaking residents of the city. Books and money continued to pour in from all over the United States and from wealthy individuals and business leaders in Chicago. On January 1, 1873, the library opened in one of the few structures which had survived the fire, an iron water tank that was no longer in use located in the Loop at the corner of Adams and LaSalle Streets. By October 1873, William Frederick Poole, one of the foremost librarians in the country at the time, was appointed City Librarian.[20]

During its first 24 years, the library moved from location to location. In 1887, the newly constructed Central Library on Michigan Avenue, between Randolph and Washington Streets, now known as the Chicago Cultural Center, opened. The library remained at this location for almost 100 years.[21]

Tim would check out a book once a week and try to read it before his next visit. This was Tim's education for the remainder of his life. Initially, Tim attempted to select his books based on his second-grade curriculum, figuring those were the subjects he was missing. Tim also would read the newspapers left behind at Mush Mouth's, typically *The Daily News* or the *Tribune*, and if a topic interested him or there was something about which he wanted to learn more, Tim would ask the librarian for a recommendation. The librarians were impressed with this young boy with the voracious appetite for reading and enthusiastically suggested books for Tim to maintain pace with his peers in school. As the months passed, the otherwise fourth-grade aged Tim was reading at a high school level. Further, Tim was blessed with a photographic memory, giving him near-total recall of anything he read.

In the afternoons during autumn, Tim usually strolled south down Michigan Avenue on his way back from the library to admire the leaves changing to glorious colors on the thousands of trees in Lake Park, later named Grant Park. He would occasionally pass by and notice a random woman who bore a resemblance to his mother or a girl who reminded him of Molly. Tim's heart never stopped aching from being separated from his family and friends. The year was 1888, and it had been two years since fleeing Queen of Heaven. Tim longed for the day he could safely return to his old neighborhood and look up Molly and a few of the Wily Boys. He hadn't heard or seen DuValle in a year since Ira beat the tar out of him. Most presumed the Devil was dead, except the boy who saw his finger twitch and the older woman who saw him crawl out of the alley in the middle of the night a day after the beating.

(1887)

DuValle lay in the dirt, unconscious, for a day. As he started to come to, excruciating pain shot throughout his head and face. He pulled the shards of glass from his cheeks and eyelids. He could only slightly open his left eye. His right eye was swollen shut from the pounding. Blood was pouring from his mouth and down his throat, making it difficult to breathe and causing him to choke and throw up blood. DuValle's brain had taken so many hits delivered by Ira that it was difficult to discern what just happened. Everything seemed to proceed in slow motion with noises, including his gasping for air, being distorted as if he was in a tunnel. Things were dire for DuValle. His brain was swelling, he suffered a concussion, he lost vision from the lens of his glasses exploding into his right eye, his breathing was critically labored, and he was losing a tremendous amount of blood. Nevertheless, the Devil's primal instincts took over, and he began to slither on his stomach through the alleyway and back to the street. It was three in the morning by the time he made it out of the alley. An unhoused woman went over to check on him, but she shrieked at the sight of DuValle's face and ran away. A couple of prostitutes walked over to the heap of a body lying in the mud. The women were horrified. "I've seen him before…that's the Mad Monk."

No one, including DuValle, knew precisely how he made it back to the flop house, but he woke up in his cot two days later. DuValle either managed to crawl back two blocks and up a flight of stairs to his room, or more likely the two prostitutes helped him. How ironic to think ladies of the evening, who DuValle loathed, judged, and scorned so vehemently during his tenure in Little Cheyenne, were the ones that showed him compassion that ended up saving his life. Blood was everywhere – the cot, the sheets, the blankets – dried blood caked his face and sealed his eyes shut. A trail of blood streaked up the flight of stairs and down the hallway to his room at the flop house. A worker at the bar in the building noticed the blood streak and followed the trail to DuValle's room. The worker must have then alerted someone at a nearby church, as two nuns with nursing training during the Civil War finally arrived later in the day and tended to DuValle, who was confined to his bed.

As an act of mercy for a downtrodden man of the cloth, the nuns visited DuValle several days in a row, cleaning wounds and changing bandages. The Sisters noticed that the Brother was mostly unresponsive and incoherent and were concerned he had suffered brain damage. They started to clean up the room but eventually gave up due to the hopeless amount of blood, garbage, vomit, and feces that covered the bed, carpet, and walls. The stench required the merciful sisters to cover their faces with perfumed scarves before they entered the room. The nuns never could determine with which parish DuValle was associated or how he ended up in this location in this condition, as everything on his person had been stolen. They reported everything to the Monsignor of their parish just north of Little Cheyenne, who thanked them for their acts of mercy but instructed the Sisters that their mission with this nameless Brother had come to an end and was no longer their parish's problem.

Washing his hands of the Brother, the Monsignor announced, "Unfortunately, many a man has been lost to the sins of Little Cheyenne. May God bless and have mercy on this lost soul." The Monsignor, of course, knew it was DuValle from a recent visit by one of the Brothers from Queen of Heaven searching for their lost priest. The Monsignor decided it was best to not publicize this fallen man of the cloth and strategically swept his story under the filthy, bloody rug.

As the weeks and months passed, DuValle managed to amble down the hallway and labor down the stairs to the bar below, where he drank whiskey and ate whatever disgusting grub they were serving. He continued to utter nonsense and uncontrollably laugh out loud, but with less vigor. DuValle was no longer capable of stringing words together to speak a lucid sentence. He would return to his cot covered in his own excrement and dried blood, where he would lay awake staring at the ceiling for hours. DuValle would seldom leave the building, and his color became ghastly pale.

Several months later, while the Mad Monk made his afternoon visit to the bar, the bartender grabbed him by the back of the neck and tossed him through the door out into the street. "Sorry, you disgusting old man, you can't come back here. That goes for your room too. Between the stench and not paying rent, we are done with you – don't come back." DuValle followed the bartender back into the bar. Before the bartender turned around ready to bounce him outside again, the Devil grabbed a large steak knife on one of the tables and held it up toward the charging bartender, who instantly stopped and held up his hands. DuValle slowly walked backwards out of the bar, all the while holding up the stolen knife and laughing.

DuValle was now penniless and lived on the streets. It was late fall in Chicago, and temperatures were about to plummet to the 30s at night, with the cold winds blowing off of Lake Michigan. The Devil was such a hideous sight with his scarred face, right eye permanently closed, mud and blood on his face, and his cassock soiled with the garbage, mud, and human waste in which he slept. DuValle foraged for food in dumpsters, fighting other folks living in the back alleys over a rotten head of lettuce.

(1890)

On his way back from the library en route to Mush Mouth's, Tim heard screaming as he approached a side alley. Tim stopped and peeked down the alley to see what the ruckus was. He saw a man sitting on the ground among the garbage cans and rodents, yelling obscenities then laughing wildly. He had a patch on his eye, and his emaciated cheeks were badly scarred. He seemed to be carrying on an unintelligible conversation and arguing with imaginary demons. This shell of a man held up a knife with both hands that he kept brandishing. Tim walked closer and saw he donned an overworn cassock now black from years of filth, and the chain around his neck was missing the gold crucifix. Tim had to get even closer and walked within two feet of him to confirm it was indeed Brother DuValle. He looked up at Tim for a fleeting second before his eyes darted away to address an imaginary ghost. DuValle wasn't even aware that Tim was standing right in front of him.

"The Devil has you by the throat, Brother DuValle. And you got exactly what you deserved, you son of a bitch." Tim walked away, feeling his constant fear of DuValle was entirely wiped away. Tim felt his shoulders lift from the relief of this burden. The terrifying demon that haunted Tim for the past four years had been exorcised, leaving DuValle with a lunatic mind, broken body, and godless soul.

Tim's plan was to stay another year or so in Little Cheyenne until he was forgotten by the cops and the Archdiocese, not knowing his case had been closed by both entities long ago. Without the hot breath of the Devil on his neck, Tim grew into a bit of a rhythm. He had two decent jobs relatively speaking for an orphan in Little Cheyenne. Maisey and Mushy looked out for him, and he had a few friends on the streets. The thing that Tim grew to cherish most of all was his freedom. Yes, he worked most of his waking hours, had little money, and worried daily about food and where he would sleep at night. But Tim really came and went whenever and wherever he wished and basically did whatever he wanted, with the only adult supervision coming from a barkeep and the owner of a brothel.

As time marched on, Tim developed, now at the age of 13, some less than desirable habits that rubbed off on him from Mush Mouth's. Tim started smoking, chewing tobacco, and drinking whiskey and beer, like 99% of the denizens of Little Cheyenne. While the legal drinking age to consume alcohol in 1890 was 21 in Illinois, Mush Mouth would serve a shot to anyone with 20 cents. The older street boys that Tim hung out with also had regular jobs and would pass around a bottle as they gathered in the back alleys to hang out at night.

Chapter 11
CORA (1891)

The interviewer was now more intrigued with Tim's story. "How are you now? Are you married? Do you have a steady gal?" Those sort of personal interview questions were commonplace in 1897. Tim was single at the time, but this provocative question brought Tim to again dream of his first love…

Tim discovered another interest while working at Maisey's. One of the new talents that started working for Maisey was Cora Zielinski, a tall and slender, blonde and blue-eyed 18-year-old immigrant from Poland. Tim was sweeping up when he first laid eyes on her. Tim froze. Cora was wearing a silk dress with a slit that showed off her long legs. His heart skipped multiple beats. Tim tried to say hello and introduce himself, but for the first time in his life he couldn't find the words.

Maisey, who was showing Cora around and making introductions to the other women, came to the rescue. "This nice young man is Tim Conlon, who has been helping us out for the last few years. And Tim, this is the lovely Cora, who is our newest lady. Tim, maybe you can show Miss Cora the upstairs." Tim managed to get out, "Will do, follow me." As Tim trailed Cora upstairs to the bedrooms, she turned toward Tim and smiled when she noticed his infatuation. Tim was amazed with how nice she smelled; it made him dizzy.

Tim told some of his older friends during one of the late evening gatherings in the alley about the lovely, attractive Cora. The teenage boys asked excruciating details about her various body part dimensions. They also provided much unsolicited advice about what Tim needed to do and how to accomplish the same. As it goes with young teenage boys, their bark was worse than their bite, and their tales of the fairer sex were greatly exaggerated, if not entirely made up. Of course, Tim did not have a father or an older brother around to tell him about the birds and the bees. Tim walked out of that bull session with the lads even more confused, more frightened, and now even a bit disgusted. "Holy smokes, a lot of that seems more like a science experiment than making love."

Cora immigrated from Warsaw to Chicago at the age of 14 with her older sister. Her parents paid for the travel expenses and arranged housing with a distant relative who lived near the Union Stockyards in the Back of the Yards neighborhood, located on the South Side between the Bridgeport and Canaryville neighborhoods. The plan was to have the sisters work and send a good percentage of their earnings back home to their parents in Poland. The hope was for the parents to save enough to immigrate to the United States as well. For a year before they left, Cora and her sister took English lessons but were barely functionally literate in English by the time they arrived. Initially, work was hard to find, even more so for immigrant women. Their cousin lined them up with jobs at the Stockyards; work was work.

Chicago's location in the center of the States and its railroad system connecting the Northeast to the West made it an ideal location for a massive meatpacking operation. Ranchers and cowboys in the Plains and the West drove livestock to railroad hubs, such as Abilene, Kansas.[22] Cattle, cows, and hogs were transported in railcars to Chicago's meatpacking distributors, known generally as the Stockyards.[23] The livestock was slaughtered, processed, and packed. Packaged meat was held in cold storage before it was transported across the United States by railroad.[24] Thus, Chicago became known as "America's Butcher."

The Union Stockyards, incorporated in 1865, covered 345 acres. Thousands of steers, cows, and hogs were herded on a nearly continuous basis into the plants of Armour, Swift, and Morris to be slaughtered and dressed. This industry relied on large numbers of de minimus wage labor performing a highly specific task in an assembly line of animals being systematically slaughtered.[25] This process was really more a disassembly line as animals were dismembered, gutted, and butchered. The workers put in ungodly hours seven days a week doing a simple and monotonous job in utterly filthy and blood-soaked conditions.

When Upton Sinclair published *The Jungle* in 1906, a horrified nation read of poisoned rats ground up for sausage and of hogs dead from cholera used for fancy-grade lard. Independent investigations confirmed these evils.[26] The outcry that followed brought passage of the Pure Food, Drink, and Drug Act.[27] The new law offered protection, and it also set a precedent for future federal oversight and of industry regulation.[28]

Cora was a natural beauty with high cheekbones and a knockout figure. She attracted constant attention from men, young and old. Two years of slaughtering pigs and cattle was all Cora could take. During a lunch break one day, a coworker mentioned a job fair downtown for people interested in office work. Cora voiced a concern that she had no secretarial skills or experience. To which the coworker replied, "With those looks, you'll have no problem getting a job downtown – as long as you wash all the blood, guts, and stink out of your hair."

Cora decided to give it a try and headed to the job fair where numerous businesses hired office staff, including secretaries and file clerks. Being a fairly honest person, Cora kept admitting her real age of 16 when she visited the various stations. Unfortunately, most of the Loop-based businesses had a minimum age requirement of 18 years old. Cora was disheartened after striking out at every interview and left the room dejected.

As Cora walked outside, she sobbed into her hands, dreading the thought of a lifetime of slaughtering livestock. Just then, a comforting hand touched her shoulder. "My dear, what is wrong?" Maisey

O'Shaughnessy would stand outside the job fairs downtown and wait for attractive young women that seemed unhappy to leave. "Let me buy you a tea next door and let's talk." Maisey was a tremendous salesperson and offered a relatively lucrative alternative to stripping intestines out of slaughtered pigs. Maisey was impressed with Cora's striking face and learned she had several boyfriends in Chicago during the past year, meaning she was presumably sexually active. Maisey too had an 18-year-old policy, based not only on the law but mainly on her sense of morality. When asked how old she was, Cora had learned her tough lesson at the job fair, so it was now easy to lie and say "eighteen." Cora would have taken just about any job offered to her. She desperately wanted to make more money to move out of the hovel in the Back of The Yards neighborhood and send more money to her parents in Warsaw. Cora reluctantly agreed to become the newest addition at The Badlands.

Tim's crush on Cora was obvious to everyone at Maisey's. All of the girls who had known Tim since he was eight thought it was sweet to watch the now 13-year-old fall head over heels for the lovely young 16-year-old Cora, who everyone thought was 18 and who could have passed for mid-20s. It was difficult for Tim to watch the nonstop assembly line of men going upstairs with Cora night after night. Although she liked the hours and the money, Cora hated what she had become. She likened the line of men to the pigs at the Stockyards. Instead of systematically pulling the animals apart piece by piece, she imagined that she was taking a piece of the soul of each man with whom she had a tryst. Cora felt that her heart too was being slaughtered and pulled apart, trick by trick. Cora's job sickened her, and she began to hate men.

Tim was different, being always overly friendly and nice. He would do favors for Cora, retrieve her meals and drinks, and most of all he would never make a pass – always a gentleman. Cora would playfully flirt with Tim, but never in a teasing or mean-spirited way.

Being only three years apart, Tim was closer in age to Cora than any of the women at Maisey's and any of the johns. Cora and Tim became friends and would occasionally go for a walk or run an errand together and talk.

One winter's night late in the evening, everyone had cleared out for the night except Tim and Cora. Tim was cleaning up, and Cora was waiting to see if any more patrons would show up, but none did due to the cold and rather snowy evening. She decided to call it a night and went to say goodnight to Tim. Cora, who was a few inches taller, looked into Tim's eyes for a brief moment. Without thinking, Tim moved in for a kiss on her lips. Cora smiled and allowed the kiss. "Not bad for a first kiss," she thought. The kiss was followed by an embrace that lasted for several minutes. For Tim, it was a kiss that lasted a lifetime. Doesn't everyone remember his or her first kiss?

Cora stopped and with a lovely smile said, "I have to go home, it's late." Tim asked to walk Cora home to her newly rented apartment several blocks away. Always the gentleman, that Tim…

When they arrived at Cora's building Tim suggested that, because the hour was late and the area was dangerous, he should walk her up to her apartment on the second floor. Cora, thinking it was so sweet that Tim had escorted her home on such a cold, snowy night, agreed. When they arrived at the door, Cora invited Tim in to warm up. She poured a glass of whiskey for herself and for Tim, then went behind a changing screen in her tiny studio apartment. She could hardly wait to remove her makeup and get out of her gown, corset, stockings, and tall skinny heels at the end of every evening and change into her pajamas. That ritual allowed Cora to treat her job as though she was an actress playing a part in makeup and costume, with the play ending once she changed clothes. Cora walked from behind the screen as a pretty, bright-eyed, rosy-cheeked 16-year-old.

Tim and Cora had talked for what seemed like hours when Cora moved over to sit next to Tim on the couch. Cora wanted to further escape from her life at The Badlands by being intimate with someone who actually liked her for who she was as a person, with no money changing hands. She realized she was three years older than the 13-year-old boy, but a few whiskeys softened her guilt. This time it was Cora who went in for a kiss. While embracing in a long kiss, with eyes closed, they rolled over to lie down on the couch. Tim was equal parts excited and nervous. "Cora, I have never done this before." Cora whispered in her sensual Polish accent, "I will show you the way, my sweet Tim."

Tim walked over to Mush Mouth's saloon the next morning with an extra spring in his step, whistling a tune all the way there. After his gig singing between rounds of the bare-knuckled fights that night, Mushy remarked, "That was one of your best nights since you started. You really hit the high notes tonight, kid."

Cora was all Tim could think about. The following day, Tim took extra time to wash himself in Mush Mouth's bathroom. He ran down the street to go to work at Maisey's even though he was an hour early. A few hours later, Cora sashayed into Maisey's. Tim had butterflies in his stomach, and in his groin, the moment he laid eyes on her. Everything else stopped for Tim as he watched Cora walk into the main parlor in slow motion. She walked over to Tim with a smile and a friendly hug, whispering in his ear, "We have to talk – meet me upstairs in ten minutes." Tim was so dizzy with excitement he nearly fainted.

After an extraordinarily long ten minutes, Tim made his way to Cora's room upstairs, where she was putting on her makeup and fixing her long blonde hair to metamorphose into her alter ego. Tim excitedly blurted out, "Cora, last night was the most wonderful night of my life."

"Tim, I had a lovely evening too. But we cannot tell a soul. If one of the girls hears about it, the news would surely make its way to Maisey. You know as well as I do that Maisey has strict rules. If she found out that one of her women had a fling with another worker, who is only 13 years old, Maisey would fire us both on the spot."

Tim almost started to cry. "But can we see each other again?"

"I'm afraid not – I made a terrible mistake. You are a wonderful boy, and we can remain friends here. I love so much your company. But as far as seeing one another as boyfriend and girlfriend, we simply cannot do. I am so sorry, Timmy." Such soul-crushing words that every male has heard at least once during their lifetime.

Tim was completely gutted but knew there was no talking Cora into seeing him again. She was right though. Maisey would fire them immediately.

Tim met up with his older friends that evening for their weekly Saturday night gathering in one of the back alleys in Little Cheyenne. Of course, the lads interrogated Tim about any progress made with Cora. The whiskey bottle was passed around, and Tim took more than his usual few swigs. As the second bottle emptied and the buzz grew stronger, Tim hinted to the lads that he kissed Cora. The lads goaded him into providing more details about his encounter with Cora by challenging and accusing Tim of being "full of shit." What put Tim over the edge was the suggestion that he was being less than manly by not making any moves beyond a kiss. Tim, feeling his manhood was being called into question, coupled with a whiskey-clouded brain, finally exposed what had transpired with Cora. All the boys were stunned and screamed out with excitement. Males living vicariously through their friend's sexual adventures existed with equal vigor in 1890 as it does today.

One of the newer guys that joined the group uttered a particularly crass comment about Cora in a poor attempt at humor. Tim, who was much younger and smaller than the newcomer, said, "What did you just say?" As the other boy looked into Tim's face and started to repeat the insult, Tim's alcohol-infused anger and occasional wicked Irish temper propelled him to wildly throw a haymaker upside the other boy's head. Boxers at Mush Mouth's had taught Tim the basics of boxing and how to defend himself in a fight.

The boy was stunned for a moment and fell to one knee. Unfortunately for Tim, the lad got up, rushed, and tackled Tim to the ground. Both boys got in several punches, and the other lads quickly intervened to separate the scrappers to break it up. Tim walked away with a bloody nose and shiner. The other boy yelled, "Are you running to your whore girlfriend for a kiss?" Tim rushed back at the boy with another punch and the whole scene was repeated. Tim got the worst of it, but both fighters had enough and went their separate ways at the group's suggestion.

Tim learned a valuable lesson of how one should never kiss and tell. A few weeks after the scuffle, the new guy saw Cora and a couple of the other Badland's ladies walking down the street. Still sore about Tim's sucker punch, he yelled out, "Hey Miss Cora, when are you and Timmy boy getting hitched?" Cora scorned in his direction, causing the troublemaker to scamper away. The other ladies quizzed poor Cora the rest of the way to Maisey's. Cora laid it off as a young boy's crush.

It was only a matter of minutes before one of the women, who was jealous of Cora's beauty and popularity, ratted Cora out to Maisey. Upon hearing this news, Maisey summoned Tim and Cora to meet at once in her office.

Maisey in her sternest voice conveyed what she had just heard. "Please tell me, Cora, that nothing happened between you and Mr. Conlon here, who I might remind you is THIRTEEN YEARS OLD!" Cora, who was brutally honest to a fault, began to confess the story, starting with the innocent kiss in the parlor a few weeks back.

As Cora was about to carry on and tell the rest of the story, Tim interrupted. "Ms. Maisey, it was all my fault. I went right up to Cora to give her a kiss and she immediately pushed me away. I quickly apologized to Cora, and we remain friends. I'm afraid I stupidly mentioned this to one of my idiot friends who drinks too much, and I understand he yelled out something inappropriate to Ms. Cora. Again, all my fault. Cora did absolutely nothing wrong."

Maisey, who had been watching the playful flirting between Cora and Tim for months, was skeptical. Still fuming, "Cora, you're not entirely innocent here, you led the boy on." Cora couldn't look either Tim or Maisey in the eye.

Tim again chivalrously fell on his sword. "No, ma'am – she made clear to me early on that we were only friends and she was not interested in any relationship with me beyond friendship."

Cora was shaking and couldn't speak. Maisey said, "I'm afraid it's time we part company, Tim. This is no place to work for a young man with raging hormones." She handed Tim $50, said she loved him, and told him that if he ever needed anything to come by and let her know.

Cora started crying. "Maisey, isn't there anything else we can do – suspend him or dock his pay a couple of weeks? Please."

Maisey's mind was made up. She hugged Tim and left the parlor. Cora, sobbing, also gave Tim a hug goodbye. "You know where to find me." Tim walked out the front door out onto the streets, completely devastated and, worse, completely alone once again.

(1897)

The interviewer was already inclined to extend an offer to Tim to fill the Research and Development position at Western Electric. But given Tim's dearth of academic credentials, the interviewer needed to drill down on Tim's work experience. "Tim, let's move on. As fascinating as your early life story is, I need to hear about your various jobs before coming to Western Electric." Tim had already discussed his boxing ring crooning and his odd jobs at Mush Mouth's Saloon Emporium. Tim wisely decided to skip the part about his part-time job at Maisey's House of Ill Repute.

Chapter 12
TIME TO MOVE ON (1891)

In 1891, now nearly the age of 14, after surviving nearly six years in Little Cheyenne, Tim sensed it was time to leave. While he would never forget Cora, Tim feared if he didn't get the heck out of the neighborhood now, he may never leave. Tim was concerned he would become trapped and morph into one of the many nameless faces wandering the streets, the regulars at Mush Mouth's, the johns lined up at Maisey's, the orphans huddled in the back alleys at night, or the mentally disturbed like Brother DuValle. All seemed to have a piece of their souls taken away with each passing day, decreasing the odds of ever leaving Little Cheyenne alive, and becoming broken beyond repair.

Tim walked into Mushy's one last time. He thanked Mr. Johnson for being the first person since his parents died that watched out for him. Mushy knew this was best for the boy. He didn't ask any questions or inquire into what had happened. Instead, Johnson went into the till for some cash and handed Tim a bunch of crinkled-up, beer-stained dollar bills. Mushy was not the most affectionate person and so he felt a little awkward when Tim ran up to him and hugged him. Mush Mouth smiled through his ever-present stogie, "You're a good kid, we'll miss ya."

According to a tip from one of Tim's older back-alley friends, the Hooley Theater in the north part of the Loop was hiring. The job entailed babysitting the children of whatever theater group or entertainers were performing and staying in the hotel above the theater. The Hooley also provided quarters with a bed for the babysitters at the end of the evening. This was a perfect place for Tim to transition out of Little Cheyenne. Located at 124 West Randolph Street, the Hooley was just a mile north of Mush Mouth's and several miles south of Tim's old family home.

Tim walked into the doors of The Hooley under its large sign, "The Parlor House of Comedy." R. M. Hooley's theater had opened on October 17, 1872. The theater was briefly called Haverly's in 1876-77, then reverted to its original name until Hooley's death in 1893. Tim interviewed with Hooley himself, who was in desperate need of someone to replace the recently fired talent babysitter who was caught stealing a brooch from one of the lead actresses. Hooley hired Tim on the spot. Tim was paid twenty-five cents a day, plus dinner and a place to sleep at night, which was essentially a cot in a broom closet. Nevertheless, it was still the most comfortable and only bed he had slept in over six years other than the one-off nights at Maisey's. Tim found chasing little kids around all night was an exhausting job, and quite boring compared to singing at Mushy's and sweeping up at The Badlands. After the children he was watching at long last fell asleep, Tim would open the door and sit in the hallway where he could listen to the performance from the theatre below echoing through the vents. These quiet times were when Tim would close his eyes and often dream of Cora. Tim heard the score of every musical that came through the theater over the next several months, including *The Mikado*, *The Pirates of Penzance*, and *Around the World in 80 Days*. Later in life, Tim would break into those songs he memorized at family gatherings or friends' parties.

Tim found the actors and actresses were very nice at a surface level but typically extremely narcissistic. After a few months that provided Tim with hot meals and a warm, mostly clean bed through the cold winter months, Tim was desperate to find a new job. He noted the Western Union couriers delivering telegrams in signature large yellow envelopes to The Hooley performers and production crew on a frequent basis. He then began to notice those messengers with their yellow envelopes made deliveries throughout the city, all day, every day.

Chapter 13
"WESTERN UNION SPECIAL DELIVERY" (1891 – 1895)

Telegraphs were the email of the mid-19th and early 20th centuries that ultimately put the Pony Express out of business. Messages of joy, sorrow, and success came in the same signature yellow envelopes, hand-delivered by a Western Union courier. Humble words typed through a telegram, cut out and pasted by hand onto a sheet of paper, was the fastest, cheapest, and most reliable way to communicate.

Samuel Morse invented the Morse code for his electric telegraph in 1842 and was granted $30,000 by Congress to build a telegraph line from Washington, D.C. to Baltimore. The first telegram sent by Morse on May 24, 1844, read: "What hath God wrought."[29]

"The telegraph was rolled out in Chicago in 1848. Telegraphy made possible instant communication, first with the East Coast and eventually with the entire country. Daily newspapers began publishing next-day accounts of important events such as speeches of world leaders and election results, all from information provided through the telegraph. Following the Great Chicago Fire in 1871, citizens lined up at a makeshift Western Union office to inform alarmed friends and worried relatives that they had survived."[30]

"Chicago quickly became the 'western' communication center of the United States and by the 1880s was the nation's second city in sheer volume of telegraph messages. The telegraph in turn promoted Chicago's economic growth. It proved critical in managing the long-distance railroad routes which made Chicago a vital link between the midwestern frontier and the East Coast. Chicago companies, serving distant markets by rail, could coordinate their operations by telegraph. Small-town storekeepers throughout the country could obtain price information or place orders with their Chicago suppliers. In 1858, the Chicago Board of Trade began receiving market news from New York City by telegraph. The Board's grain and commodity prices, now telegraphically disseminated, propelled it to national prominence as a grain market. Chicago's resources, and its importance as a center of national telegraphic activity, made it the home of Western Union's Central Division, and the city attracted and fostered a wealth of engineering and entrepreneurial talent. Chicago became a center for manufacturing telegraphic (and later telephonic) equipment when the predecessor of the Western Electric Company relocated to Chicago from Cleveland in 1870. Most railroad stations also served as telegraph offices, so residents of most neighborhoods and suburbs could send important messages anywhere in the metropolis. In 1869, private line service became available in Chicago, and the American District Telegraph Company soon offered affluent Chicagoans a home service, allowing them to summon a firefighter, private policeman, or messenger. Telegraphic communication with other Chicagoans was facilitated by the company's network of neighborhood offices and messengers."[31]

Technology continued its rapid development during the 1850s and 1860s by Western Union and several of its competitors. 1866 through the turn of the century were the Golden Years of Western Union. Yearly messages sent over its lines increased from 5.8 million in 1867 to 63.2 million in 1900. Over the same period, transmission rates fell from an average of $1.09 to 30 cents per message. Even with these lower prices, roughly 30 to 40 cents of every dollar of revenue were net profit for the company. A nickel of those rates was paid to the courier to run the telegram from the pick-up office in downtown Chicago and deliver it to the designated recipient in the city.[32]

One of the messengers that Tim intercepted on the street to obtain more information informed Tim that the couriers were insanely busy and that Western Union was looking to hire. Tim loved the idea of again roaming and exploring throughout the city, as he did with the

Wily Boys in second grade. Tim left Hooley's without even a goodbye to avoid Hooley's typical temperamental rant.

Tim arrived at the Western Union office in the middle of downtown at State and Randolph and saw the long line of couriers

Tim's ID when he worked as a courier for
Western Union in 1891 at age 13 or 14.

dressed in the WU standard blue double-breasted jackets, ties, and brimmed messenger hats. Tim went into the office where scores of other young men were filling out applications and queuing up for rapid-fire interviews. Tim overheard a couple of the other applicants discussing in the waiting room that Western Union had a minimum age requirement for couriers of 16 years old. So Tim ripped up his application, grabbed a new one, and filled it out stating he was 16 "under penalties of perjury." Although Tim was still only 13 and somewhat diminutive, he grew up quickly living on the tough streets of Chicago over the past five years, typically surrounded by adults. Consequently, it was easy enough for Tim to carry himself as mature beyond his years during the interview. Tim was hired instantly, mostly out of Western Union's desperate need, and shown the "clothing supply area." Tim picked out the smallest jacket, which was still several sizes too large, his first tie, and his very own official Western Union messenger hat.

After a brief training indoctrination with the other new hires and the clothing room lady teaching Tim how to tie a tie, he went outside to stand in line to accept his first delivery. By that time, the line had grown to at least 50 couriers long, which he eventually learned amounted to about an hour-long wait. And, of course, it began to rain. Some of the other messengers behind Tim noticed his shorter stature and likely younger age and started giving him the business. After waiting in line for 50 minutes, and about tenth in line from the front, one of the idiots behind him took Tim's nifty new hat and threw it to the side about twenty feet away. Tim ran over to retrieve it and then tried to return to his place in line. The couriers quickly filled the gap left by Tim and all shook their heads. "Sorry, sonny, the line starts back there." Too many and too big to fight, Tim walked back to the end of the line, which was now over 100 people and two hours long. Tim was reminded of another saying his dad taught him, from the Anglo-Irish novelist, Oliver Goldsmith,

> "He who fights and runs away,
> May live to fight another day;
> But he who is battle slain,
> Can never rise to fight again."

This time Tim held on to his hat until he reached the delivery window.

Tim loved the freedom the messenger job provided. He was able to again explore his old haunts north of the river, along the lakefront, and throughout Lincoln Park. Tim also loved when he had to deliver a telegram to a part of town he never frequented before. His territory for the downtown central Chicago telegraph office covered a fairly wide range, including the Loop all the way up to Lincoln Park north, to Cermak south, to the lake east, and to the Chicago River west. Over the next few years, 1891 to 1893, Tim became one of the more productive couriers, usually making at least a dozen deliveries a day. He delivered telegrams to numerous celebrities in town for the run-up to the Columbian Exposition, all of whom typically stayed in downtown hotels such as the Palmer House and The Blake, both of which remain today. Tim's delivery recipients included Potter Palmer, Buffalo Bill Cody, Annie Oakley, Diamond Jim Brady, Scott Joplin, and local politicians Bathhouse John Coughlin and Hinkey Dink McKenna. Buffalo Bill gave Tim a silver dollar for a tip, one that Tim kept in his pocket for luck.

Tim continued to try to save money, mostly for food and lodging during the cold winter months. During the rest of the year Tim mostly slept in the streets. Unfortunately, he hit a tight money spell and had to pay for a week of lodging in the dead of winter with the Buffalo Bill Silver dollar – desperate times require desperate measures.

In the mid-1890s, a tuberculosis outbreak killed one in seven people in the United States. Tim would often sit on a curb to take a break from deliveries and eat a sandwich or an apple for lunch. It was rare for a day to go by without a funeral procession passing for another victim of "consumption," as it was then called.

"Smallpox was another contemporaneous scourge that crept into the streets of Chicago in the 1890s. The smallpox epidemic was officially declared in January of 1894, and by May more than 1400 cases were known in Chicago and many more were suspected but unreported. Florence Kelley, Chief of the State Board of Factory Inspectors, presented a Special Report on July 1, 1894 to Illinois Governor John Peter Altgeld, titled 'Small-Pox in the Tenement House and Sweat-Shops of Chicago.' The factory inspectors claimed authority to report smallpox cases under the Factories and Workshop Law, requiring that every business operation be kept in a 'cleanly' state."[33]

These were dangerous times for a younger person living in Chicago. The health of children in tenements and sweatshops was abysmal for many reasons:

> "poor sanitation, open toilets, uncollected garbage full of rats, insects, and other vermin, cholera, dysentery, typhoid, tuberculosis, malaria, overcrowded living conditions without the ability to wash the body or clothes, lack of fresh running water, contaminated food and lack of adequate nutrition, living and working conditions in dilapidated buildings surrounded by dangerous machinery, parental neglect and carelessness, the hazards caused by horse-drawn vehicles and later streetcars, violence in the home and outside it, and many other aspects of everyday life faced by these children every day." (F. Kelley; "Small-Pox in the Tenement House and Sweat-Shops of Chicago"; July 1, 1894).

Tim would stand at attention, doff his messenger hat, and place it over his heart as the funeral processions passed by. He would also quietly say a prayer. Unknowingly, Tim was part of a demographic that made him a likely victim of tuberculosis and smallpox. Amazingly, though, Tim never spent a day in the hospital and didn't even see a physician until much later in life.

For fleeting moments, Tim would worry that one day the funeral passing by would be for one of his friends from the old neighborhood or for his sister Molly. He then felt a terrible dread come over him one fall day, thinking about Cora and the women who worked at Maisey's coming into intimate contact with so many different people on a daily basis. During the World's Fair in 1893, people from all over the country and the world visited Chicago. Visitors attended the White City and the Buffalo Bill Wild West show located just outside the front gates of the World's Fair, and many, while in town, also visited Chicago's infamous red light districts, including Little Cheyenne.

One day in 1893, Tim was in line to pick up his next telegram delivery, still with an unsettled feeling in his gut. He finally reached the distribution window and was handed a yellow envelope with an address three buildings down from Mush Mouth's. Tim had not returned to Little Cheyenne since leaving two years earlier. Periodically, he would have an internal debate about the pros and cons of heading back to pay Cora a visit. Each time Tim headed in that direction after convincing himself it would be good to go see Cora, he would think of all the bad experiences that occurred in Little Cheyenne. This would cause Tim to stop and turn back with slumped shoulders.

Tim thought about switching the Little Cheyenne envelope with another courier like he had done in the past, but it was always challenging to convince someone to head to that dangerous section of town. He thought, "I've been meaning to go there for too long. No time like the present. You got this, Timmy."

Tim once again entered Little Cheyenne, once again alone. Several years had passed, and through the eyes of a 16-year-old everything seemed smaller. Things also seemed much filthier. Tim knew from experience it was best to move fast in this neck of the woods. He made a beeline to the address, a tavern, and handed off the envelope to the bartender, who accepted service and signed the receipt. Many people without permanent addresses received their mail and telegrams at their regular tavern.

Tim's next stop was Maisey's. He approached the front door to the building, took a deep breath, and walked upstairs to the main parlor. Tim had rehearsed so many times what he would say to Cora, and he began to play back in his memory his best salutation to her. Tim climbed the stairs to the entryway to Maisey's. His heart stopped – there was a padlock on the front door. Tim tried in vain to rattle the door open and pounded on the door. No one answered. A million possibilities of what might have happened crossed Tim's mind. He raced into the street and headed to Mush Mouth's, a route that he could do with his eyes closed. Bursting through the swinging doors, he was met by an aged Mush Mouth and several half-drunk barflies slumped on their stools.

"Is that you, kid? Come over here and let me see you." Tim removed his messenger hat and relayed what he just saw at Maisey's. "Sit down, kid, let me get you a drink first." Tim knew it was bad, knocked down the whiskey, and braced himself for the news Mush Mouth was about to deliver.

Maisey's The Badlands, like most of the brothels, had a big uptick in business during the World's Fair. It was thus just a matter of time before someone knowingly or unknowingly sick with consumption visited Maisey's. About six months earlier, one of Maisey's older women contracted tuberculosis, and within a week three others were infected. Maisey's, being more responsible than most other houses, shut down until further notice. Unfortunately, shortly thereafter, lovely Maisey too contracted tuberculosis and sadly died within a few weeks. Maisey's was closed for good.

"What about Cora?"

"The pretty young Polish gal? I'm sorry, son, she died shortly after Maisey."

Tim put his hands on his face and wept into the bar. Mushy tried to comfort Tim by patting him on the shoulder.

Tim and Mushy sat and talked for hours, tossing back multiple drinks and catching up on everything they each missed in the other's lives. With the sun about to set, Tim headed back to turn in his delivery receipt.

"Before you leave, kid, let me show you something." Tim and Mushy left the bar, proceeded a few blocks down, and Mushy led Tim down an alley. Mush Mouth pointed toward an old, emaciated, toothless, quivering shadow of a man covered in dirt. Tim focused and saw the ghastly figure had a patch over one of his eyes and was dressed in a barely recognizable tattered cassock.

"I thought you may want to see this old wretched soul one more time. You made it out of here, son – he never will. This is his hell."

(1897)

The interviewer marveled at Tim's account of his first formal job at Western Union. Of course, he focused on Tim's meeting Buffalo Bill and the other celebrities. The interviewer did put down in his notes, "Mr. Conlon able to learn and excel at a position with little to minimal supervision at age younger than his peers."

"How long did you stay at Western Union as a courier?"

"Let's see, I was there until I was 17, so 1895."

"What did you do after that?"

"I had a brief stint at the *Chicago Tribune*…"

Chapter 14
EXTRA, EXTRA! READ ALL ABOUT IT! (1895)

It was a warm, rainy fall day in 1895. Tim was assigned his last telegram delivery of the day later in the afternoon. Tim crossed over the Clark Street bridge heading to an address just north of the Chicago River. Just ahead, a man in a suit was running toward him with a terrified expression on his face. Tim stopped and braced himself for impact when the man diverted his path at the last second and then darted to his left down an alley. Tim was about to yell out to the man to try to determine what was happening when he was interrupted by another man, taller and much heavier, chasing the other man down the alley. Tim noticed this larger guy was carrying a gun in his right hand as he passed and continued down the alley.

Tim turned to run in the other direction after seeing the pistol. Two gunshots rang out, causing Tim to hit the deck and cover his head. Then a third shot was fired seconds later. Tim looked up from the ground, petrified, and saw the larger man trot back out of the alley with his left hand covered in blood. Tim's and the shooter's eyes locked for a fleeting moment. Tim saw an angry 40ish man with a scar under his left eye, cleanshaven, his brown hair slicked back under a dark gray fedora. He estimated his height at just under six feet, and that he weighed 250 pounds. The man was breathing heavily and sweating profusely. Stopping and staring daggers through Tim, he reached his hand into his tailored gray pinstriped suit jacket, presumably to grab his recently fired gun.

By this time other pedestrians ran toward the alley after hearing the gunshots. The man aborted going for his gun, turned, and ran down the street. Tim rose and ran down the alley, where he came upon a man lying face down. Tim turned the man over onto his back to see if he was alive. The man had two gunshot wounds in his chest and one on the side of his head. Blood was oozing out through the bullet holes. The poor man lay dead on the ground with his eyes still open and a look of terror on his face.

The police showed up minutes later and took an excruciatingly detailed statement from Tim and two other bystanders who ran over just after hearing the gunshots. Tim also sat with a police sketch artist inside a nearby building, away from the light drizzle that was falling. When the sketch was complete the sergeant thanked Tim and sent him on his way. As Tim left the scene, he ran over to the curb to throw up. A young reporter from the *Chicago Tribune*, assigned to cover the activity of the near north police headquarters a few blocks away, approached Tim. "Young man, are you okay? That was quite a thing you just witnessed."

"Yes, sir, I'll be okay – it's just so upsetting what happened, I can't stop shaking."

"Let's get out of the rain, son – I'll buy you a cup of coffee."

After sitting down and having a few sips of some very black coffee, Tim took in a couple of deep cleansing breaths to calm down. He stopped shaking, and his upset stomach finally subsided. The reporter asked generally about Tim's background, and then Tim went into painstaking detail of what he had just witnessed.

The reporter was surprised with the amazing detail Tim was able to provide about both the murderer's and the victim's appearance, along with every facet leading up to and following the horrific event. The seasoned reporter had interviewed hundreds of witnesses to violent crimes. Most were able to give general descriptions of what they saw, or what they thought they saw. And many witnesses of the same crime would often provide conflicting stories. Tim's description painted a picture with clarity in sequence, and the reporter took copious notes throughout his account. Most of all, the reporter was impressed with Tim's well-developed vocabulary for a young man who never attended university, or any school for that matter past second grade. When the reporter asked how Tim had such an eloquent vocabulary, Tim responded, "I guess it's from all the books I read."

As they wrapped up the interview and finished the now lukewarm cups of coffee, the reporter suggested Tim consider a career in the newspaper business. "We are always looking for a good copy boy. That's how I started. Here's my card, stop by Monday morning."

Tim was ready for a change, and this horrific moment provided him an opportunity to once again move on. Tim met with the reporter, who lined him up with the Copy Room Head, who was responsible for hiring and supervising the copy boys. Copy boys ran errands for the newspaper, typically delivering drafts and copies of articles among reporters, writers, and editors, and finally to the print departments. Because of Tim's knowledge of virtually every block of the city from his years at Western Union, Tim became the go-to runner of errands outside the office.

Tim enjoyed the change of scenery and the slightly higher pay. It was also an exciting job, watching stories develop from a reporter's notes to an article printed in the newspaper being delivered throughout the state and across the country.

Tim also began to try his hand at writing through the reporter who got Tim the job. "Just start writing. Write a story about something you saw, something you dreamt, something you imagined." Tim took that advice to heart and started to write articles, short stories, and poems about the old neighborhood, the orphanage, Little Cheyenne, Cora, and meeting famous people delivering telegrams.

One summer afternoon, Tim had to run an errand to an editor's home in the Gold Coast neighborhood. He noticed the beautiful houses and their colorful gardens. Tim was thankful that he made it out of Little Cheyenne alive and hoped to be on the right path. He dreamt of someday living in a nice home with a garden. At that moment, he was interrupted by a man walking down the street looking for anything of value in the gutters and garbage. Tim reflected, "But by the grace of God go I." Tim sat down that night and wrote the following poem:

> Life is sweet but has no plans.
> You rise and fall like the desert sands.
> You never know 'til the game is played
> If it's ermines and mansions, or an alley slave.
>
> I stand in the garden to watch and wait,
> For the old rag picker with his weary gait.
> He travels along with a bag on his back
> And leaves nothing unturned in his crooked track.
>
> I tried hard to catch his eye,
> But never a glance as he passed by.
> His face was set as if carved from stone.
> He seemed at ease in the world all his own.
>
> His eyes were glued to the pavement floor
> As he reached for the things he seemed to adore.
> As he passed down the road and out of view,
> I thought of a friend whom I once knew.

Tim certainly followed closely the story of the murder he witnessed on Clark Street. The Chicago police were able to identify the suspect after the *Tribune* published a sketch based on Tim's description. After seeing the article, multiple tips came in. The CPD named Rocco "The Ice Man" Calabrici as the suspect. Calabrici was known as the muscle for "Big Jim" Colosimo's gang on the near South Side.

In the late 19th and early 20th centuries, organized crime in Chicago was generally made up of various street gangs controlling the South Side and North Side, as well as the Black Hand organizations of Little Italy.[34] The Chicago Outfit eventually was comprised of street crews that controlled different territories around Chicago, including

Elmwood Park, Melrose Park, Chicago Heights, Rush Street, Grand Avenue, and Chinatown.[35]

"Big Jim Colosimo centralized control in the early 20th century. Colosimo was born in Calabria, Italy in 1860 and emigrated to Chicago in 1893, where he established himself as a criminal. By 1909, with the help of Johnny Torrio, who moved operations from New York to Chicago, he was successful enough that he was encroaching on the criminal activity of the Black Hand organization."[36] Colosimo also managed to be "elected" as first precinct captain, which deepened his political connections in the organization of First Ward Aldermen Coughlin and McKenna. Colosimo became the bagman in vice-laden Little Cheyenne and later the Levee District, where Colosimo was protected by his friends with blanket political clout and protection.[37]

It turned out that the victim of the shooting was Vincennes DeLuca, who was a compulsive gambler on horses and owed Colosimo over $10,000 in unpaid betting losses. To set an example for other "customers" of the Colosimo gang, a hit was put out on Mr. DeLuca. "Ice Man" Calabrici vanished after DeLuca was whacked and was never arrested. Tim, of course, thought, "Great, my name was all over the article with the Ice Man's handsome sketch. Just when I stopped looking over my shoulder for DuValle…"

The Ice Man, having fled Chicago, walked into a dark corner of an Italian restaurant in Brooklyn. He kept his fedora on with the brim pulled down low so he could hide the signature scar below his left eye. He sat in a booth in the smoke-filled bar section with two other men in suits.

"Thanks for helping out, fellas. Big Jim and I really appreciate it, and we will be sure to return the favor." Calabrici connected with Johnny Torrio's gang in New York. Torrio and Colosimo were business partners and knew each other as young boys in Italy. One of the men Ice Man sat with was a young Al D'Aquila, who planned to move to Chicago in the coming months to better integrate Torrio into the Chicago Mob and help Colosimo rise to power.

"I probably have to lay low here for a year or so. But I have unfinished business in Chicago. I should have taken care of that kid who fingered me to the cops. That sketch of me was splashed all over the papers."

D'Aquila uttered, "I understand, Ice, but you can't go off and do something stupid, ya hear me? When the time comes, you, Johnny, and I will talk first, got it?"

Ice Man was not used to taking orders from anyone except his boss Big Jim but knew he had no choice with these guys, and nodded yes.

"No, Ice, I need to hear you say, I understand you."

Tim's face flashed in the Ice Man's mind as he clenched his fists and answered through gritted teeth, "Al, I understand you!"

One day in 1895, the copy room editor charged Tim to deliver a draft story on Chicago politics to an editor at home with a stomach bug who needed to provide final edits on the article. The address was in the Rush Street area, two blocks from Uncle Shelton's house. "Holy mackerel! I wonder if Molly and Michael are still living there..." Tim was then 17, which would make Molly 19 and Michael 21. So it was likely that Michael had moved out and was fully emancipated. Molly, as with most women of the day, would likely live at home until she married, which was typically around the age of 21.

After delivering the copy to the editor's house, Tim took a more leisurely stroll toward Uncle Shelby's and conducted one of his regular internal debates about whether he should knock on the door or bail. He found himself on the sidewalk directly in line with the front door of Uncle Shelton's house. Tim was both excited about the possibility of seeing Molly and angry that not one of them visited him at the orphanage – not once, not even a letter. Tim eventually got over the fact that he was the only one of the three Conlon children sentenced to purgatory at Queen of Heaven. But he could never understand why he was so abandoned there, causing Tim tremendous rage and, even worse, sadness to be let down by his family who he loved.

Staring at the house from the sidewalk, Tim's brain grew numb, and he walked straight up to the front door and knocked.

A female voice sang out, "I'll get it." The door opened; Tim removed his cap and smiled. Molly, wide-eyed and mouth agape, paused for a couple of seconds. Once it registered with Molly that she was staring at her 17-year-old brother, she screamed out with joy. "Oh, my dear Lord!" They hugged for the longest time. All of the anger, hurt, and disappointment was gone in an instant, replaced by joy and love.

Uncle Shelton ran to the door after hearing the scream. Tim and Shelby shook hands. The three sat in the parlor with Molly, now a pretty 19-year-old young woman, continuing to stare at Tim as if she had just seen a ghost. They sat for an hour mostly questioning Tim about his life over the past near decade. Tim patiently obliged but left out most of the darker moments, at least for the time being. Tim would try to interject his own questions on the rare occasion when Molly took a breath between her rapid-fire inquiries. Molly was newly engaged to marry in the summer. Michael had married a few years earlier to a south-sider, rented an apartment in Hyde Park, and worked for a bank in the Loop. Old Uncle Shelby remained as he was nine years ago – working, drinking, and dating a new woman every other month.

During a break in the conversation, Shelby went to the kitchen to make more tea. Tim leaned forward in his chair and asked the question that broke his heart, "Why didn't you, Michael, or Shelton ever visit or write when I was at Queen of Heaven?"

Molly knew this question was coming the second she saw Tim at the door. "I was 10, Tim; I didn't have the slightest idea of how I could visit you. I asked Shelby all the time, and he always had an excuse and would say, 'We'll go next month.' And I did write you letters every week. Because you never wrote back, I wasn't sure if you got the letters, or whether you were angry and refused to write back."

Just then Shelton, who had been listening to the conversation, interjected, "I am guilty as charged about not visiting, Tim. That was wrong and I am so sorry, Timmy. I had a full-time job, and my life was turned upside down with the adoption of your brother and sister. However, I assure you that I mailed every letter that Molly wrote to you. Why those never made it to you is beyond me. We stopped sending the letters when a Brother from the orphanage paid us a visit looking for information after you ran away. We were worried sick and sent regular telegrams to the orphanage to see if you returned for the first couple of years. I finally paid one of the Brothers a visit, who said there had been no sightings or word concerning you or the Brother who went out searching for you. I was shown a box of your possessions. The Brother apologetically said he located all of Molly's letters that were sent to the orphanage but never delivered to you. Brother DuValle had a rule of no contact with family during the first year at Queen of Heaven because DuValle believed that would encourage the orphans to try to escape back to the relatives. So, all of the letters were intercepted by the orphanage."

Sadly, Shelton confessed that Michael chose not to write Tim any letters. Molly tried to prop her absent brother back up by conveying how she and Michael had worried and prayed for him every day. "I knew in my heart that I would see you again."

All three were crying and hugged it out. Shelton offered Tim a place to stay in Michael's old room. Tim said he would think about it. He stayed for dinner and they talked late into the evening.

Tim decided not to take up Shelton on his offer of lodging for now, as he had become used to his life of total freedom. His wages at the *Tribune* were enough to afford a weekly or monthly rental of a small apartment in the Loop adjacent to the El tracks. As Elwood Blues observed in the *Blues Brothers*, "The deafening trains pass by so often you won't hear them." Nevertheless, Tim would frequently visit and spend the night at Uncle Shelby's on weekends and intervals when money was tight. Tim at long last was able to reconnect with what was left of his family, filling a large hole in his heart. On the other hand, Tim refused to reach out to Michael. When Tim visited and saw Michael was there, or if Michael was expected to stop by later, Tim would abruptly leave. The brothers never reconciled and never spoke again.

(1897)

"That's fascinating, Tim. Did they ever catch the Ice Man?" The interviewer was on the edge of his seat.

"Well, no. But several people claimed to have had sightings of Calabrici around Chicago months later. But the cops never were able to nab him or, as some have said, were paid to look the other way. That was until the Ice Man and I met one last time."

Chapter 15
ICE MAN COMETH (1896)

The Ice Man hated that he was exiled in New York. He knew Big Jim's operations were continuing to blossom, and that his own star had been just starting to rise before he was forced to flee to New York. It was destroying the Ice Man that he was missing opportunity after opportunity to move up the ranks and finally make some decent dough. As his boss had said of another mobster in his gang, who had to leave after a bank job in Chicago a few years back because Big Jim felt the hot breath of the G-Men closing in, "Out of sight, out of mind." In fact, that colleague was never seen again. What made matters worse for Rocco was that the ambitious Al D'Aquila was spending more and more time in Chicago and was starting to make inroads with Big Jim. Insanely jealous, Ice Man began to hate D'Aquila. "That should be me! I was to be Big Jim's top Capo!"

After a year of laying low in New York, the Ice Man grew antsy. He finally approached Al D'Aquila one evening at the D'Aquila "office" upstairs from a Chinese laundry.

"Al, I think it's time for me to head back to Chicago. I've been here for twelve long, boring months with my thumb up my ass. I need to get back and rejoin Big Jim and start making some plays and earning some green again. I'm sure the coppers and the G's have long forgotten about me and the hit."

"Funny you should bring this up now," D'Aquila said with his now famous smirk. "Check out last week's *Chicago Tribune*. There's an article on page three, 'The One Year Anniversary of the Unsolved Mob Hit on Clark Street'. It makes the coppers look bad that they can't find you, or worse, are looking the other way and purposely not trying to find you. The cops, even the ones on our payroll, are going to have a lot of pressure to do something fast after this article."

Ice Man grabbed the paper sitting on Al's cluttered desk, tore it open to page three, and frantically read through the article. "The only eyewitness to the murder was a young Western Union delivery boy, who worked with police sketch artists to identify Ice Man Calabrici, a reputed mob hitman for Big Jim Colosimo's gang."

Ice's heart sunk when he read his name out loud and saw his sketch prominently on the page, staring back at him.

"The answer is a big no, Ice," D'Aquila smirked again, leaning back in his chair with his feet propped up on his desk.

"Can we just whack the kid? After all, he was the only witness."

"Are you fucking kidding me, Rocco? Hit a civilian, who is a kid?! If that happens, the feds will be all over Big Jim like a cheap suit and shut our entire operation down. I think you've gone stupid!"

Ice Man abruptly left D'Aquila, completely enraged. He knew that Al would never approve the hit or his return to Chicago. In fact, Ice was worried that he might get whacked himself to eradicate the bad press that made the Colosimo gang and the cops look bad and close the case for good. So Ice Man had a Hobson's choice: stay in New York, constantly looking over his shoulder for a visit from one of Al's hitmen, or return unauthorized to Chicago to locate and take care of that messenger kid who ratted him out. No witness, no conviction. Ice Man also knew that if he headed to Chicago, he would very likely get whacked for disobeying an order and putting D'Aquila's and Big Jim's operations in further jeopardy. Ice foolishly talked himself into believing that if he killed the messenger boy, maybe the case would close and he could convince Big Jim to take him back in Chicago.

Ice Man Calabrici returned to his dingy small studio apartment in the Bronx, loaded and holstered the gun in his vest, and packed his bags. He headed straight to Grand Central Station and approached the lone open ticket booth. "When's the next train to Chicago?"

In the middle of the next night, the Ice Man arrived at Chicago's

Union Station. He knew he had to move fast as every wise guy, copper, and person who read the recent *Tribune* article would surely recognize his distinct mug. He was dressed in the least "mobster" outfit he owned. Instead of a custom-made double-breasted pinstripe suit and a fedora, he donned casual slacks, a sweater, and a worker's cap. Ice Man dabbed on some concealer that one of his molls left behind in his apartment on his cheek to make his signature scar appear less pronounced.

From a public phone booth at the train station, Ice Man called one of his most trusted colleagues with whom he kept in touch from New York. Rocco knew that it would be no more than a day or two before D'Aquila figured out that he had left New York for Chicago to rub out the lone witness. Once that happened, Ice Man would no longer be able to trust anyone. "Hey Tony, it's Rocco, sorry to call so late. I've been asked to do a thing for the Big Guy, but you can't let anyone, and I mean anyone, know I'm in town. Got it?"

"Sure, Rocco, sure. What can I do to help?"

"Nothing – just keep your mouth shut about me and let me crash at one of our spots for a couple nights."

"Got it, Ice. Go to the one on Wells and Van Buren – I'll make sure the door is unlocked."

"Grazie amico ami!"

Calabrici headed to his gang's safe house in the South Loop. The poorly lit apartment was one step above a flop house, with an old cot and a sweat-stained pillow, a tattered blanket, and a disgusting flower-print couch. The dank room smelled of cigarettes and mold. Ice unpacked, put his fully loaded gun on the nightstand, turned on the oil lamp, and began to read the handful of articles he had saved from the now-famous hit witnessed by the young messenger.

Around 3:00 a.m., just before Ice was about to retire for the night, he wandered down the hallway in his boxers and tee shirt, with his gun holstered over his shoulder just in case, to make one more call to

Tony. "Hey Tony, I got a tip from one of our copper friends. Have your guys find out where a kid named Tim Conlon lives and works. He is a teenager who was a messenger for Western Union, but I think he has been working at the *Tribune* for the last year. Find out everything you can about him. This is a top priority – I need the info yesterday."

"On it, boss."

Tim was ready to punch out for the day when his boss asked him to run one more errand. He was tasked with dropping off a draft of an article to a beat reporter who was covering a story at City Hall in the Loop and needed to edit the piece that evening. Tim's boss told him he could go home following the delivery. So, off he went.

Instead of taking the sidewalks, Tim always walked along the path of the Chicago River when he had deliveries downtown, taking in the sights of the tugboats and barges. There was a sizable population of transients camped along the river. Tim knew it was not prudent to walk along that route late at night. Even though it was only 6:00 p.m., it was near dark on this late fall day. Consequently, Tim had his guard up.

After walking several blocks along the path, he picked up a stick to throw into the river. As he did, Tim saw out of the corner of his eye a large man about fifty yards or so behind him walking down the same path. This prompted Tim to pick up his pace. After another block, Tim looked back again over his shoulder to see the lumbering figure was keeping up with Tim's faster pace. He thought, "Ok, Tim, time to start running and move up to street level now!" Access to River Street, later known as Wacker Drive, was a block away. Tim ran as fast as he could when he heard footsteps of the man chasing him clomping down the gravel path just behind. The large man, although older and overweight, was surprisingly fast and gaining speed. Tim quickly calculated that he would not make it to the street level before the man would catch up, so he darted into what was referred to at the time as a hobo camp by the path situated along the railroad tracks near River Street. A fire burned in a makeshift pit to provide warmth to a group of four men and two women surrounding the campfire. Tim whispered, "Please help." He had lived among the people who lived on the streets and knew they would always help out a younger person being chased by an adult, especially if it was a cop – that is unless they were offered money. With only a few seconds to spare, they pointed to a stack of barrels by a delivery basement entrance to the building at street level above. Tim scampered and jumped inside one of the barrels.

Just as Tim disappeared into the barrel, the large man stopped at the campsite, having seen Tim leave the path and head toward River Street. The burly man approached the men and women sitting by the fire, and breathing heavily with sweat pouring down his brow, yelled out to the hobos, "Where is he?"

None of them even looked up. Tim was inside a barrel about ten yards behind the campfire, in total darkness. He peeked his head up just high enough above the lip of the barrel to see who it was. "Oh my God, it's the Ice Man!"

The Ice Man pulled his gun from the holster inside his vest, brandishing it for everyone to see. With eyes bulging, Rocco snarled, "I said, where did he go?"

But again, none of the folks sitting by the fire made eye contact with him and instead continued to stare at the fire.

Ice Man ran over to one of the women sitting by the fire and put the gun to the side of her head. "I'm only going to ask this one more time, where the fuck did that kid run to!"

She began to shake uncontrollably and cry. The others then began to stand in protest and yell back at Rocco.

"Sit down God damn it, or I'll blow her fucking head off! Okay, good. Now someone tells where he is or it's going to get really noisy down here!" Ice Man now cocked the hammer of his pistol, which was still resting against the poor woman's temple. She was frozen in fear with her eyes closed and whispering a prayer.

The oldest member of the camp slowly stood with his hands up and said as calmly as he could muster, "Put the gun down, and I'll tell you."

Tim could hear the dialogue and began to pray the Our Father to himself, thinking his time had finally come.

"Hey old timer, I'm the one with the gun. First tell me where the boy is, and then I'll put down the gun."

Tim held out a glimmer of hope that the Golden Rule among the street people to never rat out someone would prevail. But the guy had a gun to someone's head!

"Okay, fine, mister. The boy did run in here, said nothing as he passed by, and sprinted along the basement walls back in the other direction from where you were runnin'."

"Damn it, the little shit doubled back!" The Ice Man, in a panic, immediately ran into the darkness along River Street in the opposite direction, thinking Tim had tricked him by running back the other way.

After a couple of minutes, one of the men from the campfire whispered toward the barrels where Tim was hiding, "He's gone, kid."

Tim breathed a huge sigh of relief, jumped out of the barrel, flashed a thumbs up to the camp of brave souls, and sprinted toward the access up to River Street. He thought to himself, "I'm bringing them dinner tomorrow," and thanked God that the fat slob didn't offer anyone in the camp money.

Tim made the delivery and told the reporter to whom he delivered the article at City Hall everything that happened.

"Kid, you can't spend the night at your apartment. This guy is a pro, and he'll be waiting for you. Let's not tell the cops just yet – they'll probably tip him off."

The plan was for Tim to spend the night on the reporter's couch. The reporter contacted his editor that night and wrote a story to be published in the next day's paper as a follow-up to the one-year anniversary story on the Ice Man's hit.

Back in New York, D'Aquila had one of his men go to Calabrici's apartment because he had not shown up the day before. The men reported back that the Ice Man was nowhere to be seen and that his suitcase was gone. D'Aquila immediately deduced that the Ice Man went to Chicago to kill the witness. "That Figlio di puttana! Get Big Jim on the phone now!"

Tim's boss and the reporter agreed that Tim needed to hide out in the reporter's apartment for the time being. The story ran on the attempted hit, naming Rocco Calabrici as the gun-wielding hitman trying to kill the young witness to the Vincennes DeLuca murder a year earlier. This article resulted in a citywide Chicago Police APB on Rocco "The Ice Man" Calabrici. It also got the attention of Big Jim, who was tipped off by D'Aquila the night before.

"Thanks, Alfonso – I will make the Ice Man issue go away."

The Ice Man ran a half mile down the path along the river in the opposite direction before he gave up, realizing he had been outsmarted by a punk and a bunch of hobos. He went immediately into Plan B by heading to the kid's apartment in the North Loop and waiting for Conlon to come back home. Ice stood just inside an alleyway next to the entrance to Tim's apartment building, in darkness just outside the light from the nearby streetlamp.

Big Jim's first call after he hung up with D'Aquila was to Calabrici's closest ally, Tony. Colosimo ordered, "Tony, I need you come down to the office now," before slamming the phone down.

Tony arrived at Big Jim's West Side office above a saloon and was greeted by Colosimo, who was sitting at his desk, along with two of Big Jim's no-nonsense massive bodyguards, who never spoke. "Tony, I need you to level with me. We have a potential big problem on our hands. I suggest you right now become part of the solution to this problem, and not the cause."

Tony began to shake. He knew exactly why he was summoned by Big Jim, and knew if he didn't come completely clean, he would likely not make it out of the office alive.

"I ain't gonna ask you twice, Tony. Where is Ice?"

Tony left Big Jim's office with an order that he needed to carry out immediately, and one that needed to be executed successfully or Tony would not live to see the weekend. Tony had provided Conlon's work and home addresses to Ice the day before. Given the late hour, Tony surmised that Ice was staking out Tim's apartment. Tony was begging to the stars that Ice hadn't already accomplished his evil plan to rub out the kid.

Tony briskly walked north along Wabash Avenue and slowed down a couple of blocks away from Conlon's building, crossing to the other side of the street. He slinked into the darkness on the sidewalk along the walls of the buildings, away from the light cast by the streetlamps. Once Tony was a few buildings away from Tim's apartment, he moved into the pitch darkness of a building entrance alcove. Tony scanned the street up and down over and over again, searching for any sign of Ice Man's presence. After about 15 excruciatingly long minutes, Tony noticed the shadow of a large man in a fedora and a trench coat just inside an alley directly across the street from the front door of

Tim's building. The noise and rumble of an approaching El train grew louder. Just as the train was directly overhead with an almost deafening screech, Tony saw the silhouette of a man light up a cigarette. As the match flashed, its glow lit a portion of the man's face, which revealed the hideous scar on his cheek. "There he is! Thank you, God, that Ice didn't whack the kid yet."

Tony walked one street over to Michigan Avenue and entered the opposite entrance of the alley where Ice was hunkered down. Tony pulled out his Colt .45 and slowly crept down the dark alley toward his old friend Ice. Knowing how formidable Ice Man was, Tony's hand holding the gun began to shake.

Tim spent the night on the *Tribune* reporter's couch. "Bruce, how long do you think I need to lay low here?"

Sipping some very strong coffee to get out of a fog from another long night, the reporter answered, "Probably a few more nights. The article of the Ice's failed attempted hit ran yesterday, and I'm certain it got Big Jim's and the police's attention. I'll make sure to tell your boss. I have a telephone in the apartment. I'll call with any updates."

Tim shrugged his shoulders and cleaned up the apartment after the reporter left. He also dove into some of the reporter's collection of old newspapers with historic headlines to pass the time.

Finally, the phone rang, and Tim raced over to pick it up. "Hello?"

"Hey, kid, good news. The police fished a body of a large man out of the Chicago River this afternoon. Said he had two bullets pumped in the back of his head. Also said he had a scar under one of his cheeks. One of my friends at the station confirmed the cops are very sure it is our friend Ice Man Calabrici. Seems Big Jim didn't like yesterday's article. Looks like you are back in business, Conlon."

Chapter 16
WESTERN ELECTRIC – ON THE BELL HIGHWAY (1897)

The interviewer wrote down, "Applicant very descriptive writer, with advanced vocabulary – worked at the *Tribune* for a year and a half in the copy room. May be of great use assisting writing patent applications."

"That brings us to your current position here. How do you like working for Western Electric?"

"Well, as we discussed earlier, after seeing the Western Electric technology on display at the Columbian Exposition I focused all of my energy on figuring out how to work for Ma Bell. I read the paper every day and saw Chicago Telephone had an opening for a Student Repairman at the main office. I had no idea what that job entailed, but it got my foot in the door. I left the *Tribune* and came to Western Electric to work nights for a year and learn everything I could about all the equipment, the lines, and how everything fit together in the operations."

Tim explained how he eventually learned all the intricacies of how a call in one location is connected to another. "I am fascinated by the technology and have so many ideas of how we can improve various aspects of operations."

The interviewer put in his notes, "Applicant's enthusiastic knowledge of operational technology greatly outweighs his lack of pedigree – must hire. Find role for him."

At the time, the demand for telephones was growing exponentially. "In 1882, Western Electric and Bell signed an agreement that made Western Electric the exclusive manufacturer of telephones for Bell in the United States, while Western agreed to sell only to the American Bell Telephone Company (which in 1899 became AT&T), which then leased the phones to regional 'operating' companies, who in turn leased the phones to end users. Those two contracts combined with AT&T's agreements with its licensees to form the nascent Bell System, and provided its organizing principle for what would emerge the next century: long distance service."[38]

These contracts alone would have meant little without a source of innovation for the development of new products and the improvement of existing ones. There were two directions Bell could go for technical innovation after 1894: depend on outside inventors for innovation by purchasing their patents, or establish an in-house research organization to cultivate invention. An 1896 memo from AT&T's chief engineer to the president of the company shows the direction in which Bell initially moved: "Every effort in the Department is being executed toward perfecting existing engineering methods. No one is employed who, as an inventor, is capable of originating new apparatus of novel design."[39] This quickly evolved to an effort to form an internal department to create and advance new technologies, a wonderful opportunity for Tim.

To further this new AT&T corporate goal, Chicago Telephone was working in collaboration with its sister company, Western Electric, to form an ad hoc research and development department. It began recruiting top engineering students from the University of Chicago. This early group of engineers and inventors from Chicago Bell and Western Electric was the forerunner to what would later become Bell Labs, one of the preeminent research organizations in the world. While the new group was having success in hiring great engineering minds, they lacked someone with hands-on, detailed knowledge of the existing operating equipment, its weaknesses, and areas that needed improvement.

The interviewer knew they had to find a spot for Tim to plug into this role. Because of budgetary constraints for this newly created innovative department, the company could only pay Tim as a part-timer. Tim was elated to receive the offer but couldn't afford to take a pay cut. The solution that Chicago Bell came up with was for Tim to continue as a repairman but move from Western Electric to the Toll Department of Chicago Bell, which later became Illinois Bell. The Toll Department was responsible for all calls to and from outside the greater Chicago area, which were starting to boom as more and more long-distance telephone lines spread across the country. The Toll Department was in desperate need of an operational repairman, and with Tim's glowing reviews from his supervisor in the main office Tim was quickly hired to that role as well. Consequently, Tim worked three days a week with the new Research and Development group and three days a week with the Toll Department. Unfortunately for Tim, the demands of both roles were great, and he seemed to be working two full-time jobs, putting in many days and nights and seven-day weeks.

Tim's time working in the R&D group was far more gratifying to him than the repairman job. He enjoyed collaborating with inventors from Western Electric and Chicago Bell and meeting the bright new engineers from the University of Chicago. Tim's hard work and in-depth knowledge of the Bell operations systems earned him the respect of the others in the group. Tim used to laugh to himself over the numerous diplomas and degrees on display in his coworkers' offices. One night at a bar, a drinking buddy of Tim's presented him with a diploma from "The School of Hard Knocks." Tim prominently displayed the faux sheepskin in his work area.

Tim shared several of his ideas during initial brainstorming sessions with the engineers and inventors. One of his ideas involved a trunk line for Chicago Telephone's Toll Center calls, which ended up being Tim's first of 22 patents. The interviewer who hired Tim, having heard this amazing news, sent Tim a note, "Congratulations, Tim! I had every confidence that you were the man for the job. A degree does not define a man's intelligence. Truly amazing what you have accomplished – well done."

Chapter 17
HELEN MAE McEWEN

Tim still had a heavy load to handle as Toll Department mechanic. One morning, he received a note that one of the toll operator's switchboards was acting up. In 1900, the Toll Department had a dozen or so young women switchboard operators handling all toll calls, either inbound or outbound, from outside of Chicago. Chicago Telephone had strict rules against employees conversing among themselves during work hours, other than for exclusively work-related communications. This was due largely to the heavily male-dominated workforce at the main offices of Chicago Telephone on Washington and Franklin in the downtown business area. When the 15- to 18-year-old boys, who were the original operators, began to be replaced by young 18- to 20-year-old women due to new company minimum age requirements, the new switchboard operators received constant and intense attention from their male coworkers. When it got to the point that the continuous social visits to the switchboard room impacted the operators' productivity, the draconian "No Talking With Coworkers" rule went into effect.

Tim strolled into the switchboard room and made his way toward Operator Station 8, which was reportedly on the fritz. Tim didn't realize this routine event was about to be a life-changing moment. When he laid eyes on the operator at Station 8, time stood still. Tim couldn't see the switchboard, could no longer see the other operators, and frankly could not even recall where he was or why he was there. Tim only saw what he described for the rest of his life as "the most beautiful girl on the planet."

Helen Mae McEwen was a beautiful, dark-haired, dark-eyed, petite-framed 18-year-old toll operator. Her arms were crossed and her brow frowned as she sat staring at the switchboard, upset that her "machine" was broken, and she had nothing to do but sit and sulk. Mae turned to look at the repairman, who had stopped dead in his tracks, holding tightly onto his toolbox, and was staring at her. "Are you the nice man who is going to fix my board?" Tim didn't respond but just kept staring at her. The other operators witnessing this spectacle began to giggle at the flushed, gawking repairman. "Hellooooo...sir, are you just going to stand there all day or are you going to help me?" This prompted more muffled laughter from the peanut gallery.

"So sorry, miss, I, um, was, ah, just trying to, um, remember which, ah, switchboard needed to be fixed, and..." Tim's voice trailed off into a mumble as he tried to come up with an excuse for his strange behavior.

"It's this one right here in front of me," Mae said with a big smile as she flashed her gorgeous sparkling eyes. Mae's smile nearly caused Tim to pass out. Fortunately, he snapped out of his head spinning trance and walked over to Station 8. He plunked his tools on the floor and went to work. Mae pushed her chair back to make room for Tim, crossed her legs and smiled patiently as the repairman toiled away.

"There you go – just like new, ma'am."

Mae thanked the helpful, awkward repairman, put her headset on, and went back to work, with her pleasant, "Operator number 8, how may I help you place your call?"

As Tim walked away, he turned to look back at Mae one more time and thought, "I'm going to marry that gal."

Tim thought of little else the next several days. He kept thinking of ways to see Mae again. "I will try to get to know her and maybe, just maybe, muster up enough courage to ask Mae out on a date." Tim waited until Mae left for the day when her shift was done. With the flick of a switch Tim was able to disconnect Station 8 from the Master Operators Board, thus disabling Mae's work station. Sure enough, when Tim arrived at work the next morning, he had a message that Operator's Station 8 was inoperative again. Tim smiled, grabbed his tools, and proceeded to the toll operators room. He thought, "My God, she's even prettier than before…"

With slightly more confidence this time, Tim walked over toward Mae's desk. Mae put her hands in the air, smiled, and said, "I swear it wasn't anything I did – the blasted machine simply won't turn on again."

Tim politely laughed and said, "No worries, these new toll switchboards can be very sensitive, especially when they are touched by such a pretty angel."

Mae rolled her eyes. "Do you have a name, Mr. Repairman? I'm Mae McEwen."

"What a beautiful name. So glad to meet you, Mae. I'm Tim Conlon."

They chatted a few more minutes as the other operators eavesdropped. Finally, Agnes, the supervisor across the room, arms crossed, tapped her large right pump on the floor and with a stern look through some awfully thick glasses yelled, "Mister, you are distracting all the girls with all your chit chat. PAH-LEASE fix the board and move on so Miss Mae can go about her business and our waiting customers can place their calls! And Miss Mae, I'm certain you are well aware of the No Talking policy…"

Tim fell on his sword. "Sorry, ma'am – that is all on me. Sometimes I just can't stop talking. Like right now, I should pipe down. But I keep on blabbing, blabbing, blabbing. Maybe I should see the company doctor about this incessant blabbing."

All the operators and Mae tried to stifle their smiles and giggles, realizing Tim was purposely testing the supervisor Agnes's patience.

"Enough or I'm writing you up!" snapped Agnes.

Tim didn't want to push it, so he playfully grimaced to Mae, winked, and went to work. He made his way to the back of the switchboard and pretended he was tinkering and trying to diagnose the problem for a few minutes before flipping the override switch back on. Mae smiled and mouthed, "Thank you, Tim."

Another week passed, and Tim simply could not shake Mae from his thoughts. Time again for the old Master Board Override Switch trick. As expected, the work order came in the next morning for Operator Station 8. Agnes glared at Tim when he entered the room. "You again? This better be fixed properly this time or I'm talking to your boss." Being mindful of the ridiculous No Talking rule, Tim smiled and flashed a big thumbs up. Several women tried to stifle their laughter. Mae smiled and, wagging her finger at Tim, whispered, "Tim, if I were you, I'd try really hard to fix it for good this time."

Tim knew that this was the last time he would be able to rig the machine so that it needed "repair" or he would potentially get reprimanded or written up by his supervisor. Tim studied the board and feigned taking notes. In reality he wrote a personal note to Mae, "I'd really get a kick out of having a soda or a coffee with you sometime – would love to get to know you. How about tonight after work? Give me a chance, as your supervisor would say, PAH-LEASE."

Tim threw the switch back on and discreetly left the handwritten note on Mae's desk. Mae picked up the note as Tim walked away. Just before he left the toll room, he turned back to have one more look at Mae. Their eyes met, and Mae nodded and imitated Tim's thumbs up. Tim raised his hands above his head as he exited the door as if he had just won a championship bout and was leaving the ring.

Tim began waiting outside the main door of the Chicago Telephone building 15 minutes before Mae's shift ended, not wanting to be one second late. Finally, Mae walked through the door. Tim immediately got butterflies, and his heart was beating like a racehorse.

"Hi Tim. I almost didn't recognize you without your toolbox." They laughed and strolled down the street, both smiling from ear to ear. They came upon an ice cream shop and walked in for a quick soda as Mae had to be home by 7:00 p.m. or her mother would begin to "worry sick" about her.

(1859 – 1899)

Helen Mae McEwen was born on December 18, 1882 in Chicago. Because the McEwens called their children by their middle names, she went by Mae. Her father was William Robert McEwen, who was born in 1859 on an empty cargo ship deadheading from Aberdeen Harbor, Scotland en route to Prince Edward Island, Canada. Apparently, obstetrics wasn't advanced enough in 1859 to accurately predict the arrival of a child, so baby William arrived a wee bit early.

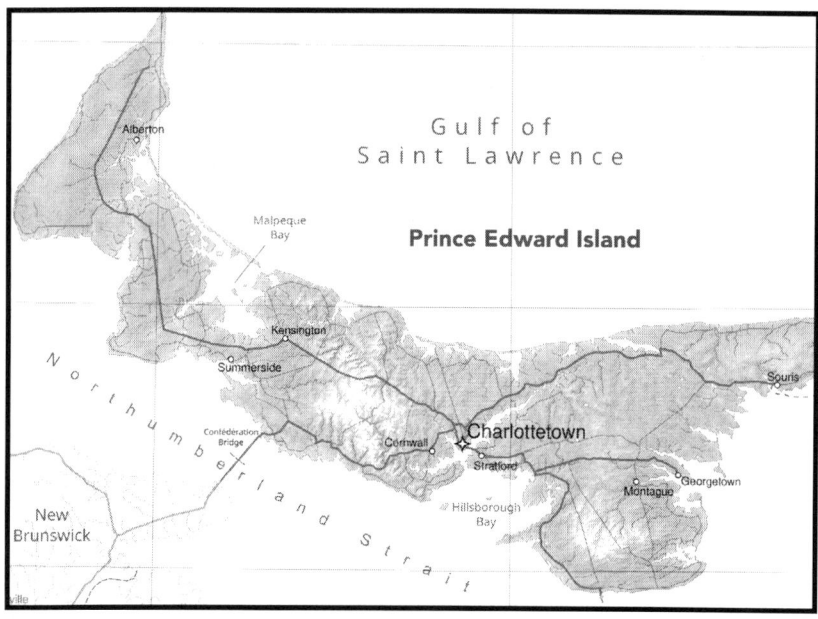

Map of Prince Edward Island; March 18, 2013;
Commons Wikimedia Org.; Permission to Use Creative Commons Attribution – Share Alike 3.0 Unported.

"In the early 1800s, a journey from Europe to America was long and difficult. Immigrants first traveled by foot or cart to the nearest port and waited for a sailing ship to transport them to America. Poor immigrants traveled to America on unloaded cargo ships that were making their return voyage after having carried tobacco or cotton to Europe", as was the case for the McEwens. "The voyage lasted between 40 and 90 days, depending on the wind and weather. In steerage, ships were crowded, each passenger having about two square feet of space, and dirty with a spate of lice and rodents. Passengers had little food, water, or ventilation. 10-20% of those who left Europe died on board before they reached North America."[40]

"In the 1840s, steamships began transporting wealthy passengers, while poor immigrants still made the voyage to America by sailing vessels. Beginning in the 1860s, transatlantic journeys became shorter and less dangerous when railways enabled an easier trip to ports of departure and steamship companies improved their accommodations to attract immigrants as passengers. Conditions in steerage were still harsh, but steamships began to run on regular schedules, and crossing time was dramatically reduced to seven to ten days. In the 1860s and 1870s, the size of steamships increased, and companies began to transport poorer families in steerage at a low cost."[41]

With increasing numbers of Europeans immigrating to North America, there was a coinciding increase in the number of children being born during the transatlantic passage. William was the first of the McEwens born outside of Scotland during his parents' immigration to Canada.

The McEwens had saved a modest sum of money from the sale of their land in Scotland shortly before they departed their homeland. After landing in Prince Edward Island, the McEwens settled near Alberton and eventually purchased a home with a nice stretch of land for farming in the Tignish region at the northern tip of the island. Ultimately, the family started a fox farm, which was part of a growing industry in Prince Edward Island and which constituted a large portion of its economy in the late nineteenth century. Fox pelts made into stoles with the fox head intact became the rage in England in the latter half of the 1800s and quickly spread throughout Europe. By the year 1900, there were more than 8,000 fox farms on the relatively small island.

Young William McEwen served as the family fox hunter/trapper under the tutelage of Old Man LaTrec, a French-Canadian fur trapper whose job it was to snare foxes in Quebec and Newfoundland for his stable of independently owned fox farms on Prince Edward Island. William at the young age of fifteen accompanied LaTrec on several expeditions outside of Prince Edward Island for weeks at a time to learn how to trap fox at the feet of the seasoned professional.

William's time with LaTrec gave him an appreciation of the outdoors. He soon became addicted to the adventure and the freedom experienced during the expeditions. Nonetheless, William wanted to see the world outside Prince Edward Island, which seemed smaller to him with every passing year. Without warning to his family, after saving money by selling some fox pelts from his tours of duty with LaTrec, the free-spirited 16-year-old William left Prince Edward Island for America. In 1886, he landed in Chicago, where several of his relatives had immigrated from Scotland. In the first month of living with his aunt in Chicago, William met his future wife, Cecilia Kelty. The two 16-year-olds fell in love and instantly became inseparable.

Cecilia Kelty was the daughter of James Kelty and Mary Jane Dowling Kelty. The Keltys were of Irish descent and moved to Lancashire, England in the mid-1850s as a result of the Potato Famine. Mae's mother, Cecilia, was born in Lancashire in 1859. The Keltys managed to retain ownership of their land in Ireland, which was leased to a wealthy English family that wanted to ultimately purchase the tract, but with the uncertainty created by the famine entered into a long-term lease instead. The Keltys also owned a very successful millinery shop which designed, made, and sold elaborate fancy women's hats and headdresses. Between their millinery and rental income, the Keltys became relatively well off. As a rather ambitious couple, James and Mary Jane decided to expand their millinery business to the United States. Believing New York was already saturated with women's fashion shops, they thought that the up-and-coming midwestern hub of Chicago would be a lucrative location for their U.S. millinery business.

When the Keltys arrived in Chicago in 1865, they were gravely disappointed when they first laid eyes on the muddy streets lined with dilapidated buildings and wooden shacks. It was a startling contrast to what they hoped and expected would be a city resembling London, and a shocking departure from their quaint village in Lancashire. The Keltys settled just north of Division Street on Schiller Street, now Chicago's Gold Coast, where they could see Lake Michigan from their second-floor bedroom window.

It was difficult to assimilate into the Chicago fashion community, which was very new, and stores were scarce. The search for the right location for their millinery shop took longer than expected due to a lack of storefront buildings in an area that women would feel safe to frequent. Ultimately, they entered into a lease near the theater district in the Loop for a fairly sizable rent. Young Cecilia and her mother, Mary Jane, spent most of their time setting up the hat-making operations. James made several long trips each year to collect rents from their farm in Ireland and then travel to England to check on their store in Lancashire. Despite these busy times, with many long stretches living apart, Mary Jane managed to become pregnant on multiple occasions. Sadly, due to the primitive medical care in Chicago in the 1860s, she suffered several miscarriages.

In 1868, Mary Jane "Molly," Cecilia's first and only sister, was born. Two years later, brother Christopher entered the world. Things were happy again in the Kelty household. The store was taking off, and James stayed in Chicago, shelving his regular European trips to lend a hand with the new babies. At the age of eleven, Cecilia was relied upon to care for her younger siblings and run errands for the shop. The Keltys were living the 19th century American dream, but as was typical in harsh Chicago in the 1870s, their peaceful and tranquil life was interrupted by tragedy.

The Chicago Fire raged on October 7, 1871, killing more than 300 Chicagoans (a number many believe was vastly underreported) and leaving one third of the city's population homeless. Countless others died from smoke inhalation in the days and weeks that followed. As the fire raged north and east from its originating point in Chicago's Southwest neighborhood, information spread mostly by panicked word of mouth that the Loop was directly in the conflagration's path. The Keltys left their three children with their next-door neighbor and drove their horse-drawn carriage apace toward their millinery store downtown. By then, firefighters and police blocked anyone from entering the downtown business area from north of the river. Business owners were allowed to pass, but it took many precious minutes for the Keltys to convince one of the officers that they were indeed legitimate downtown business owners.

When the Keltys arrived at the millinery in the early evening, the smoke was horrendous and they could see several nearby buildings ablaze. Scrambling, John and Mary Jane grabbed whatever merchandise and inventory they could in the twenty or so minutes they had before the thick black smoke became too much for them. They began to feel the extreme heat from the fires coursing down the streets in their direction. The Keltys could barely breathe from the even worse bellowing smoke that was infiltrating through the handkerchiefs around their faces. The horses too began to panic as they mounted the carriage and headed back north in a gallop, just as the building next door to their millinery was engulfed in flames.

By the time the Keltys arrived home, neighbors were beginning a mass exodus toward Lake Michigan near what is now known as Oak Street Beach, a few blocks east of their homes. Mary Jane grabbed their children and James rushed for valuables and heirlooms to add to their carriage. The pilgrimage to the lake consisted of wall-to-wall people and carriages. Kelty parked the carriage as near to the shore as he could and walked his two horses to the nearest hitching post, thinking he would run and untether them if the fire continued to spread that far.

The night sky flickered amber, yellow, and orange. Reports of the fire's progress were sporadic and inconsistent through the night. Around 3:00 a.m., the first flames were visible by Chicagoans taking refuge at the edge of Lake Michigan. Women began to scream, and children cried out from the terror. As the fire's edge seemed to be less than a half mile away, smoke on the beach thickened, burning peoples' eyes and causing many to cough and choke, their lungs screaming for fresh air. This caused a chain reaction of the now panicked crowd of thousands to walk into the water of Lake Michigan up to their waists. James held Cecilia in his left arm and baby Christopher in his right, while Mary Jane hugged Molly as they waded into the cold water. The Kelty family turned back toward the shore and watched Chicago burn through the night while they were half submerged in the frigid October waters of Lake Michigan.

The aftermath of the Great Fire was dreadful for the 300,000 citizens of Chicago. Worries abounded about their homes, businesses, and loved ones. For the Keltys, their house was spared but the building where their millinery was located was destroyed. Most concerning, however, was Mary Jane's severe cough that lingered for days after the fire. Her cough worsened with time and eventually caused her to be bedridden. A doctor making a home visit provided news that James and Cecilia were dreading – Mary Jane had suffered irreparable lung damage from inhaling toxic fumes from the smoke during their attempts to salvage what they could from the store. Sadly, Mary Jane Dowling Kelty perished a week later, leaving her husband John and three children. Cecilia took over responsibility for caring for her siblings at the age of eleven, while her father tended to his various business dealings and even during his extended trips to Ireland and England.

Photo of Chicago Fire Aftermath;
Public Domain; Commons.Wikimedia.org; Circa 1871.

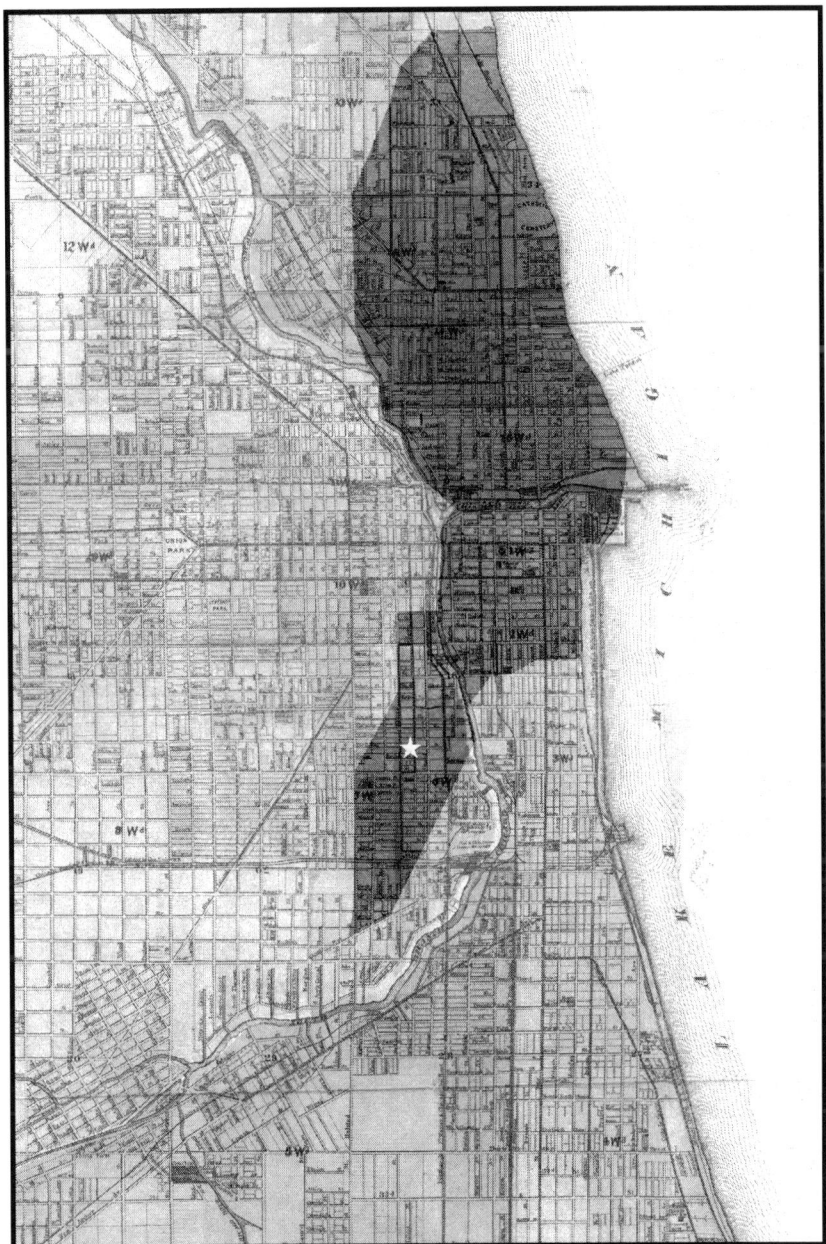

Map of Chicago, showing the burned area after the Great Chicago Fire in 1871, including the starting point of the O'Leary's barn (white star);
Unknown author; Public domain; Common.Wikimedia.org; 1871.

In 1876, Cecilia and William McEwen married at the age of 17. Cecilia became pregnant 12 times, with only five reaching full term. Annie was their first child born in 1878, followed by Mae in 1882. Corina, Loretta, and Roy followed over the next ten years. William took on many different jobs trying to provide for his full house of children, including working as a conductor of streetcars which were driven by horses before they were replaced by electric powered trolleys in 1906. Cecilia put great importance on education and made sure her children attended the best schools they could afford. Cecilia also emphasized the arts by ensuring her children were enrolled in voice, piano, theater, and art lessons. In adulthood, Corina was an artist, Roy played multiple instruments, and Loretta became a professional actress.

In 1898, at the age of 40, Mae's father William received a telegram that both of his parents had passed away and bequeathed him a share of the McEwen fox farm. After several trips to Prince Edward Island to meet with his siblings about the future of the family business, William once again enjoyed the freedom of the outdoors that he missed so dearly since transplanting to Chicago. While traveling, William was able to escape the stress and claustrophobia of a 9 to 5 routine and a household full of noisy children.

William and his brothers decided to try and expand their fox farm business to the States, with William happily in charge of heading to the western states in search of a site for the new McEwen stateside fox farm. Following some research and meetings with others in the business, the McEwen brothers identified Steamboat Springs, Colorado as a prime location. Foxes were reportedly still in abundance in the mountains surrounding the town, there were several competent fur trappers in the region that could be employed to gather inventory, and land in Colorado was still relatively cheap.

William immediately left for Steamboat Springs with little notice to Cecilia, who was already angry with his frequent absences from their home and five children.

During William's first trip out West, he rented a horse-drawn carriage to drive into the mountains to survey the fox population. William instantly fell in love with the breathtaking mountain views. After the second day, a significant blizzard hit Steamboat Springs and the surrounding mountains. Initially, William tried to ride out the storm in a small tent pitched alongside the carriage. Worried about the horse and the increased intensity of the storm on the third day, however, William decided to risk heading back down the mountain to Steamboat. He, of course, was unfamiliar with the mountain trails, and the blinding snow made it impossible to see more than a few feet in front of the carriage. Controlling the nervous horse was also proving to be extraordinarily difficult. William tried desperately to keep up the pace and forge ahead through the heavy snow front with the hope that crossing to the other side of the pass would provide relief from the storm.

As the horse was encouraged to reach a cantor through the blizzard, unbeknownst to William the carriage was heading down a path perilously close to a cliff with a 500-foot drop. The horse stumbled over a log covered by feet of snow and slid to the left, taking the carriage sharply toward the cliff. William held on tightly to the reins and rode the horse and carriage off the cliff, falling 500 feet to his death.

After William perished, the family suddenly needed financial support, prompting Mae and her sister Agnes to join the workforce. Mae left school at Lady of Sorrows parish on the near West Side of Chicago at the age of 15 to work at the new Carson Pirie Scott department store at State Street and Madison Avenue. Cecilia was fiercely protective of her attractive daughters. She accompanied them and sat in during her daughters' job interviews so that she could assess whether a prospective employer was a good and safe place to work.

Mae worked for a year at Carson's department store as a messenger/clerk and practiced typing during her lunch hour to hone

HELEN MAE McEWEN (Approximately Age 18); 1900.

her potentially more lucrative secretarial skills. Mae walked 20 blocks to and from work every day on the wooden sidewalks and sloppy, muddy streets in heels and a high-collared dress because Cecilia refused to allow her daughters to ride in a horse-drawn streetcar with scores of men.

In 1899, at the age of 16, Mae heard of a higher paying opportunity at Chicago Bell as a toll call operator at a location four blocks closer to her home. Mae took to the position quite nicely and passed the training sessions with flying colors. The toll room was isolated from the rest of the offices but was frequented all day, every day by random male coworkers who had no legitimate business reason to visit. Mae and the other toll operators amusingly kept a list of excuses provided by the gawkers looking for a date. Mae stopped keeping her list the minute she was asked to go out on a date by the nice and ruggedly handsome repairman, Tim.

On their first date, Mae and Tim chatted until late in the evening, laughing and trading stories about their respective pasts. They were interrupted by the soda jerk who informed them the shop was closing in five minutes, at 9:00 p.m. "Nine o'clock! I was supposed to be home by 7:00. My mother will be beside herself. She probably has already contacted the police who will be out searching for me."

Tim tried to reassure Mae that all would be okay and said he would escort her home given the late hour. They continued their lovely exchange of stories as they strolled to the McEwen's cottage at 1340 West Congress. Tim walked her to the front door and said, "Good night, my dear Mae, I had such a pleasureful evening." He extended his arm to give her a good night handshake. Mae artfully moved his arm aside and moved in to give Tim a gentle kiss on his cheek. "Good night, Tim."

With a happy grin, Tim felt as though his feet didn't touch the ground on his walk back to his downtown apartment. Tim felt so blessed that the winds of fate blew their two souls' paths together. What if the Conlons, the Gillens, the Keltys, or the McEwens had not survived the potato famine and immigrated to Chicago, or if Tim had not successfully escaped from Queen of Heaven, or if Mae's father had been able to negotiate the turn in the blizzard which would have allowed Mae to stay in school and not go to work in the toll room. It boggled Tim's mind how infinite decisions made and random forks in the road down which ancestors chose to travel since the beginning of time ultimately presented the opportunity for Tim and Mae to meet. Tim thought of the fork in the rail tracks that he and Billy happened upon and Tim's split decision to travel down the tracks leading to Chicago all those years ago. He wondered if it was meant to be, whether a plan was mapped out by some greater being or by spirits guiding Tim's and Mae's lives to intersect, or whether it was just pure dumb luck. Tim was never able to explain his feeling of being struck by a lightning bolt when he first laid eyes on sweet Mae, and had said to himself, "I'm going to marry that gal."

Years later, when Tim happened to pass Mae's childhood home, reflecting on her separate life before they met, he wrote a poem he titled "Romance On The El":

> I saw the old home yesterday
> While riding on the El.
> I would like to hear the secrets,
> The bricks alone could tell.
>
> The train stopped for a moment,
> While going around the curve,
> And I saw a woman sitting
> In the window with a girl.
>
> I knew that many years ago
> A little brown-eyed maid

Was sitting in that window
Underneath the shade.

Dreaming of the future
Thinking of the past,
Sometimes counting El cars
As by her home they'd pass.

I saw the fence and saw the yard
And saw the timeworn stairs,
Where she had sat for many a day
To dream away her cares.

The friends who gathered around the place
And pass through the open door,
Somewhere some are thinking
Of the days that are no more.

I'll dream again of her childhood scenes
That stretch from sky to sky,
And the little "McEwen" cottage
Where the cars go rolling by.

Their courtship continued for the next several months, with visits to the malt shop, walks during their lunch hour, and dinner dates on

McEwen Cottage

Saturday nights. They became closer and closer with each date.

Other young men also pursued the pretty young Mae. As is inevitable in human relationships, there were rocky times resulting from Tim misinterpreting how Mae was paying too much attention to someone else or not enough attention to him. This prompted Mae to let Tim know how she felt about his jealousy and lack of trust in her. The two lovebirds didn't speak for a few weeks. Tim fell into a depression over the ridiculous spat that had escalated into a mutual silent treatment. Tim finally relented and apologized profusely for his irrational jealousy. Mae, tiny in stature at barely five feet tall and 98 pounds, was one tough cookie. She didn't want Tim to think he could just waltz in, say he was sorry, and all would be forgiven. A stubborn Irish woman – this could last awhile or worse…

Tim poured out his emotions in a poem that he left on Mae's workstation one morning before she arrived,

> Sweet Girl of My Dreams
>
> Although you are my sweetheart
> And letters we exchange,
> I never meet you anymore
> Now doesn't that seem strange.
>
> You hold a place within my heart,
> Unusual and unique,
> We share ideals and special dreams,
> But still, we do not speak.
>
> I picture of what I think of you
> Perhaps you picture me,
> Peculiar game for both of us
> Of someone you don't see.
>
> So, for the love that we possess
> We owe the mail a debt,
> Perhaps its charm lies in the fact,
> That you are my best bet.

Mae read the poem at her desk and her eyes welled up a bit. She felt his presence in the toll room, turning back to look toward the door to see Tim standing nervously with teeth gritting and hands wringing. Mae smiled and nodded her head. Tim, as he did after Mae accepted his invitation for the first date, again raised his arms with clenched fists over his head and trotted out the door. All was right and good again in Tim and Mae's world.

Ever since Mae was a teenager, she could sense when someone was about to enter the room. Mae was able to guess correctly who it was that rang the bell before she answered the door, or who was calling the house phone before it was picked up. Mae was also the first one to know when someone in the family was feeling blue, without saying a word, and provide a comforting hug.

Mae's mom, Cecilia, told stories of her mother, Mary Jane Dowling Kelty, who also possessed a special gift. Mary Jane had an incredible knack of sensing what the future held for her family and friends. Irish culture being spiritual and full of superstitions in the 1800s was particularly susceptible to believing that some were born with an ability to see the future or speak to the spirit world. Before her family immigrated to Lancashire, Mary Jane's reputation in the village of Rathsowney, County Laois, for predicting the future had become well-known in the form of interpreting the 'tay'. Tea reading was a very common and accepted practice in Ireland. Cecilia, too, practiced the craft of tea reading but would always say that it was Mae who truly inherited Grandmother Mary Jane's gift.

The custom of drinking tea dates back to 2,500 BC in China. Tea finally reached Europe in the 16th century when Portuguese and Dutch traders imported the leaf-based beverage. England's influence on China and India in the 1700s led to the British East India Company acquiring a monopoly on the tea trade, making tea the most popular drink in Ireland due to the Anglo-aristocracy that had settled on the island.[42]

Contemporaneously with the new massive popularity of tea in Europe, the work of Sigmund Freud spawned immense interest in psychoanalysis during the mid-1800s. "What began as a parlor game, discerning patterns and symbols in random clumps of soggy tea leaves, was soon adopted as a new form of divination that evolved along with new interest in psychoanalysis. With an interest in oracular consultation that spanned several generations, Irish tea drinkers quickly became proficient at the practice, identifying and interpreting hundreds of shapes that wet tea leaves might produce. Some tea readers, for whatever reason, were consistently accurate, leading the particularly accurate predicters of fate to become the Village Tay Reader."[43]

The tea reading process was precisely prescribed. "After a cup of tea has been poured, without using a tea strainer, the tea is consumed or poured away. The cup should then be shaken well and any remaining liquid drained off in the saucer. The diviner now looks at the pattern of tea leaves in the cup and allows the imagination to play around [with] the shapes suggested by them. They might look like a letter, a heart shape, or a ring. These shapes are then interpreted intuitively or by means of a fairly standard system of symbolism, such as: snake (enmity or falsehood), spade (good fortune through industry), mountain (journey of hindrance), or house (change, success)."[44]

At the age of eighteen, Mae's reputation for accurate tea readings was widespread in her West Side mostly Irish neighborhood. Her insight was described as "impeccable," and Mae was said to have correctly seen in the tea leaves impending marriages, pregnancies, and new careers. Word traveled fast and farther, with people from around the city paying Mae a visit for a reading.

Mae surprised Tim during one of their first dates with the prediction that he was going to have a job promotion soon. Sure enough, the very next week, in recognition of Tim's first patent for Illinois Bell/Western Electric, Tim received his first promotion since joining the R&D Department. Mae had a difficult time explaining how she connected with a person to perform a reading, but she would be overcome with visions or sensations once she concentrated on nothing else but the person for whom she was reading. Mae described it as almost falling into a trance during a reading. Other times, premonitions would come out of absolutely nowhere while she was walking down the street or shaking hands to greet someone. Tim was a little spooked by this revelation, but it paled in comparison to Mae's dire warning a few months later.

Chapter 18
IROQUOIS THEATRE
(December 30, 1903)

Tim planned a special date with Mae during the holidays in December, 1903. They had been dating for a few years, and Tim was starting to consider proposing on the four-year anniversary of when they met in 1899. They both loved the theater. Tim knew so many showtunes from his time babysitting actors' children at the Hooley theater as a teenager, and Mae's sister Loretta was a professional theater actress. Mae loved to hear Tim croon showtunes as they sat on the front porch of the McEwen Cottage in the evenings.

The talk of the town was the recent opening of the Iroquois Theatre, located at 24–28 West Randolph Street, between State and Dearborn Streets. The Iroquois was two blocks from Mae's grandparents' former millinery store before it was razed in the Chicago Fire and was three blocks from the old Hooley theater. The group of investors that financed the Iroquois construction chose the downtown location to attract out-of-town women visiting Chicago who would be more comfortable seeing a play at a theater near the heavily police-patrolled shopping district.[45] The Iroquois opened on November 23, 1903, after numerous delays due to labor unrest and the unexplained inability of architect Benjamin Marshall to complete required drawings in a timely fashion.[46] Following its grand opening, theater critic Walter K. Hill wrote in the *New York Clipper* (a predecessor of *Variety*) that the Iroquois was "the most beautiful ... in Chicago, and competent judges state that few theaters in America can rival its architectural perfections ..."[47]

Tim was always thinking of gifts at the last minute. By the time Tim got around to looking for tickets to the Iroquois play during Christmas week, all the evening performances were sold out. There was, however, availability for a few matinee shows.

After checking with Mae to make sure she had the week off for the holidays, Tim bought two tickets for the December 30, 1903, Wednesday matinee performance of the popular Drury Lane burlesque musical of the traditional *Mr. Blue Beard*, which had been playing at the theater since opening night. Attendance at the performances since the premier had been disappointing, mostly due to people having been driven away by the particularly rough winter weather. The December 30 performance at last drew a sellout audience. Two thousand tickets were sold for every seat in the house, including hundreds more for the "standing room" areas which were supposed to be behind the last row of seats at the back of the theater. The standing room areas became so crowded that patrons were forced to sit in the aisles, which in turn blocked the exits.[48]

On Christmas Day, Tim surprised Mae with the tickets to the December 30 matinee. They were both so excited to see the new theater about which the papers were marveling with its wonderful ornate architecture. They had lunch near the Iroquois before the play. During lunch, Tim noticed that Mae wasn't herself, being unusually serious and less talkative.

"What's the matter, my dear Mae?"

"Ever since you handed me my ticket for the play, I have had a horrible feeling of dread. I can't explain it – I'm so sorry, I truly am excited about going to the Iroquois. But every time I touch the ticket, I feel terribly anxious. Tim, I really don't think we should go. Please don't be angry."

"Mae, I'm sure everything will be fine – we can leave after the first act if you still feel uneasy."

"Tim, no. I just know something awful is going to happen there."

Tim thought back about Mae accurately predicting his job promotion out of the blue and, though disappointed, quickly capitulated.

"No worries, my sweet. I hear it's sold out and they are selling Standing Room Only seats. I'm sure we can wander over there and exchange our tickets for another day." Tim and Mae turned in their tickets in short order and headed back to Mae's house for tea to shake off the frigid Chicago winter's chill. Little did they know, a tragedy of horrific proportions was moments away.

The eager crowd of more than 2,000 patrons, many of whom were teachers, mothers, and children enjoying their holiday break, could not have suspected that more than 600 of them would perish later that afternoon in "a calamity which…bereft hundreds of homes of their loved ones and made Chicago the most unhappy city on the face of the earth," as *The Great Chicago Theatre Disaster* would later recount.[49]

As the show began its second act at 3:15 that afternoon, a spark from a stage light ignited nearby stage drapery.[50] Attempts to stamp out the fire with a primitive fire-retardant blanket did nothing to halt its spread across the flammable decorative backdrops.[51] One of the lead actors attempted to calm the increasingly frightened audience by telling the orchestra to continue playing to soothe the crowd as stagehands attempted to lower a flame-retardant curtain, but the rope snagged on one of the pulleys and was never deployed.[52]

The fire raged and continued to spread. Terrified patrons ran towards the handful of exit doors that were visible, as most were hidden by curtains.[53] The exit doors were equipped with metal accordion gates, which Iroquois staff kept locked to prevent those in the "cheap seats" from entering more expensive main floor seats after the house lights dimmed once the performance began. Most of the frantic audience members were routed down clogged aisles to locked exit doors. Quickly the scene changed "from mimicry to tragedy," as one survivor said.[54] Watching from the stage, actor Eddie Foy wrote in his memoirs that he saw in the upper levels a "mad, animal-like stampede – their screams, groans, and snarls, the scuffle of thousands of feet and bodies grinding against bodies merging into a crescendo half-wail, half-roar."55

Several stage crew and actors opened a rear stage door to escape. Once the large stage door was opened, a backdraft created an explosive ball of flame that blasted through the main floor, killing many that were entrapped in the balcony sections. The explosion blew open an exit door in the rear of the theater, providing a fortuitous escape route for many. A lucky group happened upon a lone exit on the top level of the theater which was unlocked and led to a fire escape. As the patrons rushed onto the fire escape, they quickly noticed there was no exterior ladder down to the street. Now stuck on an exterior fire escape four levels above ground, the patrons screamed for help. Fortunately, their cries for help caught the attention of workmen in a building across the alley who "cantilevered planks to create a heart-stopping makeshift bridge, saving a handful of patrons after the first two who attempted the crossing slipped and fell to their deaths."56

Conditions inside the Iroquois were utter chaos. Those still alive and trapped inside attempted to scale over heaps of dead bodies. "Corpses were stacked ten feet high around some of the blocked exits. The victims were asphyxiated by the fire, smoke, and gases, or were crushed to death by the onrush of other terrified patrons behind them. It is estimated that 575 people were killed on the day of the fire; at least thirty more died of injuries over the ensuing weeks. The Great Chicago Fire, by comparison, killed … an estimated 300 people."57

Within a few moments, patrons desperately searched for an egress in vain, and hundreds of bodies began piling up inside the theater. They had died before firefighters arrived on the scene. *The Great Chicago Theatre Disaster* described what awaited the firemen arriving at the Iroquois as worse than that "pictured in the mind of Dante in his vision of the Inferno."58

The diner next door to the Iroquois, where Tim and Mae had lunch before the matinee, became a makeshift morgue and triage emergency room for the injured fortunate to make it out alive. "Panicked family and friends soon began descending on the restaurant to see if loved ones had escaped. As word of the staggering death toll spread, the city was overcome by a state of collective mourning."[59]

The fallout from the Iroquois Disaster was rapid and far-reaching. The city ordered all theaters closed until they were inspected and confirmed up to code. The tragedy made national headlines, prompting cities, large and small, across the nation to conduct safety and building code inspections of theaters. Chicago's City Council quickly enacted a building ordinance that included "new standards for aisles and exits, the use of fireproofing solution on scenery, connected fire alarms, limits on occupancy, the elimination of 'standing room' tickets, changes to sprinkler requirements, and rules for rooftop flues like those shockingly nailed shut in the Iroquois. Another result was a law that all doors in public buildings must open outward, in the direction of the egress, and widespread implementation of the 'panic bar.' Because the Iroquois exit doors opened into the theatre, as people rushed to get out it was impossible to open the doors against the weight of the stampede."[60]

The new ordinance included an important requirement that has been implemented in today's theaters – the requirement that "a red light is to be kept burning over the exits" during performances. This echoed the words of an electrical engineer who had advocated for signs to be illuminated by "a source of light independent of the theater lighting system."[61] This part of the ordinance was in response to the Iroquois's electricity going out during the blaze. The April 1904 edition of Western Electrician highlighted the adoption of "exit lights [which] are also supplemented by sperm-oil lamps" in the event that "the current supply is interrupted." Although technology has evolved, signs like these were the forerunners of the glowing red exit signs now prominently illuminated in modern theaters.[62]

Iroquois Theatre Before The Fire; 1903;
Author Unknown; http://Fire-Truck.Ru; Public Domain; Wikimedia Commons.

Iroquois Theatre Post Fire;
http://Fire-Truck.Ru; Public Domain; Wikimedia Commons.

Upon hearing the news later that evening, Tim and Mae held each other tightly and cried into the wee hours of the night. For years Tim wondered over and over again, "Why? Why did this awful tragedy happen? Why were he and Mae spared?" They were filled with sadness for the families and guilt for surviving every time those horrible memories floated in.

As to the first question of why this happened, the answer that came to light in the aftermath was that the tragedy was due in part to building inspectors and local politicians allowing the Iroquois to open despite numerous fire code breaches. Tim never lost his rage at crooked politicians for the remainder of his life, as can be detected in his poem:

> A grafting politician found a piece of gold,
> He put it back again, said it was too cold.
> Then he found another piece, put it in his pot,
> Now he wants to lose it, because it's getting hot.
>
> He's got automobiles with horns that make a screech,
> And when dreary cold winter comes, he drives to Palm Beach.
> He eats at all the best hotels, and tries to butt right in,
> But the only ones he blends in with are the peddlers of the gin.
>
> But don't forget old timer, right now you are sailing high,
> As time goes on so swiftly, 'twill soon be time to die.
> And then you'll sit alone oh boy, remorse will have his day,
> And friends won't come to greet you, but travel on their way.
>
> Remorse is a great old fellow, who seems to come in the night,
> When the rest of the world is sleeping, he seems to be at his height.
> He turns you over on your side and puts you on your back,
> And wakes you up most every night until your brain he racks.
>
> What's that noise? A buzzing sound sailing 'round through space,
> I seem to hear it all the time, and look! A smiling face.
> Gosh, it's Jake, and he smiles on me, he thinks I'm still on the square.
> Gee, how could I trim a sport like him, no wonder the folks all stare.

Chapter 19
TIME TO GET HITCHED
(February 8, 1905)

A lovely romance continued to grow for Mae and Tim. They became closer and closer every day. Tim couldn't believe he had found the girl of his dreams and, even more shockingly, she loved him back.

Before they met, Tim had lost faith in the concept of love because everyone in his life, whom he had loved unconditionally, had abruptly and unceremoniously left him alone. Tim had given up on love, trying to protect his heart from further devastation. He buried himself in books, novel after novel, and in working 14-hour days, week after week. It's easier to forget all the pain in your heart and soul when you fill your days with activities that keep your mind otherwise occupied. That is, until nighttime arrives. Then Tim would lay awake thinking about his parents, his siblings, the Wily Boys, Billy from the orphanage, Cora and Maisey. It was difficult for Tim to sleep and he seemed to be drinking more and more at night to self-medicate his sadness, but that only exacerbated his depression.

Then that fateful day arrived when Cupid's arrow shot him right between the eyes when he gazed at Mae for the first time. Whether it was serendipitous or meant to be, Tim didn't much care. However, following Mae's premonition about the Iroquois Theatre fire, Tim thought there may be a purpose to his life after all. Tim felt he finally found what he was searching for since escaping from Queen of Heaven all those years ago – not that his journey was over, but that it was just beginning. Tim wanted to spend the rest of his life with sweet Mae, have children, work hard, buy a home, and grow old together as a family. The American Dream – the Keltys, McEwens, Conlons, and Gillens were all striving to achieve exactly this for future generations when they took that leap of faith by leaving the homeland they loved and immigrating to North America. Tim was so proud of his ancestors for presenting this opportunity, but also was proud of himself for never giving up and seizing the opportunity.

One day in 1904, Mae sat down at her station, turned on the switchboard…and nothing – broken again. "Are you kidding me? Not again!" Agnes, the supervisor, rang up maintenance, and although Tim had been promoted and was now working exclusively in the Research Department, he showed up with his old tool box dressed in a suit. Agnes smiled and winked at Tim. Mae finally noticed the repairman was Tim. "What are you doing here?" Tim, grinning, reached around the switchboard. "Ah, here's the problem…there was a small box stuck in your switchboard." All the other operators, with hands over their mouths along with Agnes, gathered around Mae's desk. Tim grabbed the box, got on one knee, looked at Agnes, and asked, "Can I violate the No Talking rule for a minute?" Agnes, with tears in her eyes, nodded in approval.

"My sweet Mae, nearly five years ago I saw the love of my life for the first time. I thought I was dreaming because you were the prettiest girl I had ever seen. I later learned that you have the kindest heart, making you equally beautiful on the inside. I can't imagine living another day of my life without you. Will you marry me, Mae?"

Mae smiled and gazed at Tim with tears of joy in her sparkling dark brown eyes. "Oh Tim, it would be an honor. Yes!" The toll room erupted in cheers and applause. Tim, for the first time since he was eight years old, did not feel he was alone.

Tim and Mae married on February 8, 1905, at Holy Name Cathedral at 735 North State Street, where it remains today. Holy Name is the seat of the Archdiocese of Chicago, one of the largest Roman Catholic dioceses in the United States. Dedicated on November 21, 1875, Holy Name Cathedral replaced the Cathedral of Saint Mary and the Church of the Holy Name, which were destroyed by the Great Chicago Fire of 1871. Holy Name Cathedral was built in the Gothic revival architectural style. The church can seat 1,110 people, with a ceiling height of 70 feet high and a spire that reaches a height of 210 feet.[63]

Mae was stunning in her classic white lace wedding gown. Tim's dream came true. Their wedding reception was a modest affair with fifty or so family and close friends. The honeymoon was a long weekend at the Palmer House Hotel downtown.

The first order of business following the honeymoon was to move into their first apartment, located west of downtown near Laramie and Monroe. Mae and Tim had picked out their first home a few months before their wedding. Of course, in 1905, it was very rare for couples to move in together until they were married.

Mae Conlon in her Wedding Gown – 1905

A year later, Mae was pregnant with their first child, Dorothy, who was born at home in 1906. Due to the extraordinary muddy conditions of Monroe Street near the Conlon apartment that spring, the doctor had to park his horse and buggy on Madison Street and walk a block, arriving just in the nick of time.

In 1908, after their second child, Richard (Dick), was born, again at home, the Conlons were quickly outgrowing their tiny home. Although Mae had stopped working shortly before Dorothy was born, Tim continued at Chicago Bell. After successfully coming up

(Picnic – 1906)
Pictured are Mae (6th from left) holding baby Dorothy, next to Tim Conlon (seated to Mae's left/7th person from the left of the picture), Aunt Corina McEwen McGinnis (Mae's sister standing with big hat two down from Tim), Mae's mother Cecilia Kelty McEwen (standing next to Corina), Mae's sister Annie McEwen (standing next to Cecilia), Tim's sister Molly Conlon Golden (standing on the right side with feathers in her hat), and Mae's youngest sister, Loretta McEwen Bertaux (far right side eating a cookie)

with and being issued 22 patents on behalf of Western Electric and Chicago Bell during his tenure in the Research and Development Department, Tim was promoted to Chief of Chicago Area Toll Lines. As such, Tim was responsible for operating and maintaining all of the toll lines connecting calls made to and from Chicago. Whenever a call could not be placed or was dropped, Tim's department was responsible for determining the cause and making necessary repairs to the line.

Despite the increasingly tight quarters, Lucille was born in 1912 and Robert (Bob) in 1915. With four children under the age of eight, the full Conlon house was always abuzz with activity. Mae kept the house immaculate and the children clean and in order. She also made time to continue her tea reading for her friends and family, and the occasional client who heard about Mae through the Irish-American Chicago community. This, however, came to an end after one fateful session.

One summer afternoon, a few months after Bob was born in 1915, Mae had a group of friends over for a visit. Then, as was the protocol, the women gathered in the parlor for tea and the women asked politely for their tea to be read. Mae, according to tradition, would never read the tea until specifically requested to do so by her guests.

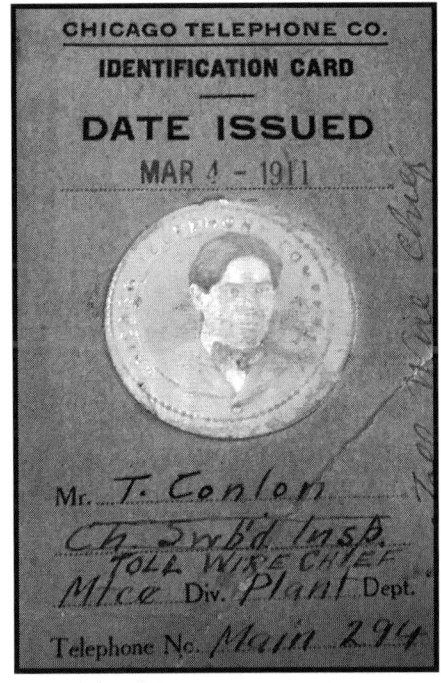

Chicago Telephone Co. Tim Conlon ID Card from 1911.

The first to ask for a reading was Rose O'Reagan, a friend of Mae's who lived down the street in the Conlon neighborhood. The tea was sipped by Rose, who handed the ornate porcelain cup to Mae when she was finished. Mae took a deep, slow breath while closing her eyes. Then, Mae tilted the cup and swirled the cup in a clockward movement so that the remaining drops of tea disbursed the tea leaf remnants along the wall of the cup. Mae emptied her mind of all other thoughts and focused exclusively on Rose's tea leaves. Mae instantly saw a long dark leaf trail at the very bottom of the cup with a stark break near one of the ends. Mae's heart raced, and she started to hyperventilate. The women, leaning in waiting for Mae's reading to begin, noticed the change in Mae's now ashen face. Mae had not seen this configuration in the tay before but immediately knew what it meant for Rose – impending death. Mae couldn't speak.

Rose, now frightened, inquired, "Mae, what is it? What do you see?"

Mae was able to shake the fear and regain her composure. "I see exciting things in your future…," proceeding to feign a very beige, positive reading. Mae, as most tea readers, would never relay such a horrid reading during a friendly, socialized session. Rose and the other women seemed to breathe a sigh of relief and the readings continued in a more normal, light mood.

After the women left, Mae sat in her kitchen by herself and began to sob. Mae faced the dilemma of revealing the premonition, which would cause tremendous stress and certainly frighten Rose and her family. In reality, while Mae had accurate premonitions often, sometimes readings didn't come to bear. "What if I revealed what I saw to Rose and I was wrong – the fright alone would probably kill her…" The last time Mae had such a strong negative feeling course through her entire body was when she had a foreboding about the tragic Iroquois Theatre fire. Mae was convinced Rose was going to die soon. Mae ran into Tim's arms when he returned from work and walked through the door that evening. Tim and Mae discussed the reading and what, if anything, to do about it well into the late hours. After weighing the numerous pros and cons of the various options, they concluded that Mae ought to pay Rose a visit and reveal that she saw something in the leaves that indicated something bad might happen and that she should be extra careful in the coming days.

After having breakfast and seeing Tim off to work and the two older children to school, Mae grabbed baby Bob and toddler Lucille to walk down the street to visit Rose. As Mae approached the O'Reagan house, she noticed a policeman leaving the house as Mr. O'Reagan shook his hand, and overheard that Father McGivern was en route to the house. Mae ran to the officer, who was now at the sidewalk. The officer informed Mae that Rose had tragically died in the middle of the night from what they believed was a heart attack. Mae fell to her knees, breaking down in tears.

Mae never revealed her premonition to anyone except Tim. Although some of the women who were present during the reading noted the uncomfortable demeanor Mae presented during the reading, Mae consistently denied she saw anything concerning. Mae officially retired from tea reading.

Mae's premonitions, however, continued regularly, usually when she least expected it. An image of her childhood friend Colleen, who she hadn't seen for years, would pop in her head, and then a half hour later Colleen would knock on her door for an unannounced visit. Fairly mundane episodes occurred for the next several years, until the evening before the Western Electric annual family outing in the summer of 1915. Mae felt an electric shiver through her entire body as she was packing a picnic basket for the family on the eve of the day-long outing. Mae dropped the silverware and dishes, which smashed on the kitchen floor. She then fainted and crashed to the floor herself. As Mae was falling, she heard a horn that began faintly then grew to a deafening blare.

Moments later, Mae began to hear Tim and daughter Dorothy rushing to her side, but she couldn't move and fell deeper into a state of unconsciousness. Mae initially saw total darkness and felt cold. Mae's dreamlike state evolved to where she was under water and began to panic as her lungs seemed to be running out of air as she frantically searched for the surface. Tim's voice was muffled at first, then slowly grew louder until Mae made her way to the surface and came to gasping for air.

Chapter 20
THE SS EASTLAND[2] (July 24, 1915)

The Conlons were excited to attend the fifth annual Western Electric Family Picnic. Several Illinois Bell employees and their families who, like Tim, interfaced with the Western Electric Research and Development Department, were also invited to attend. The Hawthorne Club, made up of Western Electric non-executive employees, planned several social and educational events throughout the year for the more than 20,000 employees of the Western Electric Hawthorne Works in Cicero, located just west of Chicago. The annual Family Picnic drew 3,000 participants the first couple of years and, due to the enthusiastic reviews of those attending the event, soon grew to more than 7,000 attendees.[64]

This year's outing was planned for July 24, 1915, a Saturday, which meant most of the attendees got the day off from their typical six-day work week. Each year, the picnic started by boarding one of five boats docked along the banks of the Chicago River at the Clark Street Bridge wharf. The patrons traveled on the vessels that were towed by tugboats down the Chicago River to Lake Michigan. Once out on the lake, the boats made the approximate two-hour journey over 38 miles southeast to the port in Michigan City, Indiana. From there, the people would walk several blocks to the location of the Family Picnic at Washington Park, located along the shores of Lake Michigan. Washington Park was a popular destination for Chicagoans to spend the day and enjoy the rollercoaster, electric merry-go-round, dancing pavilion, baseball park, picnic grounds, bandstand gazebo, beaches, and bathhouse. Young couples took leisurely strolls through the wooded area of the park leading to tall sand dunes. The Hawthorne

---

2   Much of the factual information in this chapter is attributable to the excellent Eastland Disaster Historical Society website (EastlandDisaster.org) and Susan Stranahan's article in Smithsonian Magazine.

Club had a full day of activities for the families with games, lunch, and bands playing on the transport vessels and at Washington Park.[65]

One of the ships that was chartered for this year's trip had also been commissioned for the previous two years. Because this particular ship was larger and particularly slower than the other vessels, it had lagged behind by nearly an hour at the previous two outings. Consequently, the organizers decided that this year she should be the first of the five chartered vessels to leave port and transport the 7,000 plus people across the lake to Indiana. The ship was the SS *Eastland*.[66]

Tim decided to sign his family of six on the first boat leaving that day, because he wanted to get a good picnic spot near the band gazebo. Tim was an early riser, as were his four children, all under the age of 9. "We are early risers anyway, Mae; we might as well get up and at 'em." The Conlons had not attended previous Family Picnics, but Tim had heard how much fun they were from coworkers. The children were so excited as the big day approached.

The *Eastland* was designed by an engineer who had to that point exclusively designed freight ships, which are typically specified to carry loads low in the ship's hold, which creates a lower center of gravity. The *Eastland* was the designer's first, and only, passenger ship. It was designed and built in 1902 with a maximum capacity of 500 passengers for lake excursions to Indiana, Michigan, and Wisconsin, and hauled produce on the return trips to Chicago.[67]

The boat was designed with no keel, was top-heavy, and relied on poorly designed ballast tanks in the hold to keep the ship upright. Subsequent modifications increased the vessel's speed and passenger capacity, but design "improvements" actually made the vessel less stable. In all, the *Eastland* was modified and retrofitted five times from 1902 through 1915 to increase the ship's passenger capacity to 2,500 souls.[68]

Tim carried Mae to the couch in the family room and had Dorothy run to the kitchen to retrieve a glass of water. "Mae, you fainted. Are you okay?"

"I don't know, give me a minute." Mae was still breathing heavy and was lightheaded. After taking a few sips of water, Mae was still very frightened. "It was pitch black – I was cold. It was as if I was underwater, trying to surface so I could breathe." Mae then broke down crying, "I thought I was going to die!"

"What did you see, Mae?"

"Nothing, but I most definitely was underwater."

"What were you doing right before you passed out?"

"I was packing the picnic basket for tomorrow."

"Did you see or hear or feel anything right before you blacked out?"

"I had a shiver course through my body, the room started to spin. And, yes, I did hear a loud horn blast just as I slipped away."

"What sort of horn – a car, a train?"

"Loud like a train, but not a train whistle – it was deafening."

"Like a ship's foghorn?"

"My God – yes, that's exactly what I heard. Tim, we can't take our family on that boat tomorrow."

Tim was now frightened. There was no way he was not going to take Mae's premonition seriously. He and Mae stayed up discussing what had happened and what they should do or not do. Given the late hour, Tim made a couple of phone calls to members of the Hawthorne Club to get more information on the boats and whether there were other vessel options available for his family. He was, however, unable to reach anyone. Tim did finally connect with a couple coworkers to mention Mae's episode as a warning and to seek their advice on what to do. Both of the coworkers, while sorry to hear that Mae fainted, were unaware of Mae's uncannily accurate premonitions and mostly laughed off the foreboding and pointed out that Western Electric had chartered the same ships last year.

One friend noted, "Tim, we are going across the southern tip of Lake Michigan. If there are any signs of trouble, we'll only be ten miles or so from the shore."

Another friend remarked, "Since the *Titanic* sank in 1912, there is a new Maritime Law requiring enough lifeboats to accommodate every passenger. So, there is nothing to worry about. I mean, really, what could possibly go wrong?" Tim had learned at an early age that is a question that should never be asked.

Tim, of course, was extraordinarily apprehensive about participating but felt some pressure to attend this year's event from company management. Having missed previous years' outings, along with receiving several of the higher-ups' missives that everyone should make every effort to attend, Tim thought he should make an appearance this year. But he and Mae certainly did not want the children to go given Mae's premonitions of danger. Though the children were terribly disappointed, the plan was for Tim to go alone while Mae would stay home with the kids under the pretext that the children all came down with the bad summer cold that was going around.

Tim woke up extra early the next morning so he could make his way down to the wharf and explain to the organizers that his family would not be attending and, importantly, that he was not boarding the *Eastland* as he was traveling instead with coworker friends on a later departing ship, the *Theodore Roosevelt*. Arriving at the wharf adjacent to the Clark Street Bridge at 6:30 a.m., Tim saw there already were hundreds of people lined up to board the *Eastland*, which was scheduled to depart at 7:30 a.m.

Tim looked toward River Street, adjacent to the wharf about a block downriver, and recalled the hobo camp that had helped him escape from Ice Man decades earlier.

It was a cloudy summer morning with light drizzle falling. After informing one of the organizers of his change of plans, Tim spotted the *Theodore Roosevelt*, which was scheduled to depart fifteen minutes after the *Eastland* launch, with boarding to begin at 6:45 a.m. Tim boarded the *Roosevelt* and eventually located one of his friends and his wife, who were standing outside on the top deck. They perched themselves by the railing, which provided a bird's-eye view of the masses boarding the *Eastland*, which was docked 30 yards in front of the *Theodore Roosevelt*.

Tim was surprised at the number of people who were lined up for the *Eastland*, thinking there was no way you could fit 2,500 on board. "They'll be packed in like sardines – boy, I'm glad Mae and the kids took a pass."

Boarding for the *Eastland* began, with a rate of 100 passengers per minute. Two children were counted as one passenger, and infants were not counted toward the capacity quota. The cost was $1 for an adult. Considering the average pay at the Hawthorne Works for a line worker was $17 per week, the fare was not exactly cheap, relatively speaking. The top deck quickly filled to near capacity, and passengers started to trickle down to the first deck below where a band was playing ragtime music. Many of the younger couples began dancing as the boarding continued.[69]

Prior to boarding, Captain Harry Pederson ordered all of the ballast tanks to be emptied because he thought the weight of the maximum capacity passengers would lower the ship's hull enough for proper stability. Just before 7:00 a.m., Tim noticed that the *Eastland* began to list starboard toward the wharf. Tim and his friend surmised the listing was due to the multitude of boarding passengers on the starboard side from the pier. Tim was relieved when the ship straightened, but it did so only for one or two minutes before it then began to list to the port, out toward the river and away from the wharf. Most of the passengers seemed to laugh nervously at the ship's rocking back and forth. The first officer immediately ordered to level the *Eastland*, and she was righted again, causing Tim, who was already on high alert, to breathe a sigh of relief.[70]

By 7:00 a.m. approximately 1,000 passengers had boarded. The *Eastland* again listed, this time again slightly to the port side. At this point the captain ordered the engine room to start the engines. By 7:15 a.m., the *Eastland* reached its maximum capacity of 2,501 passengers. The crew terminated boarding and directed the people remaining in line to board the *Theodore Roosevelt*. As the crew started to stow away the gangplank, the already listing port-ward ship tilted several degrees more to the left due to a majority of the passengers walking to the port side of the top deck after boarding to make way for the last of the passengers. The crew attempted to move many of the passengers back to the starboard side of the *Eastland*, but it proved difficult to persuade the passengers as they wanted to have a nice view of the river side as opposed to the starboard where the *Eastland* was still moored to the wharf.[71]

At 7:20 a.m., Tim became gravely concerned to observe the *Eastland* list even further port to an estimated 15 degrees. Captain Pederson, also bothered by the continued list in spite of the weight of 2,573 passengers and crew, ordered the engineers to open the valves to fill the No. 2 and 3 starboard ballast tanks. But it takes nearly five minutes for the ballast tanks to fill. This maneuver facilitated the *Eastland* to right itself, but the ship was still unstable.[72]

The *Eastland* then quickly again listed back to port, even though most of the passengers had been asked to move near the starboard rail. Tim and his colleagues noticed water began to enter the main deck through a port side scupper, and the captain ordered the engine stopped. The captain quickly tried to problem solve in his head and concluded the ship would correct itself once they departed from the wharf and motored forward. So the crew was again ordered to initiate final preparations for departure.[73]

At 7:25 a.m. Tim observed that now almost all of the passengers on the main deck and below were again being instructed to move to the starboard side. This ploy did not correct the port side list. Tim's friend shouted, "Look at the gangways on the left! There is water rushing into the *Eastland*!"[74]

A warning signal blared out from the *Eastland*. Tim whispered to himself, "Mae was right – this is the horn she heard just before she fainted. God help them all." Captain Pederson sent an urgent "stand by" on his engine room telegraph. Tim could see the stern of the *Eastland* drift away from the wharf toward the river, causing the bow to move closer to the wharf. This movement resulted in the boat rocking back toward the center. As the *Eastland*'s rear drifted from the wharf, passengers on the upper decks, thinking that they were now departing, decided to rush away from the crowded starboard rail. This was the first substantial move made by the passengers to the port side. The ship, however, was still tethered to the wharf. This en masse move away from the right side resulted in the *Eastland* listing to port its third and final time.[75]

Just before 7:30 a.m., the *Eastland* port-ward list was an estimated 30 degrees. Engineers in the boiler room and crew below deck began to run up to the main deck, sensing disaster as water started gushing into the ship. The crew requested passengers on the hurricane deck to head toward the starboard side. The now 45-degree list to port made it impossible for the passengers to comply due to the sharp angle and wet, slippery deck from the morning rain. Because the boat's planned journey was a short trip across Lake Michigan, nothing was battened down as it would be on a rougher day or during a longer journey such as a lake crossing to Grand Haven, Michigan. The stark list caused everything on shelves, racks, cabinets, and drawers to slip off, with many items striking passengers. The piano on the promenade deck rolled violently and crushed two women. The refrigerator behind the bar fell onto one of the bartenders.[76]

Water was now flowing in through the aft port gangway and

portholes on the main deck. Passengers on the main deck sensed impending disaster and began to panic. Passengers in the lower-level decks ran to the staircases leading up to the 'tween deck, which caused a logjam from which many never escaped. The few passengers and crew members that were able to crawl their way up the 45-degree wet bank to the starboard side tried to jump to the wharf, some landing on the wharf, but many falling into the river. The *Eastland* now listed 60 degrees to the port side, as she was being further lightened as passengers jumped from the ship.[77]

The wreck of the SS *Eastland* came at 7:30 a.m. as it rolled quietly into the Chicago River and came to rest in the mud at the bottom. The *Eastland* rolled over, as reporter Carl Sandburg wrote for the *International Socialist Review*, "like a dead jungle monster shot through the heart." The *Eastland* disaster took place in 20 feet of water and less than 20 feet from the wharf, still tied to the dock.[78]

"When the boat toppled on its side those on the upper deck were hurled off like so many ants being brushed from a table," wrote Harlan Babcock, a reporter for the *Chicago Herald*. "In an instant, the surface of the river was black with struggling, crying, frightened, drowning humanity. Wee infants floated about like corks."[79]

Photo of Eastland Disaster;
Permission Granted By Eastland Disaster Historical Society; Public Domain; July 24, 1915.

Photos of Eastland Disaster;
Permission Granted By Eastland Disaster Historical Society; Public Domain; July 24, 1915.

The captain of the *Kenosha*, the tugboat assigned to tow the *Eastland* down the river to Lake Michigan, cleverly maneuvered his boat in between the wharf and the *Eastland* so as to create a makeshift bridge for those that were able to crawl from the top starboard side of the *Eastland* and walk to safety, saving many without getting their feet wet, including Captain Pederson.[80] "The captain goes down with the ship" is a long-held maritime golden rule, meaning the captain of the vessel bears full responsibility for the ship, its passengers, and crew. In an emergency, the captain must exclusively devote his or her time and energy saving everyone on board or die trying. Old Captain Pederson apparently missed that lecture in captain's school.

In the early 1900s, many people in the United States, especially those living in large cities, were weak swimmers if they had learned to swim at all. Consequently, many of the passengers that fell into the river or those that escaped from inside of the *Eastland* into the river were not proficient swimmers and struggled to survive. Many passengers who were unable to swim grabbed others in the water who were able to tread water, putting both lives in jeopardy.[81]

People from the nearby Clark Street Bridge and those along the wharf grabbed boxes, crates, ladders, wood planks, and anything they thought would float and threw them into the river toward those thrashing in the water trying to stay afloat. Tragically, it was reported that some of the wood crates and pallets struck some passengers in their heads, either killing them instantly or knocking them out. While there was an abundance of life jackets on board the *Eastland*, none were taken out of storage because the vessel was still tethered to the pier. Nor was there time to deploy the numerous lifeboats and rafts, which were required on all passenger ships following the demise of the *Titanic*.[82]

Three years earlier, the 1912 sinking of the *Titanic* prompted a "lifeboats-for-all" law among marine safety officials. "The United States Congress passed a bill requiring lifeboats to accommodate

75 percent of a vessel's passengers, and in March 1915, President Woodrow Wilson signed what became known as the LaFollette Seaman's Act. During the debate over the bill, the general manager of the Detroit & Cleveland Navigation Company had warned that some Great Lakes vessels, with their shallow drafts, 'would turn turtle if you attempted to navigate them with the additional weight of lifeboats on the upper decks.' Too few legislators listened. By July 1915, the *Eastland*, which had been designed to carry six lifeboats, was carrying 11 lifeboats and 37 life rafts, each weighing about 1,100 pounds, and enough life jackets, each approximately six pounds apiece, for all 2,573 passengers and crew. Most were stowed on the upper decks. No tests were ever conducted to determine how the additional weight affected the boat's stability – even though the *Eastland* already had a troubled history of instability."[83]

Ironically, ensuing investigations concluded that the additional life rafts intended to promote safety in fact made the *Eastland* more top-heavy and more unsteady and were a contributing factor to the disaster.[84]

Tim and his friends scrambled to grab every life jacket they could on board the nearby *Theodore Roosevelt* and threw them toward those treading water. Other nearby boats also deployed their life rafts and paddled over to rescue the people that were still alive.

Anna Repa, a Western Electric nurse who was a passenger on the *Eastland*, made it safely to the pier and immediately went to work triaging survivors brought back to the pier. "People were struggling in the water, clustered so thickly that they covered the surface of the river," she would recall. "The screaming was the most horrible of all." Anna would stop cars driving by on River Street running parallel to the Chicago River, now called Wacker Drive, and plead with the drivers to transport them to nearby hospitals with specific instructions on the survivors' conditions. Anna told a reporter later that day that every one of the fifty or so drivers she stopped willingly complied.[85]

CPR and mouth-to-mouth resuscitation were not well known in 1915. Certainly, none of the 75 police officers that arrived on scene had any such knowledge or training.[86]

The Clark Street Bridge operator, who was standing by to raise the bridge once the boats departed, immediately climbed down the bridge tower and jumped into the bridge's dinghy. He was the first rescuer to paddle over and was responsible for saving several passengers.[87]

Chicago firemen were also quickly sent to the scene. Other off-duty fire personnel heard the news of the disaster and ran over to provide assistance. A CFD fire boat, the *Graeme Stewart*, arrived within minutes of the capsizing of the *Eastland*, saving many lives.[88]

Seventeen-year-old Reggie Bowles was driving by on his scooter on his way to work. Reggie happened to be an accomplished competitive swimmer. Without hesitation, Reggie stripped down to his underwear and jumped into the river. Reggie saved several, and also held his breath for long periods while he swam into the hull of the capsized Eastland trying to locate survivors stuck inside the ship but still with access to rapidly depleting oxygen. Based on Reggie's heroic efforts, nearby construction workers with acetylene torches cut holes in the hull where Reggie estimated survivors were located.[89]

While the workers were cutting holes in the hull, Captain Harry Pederson, who managed to make his way to the safety of the pier just as the ship capsized, screamed at the workers to stop. "You are ruining my ship!" The police quickly arrested Pederson, which was actually fortunate for him because the angry mob witnessing the captain's antics wanted to tie a cement block around his neck and throw him in the river! The workers either ignored Pederson or told him where he should go, and continued to torch holes in the hull. Ten survivors escaped and reached safety through these escape holes.[90]

Thirty minutes after the *Eastland* tipped over on its side, at 8:00 a.m., the rescue efforts turned into a recovery operation. All of the victims that were thrashing in the water and those that somehow escaped from the hull were on the wharf side. The rest perished from drowning in the river or being trapped inside the *Eastland*. Rescue efforts proceeded round the clock for several weeks. The Bear Trap Dam in Lockport located 40 miles upriver was ordered closed to slow the current of the river from 8 miles per hour down to 2 miles per hour, so as to keep bodies from flowing down the river and into Lake Michigan, where they would likely never be recovered.[91]

Eight hundred forty-four souls were lost that morning, including 22 entire families. Seventy percent of the victims were under the age of 25. The Eastland Disaster was and remains the deadliest shipwreck in Great Lakes history. Seven priests were on site administering confessions and last rites as victims in various states of consciousness were brought onto the pier.[92]

Harlan Babcock, reporter for the *Chicago Herald*, wrote "That silently sad procession of policemen and firemen and others bearing in fours, each a body on a dripping stretcher – mute evidence of the terrible toll of the waters. Solemnly, the stretcher bearers walked down the hull of the steamer onto the dock with their inanimate burdens of humanity that a brief half hour or hour before had scurried laughing to the death craft."[93]

Tim and his friends remained at the dock long into the afternoon doing what they could to help along with hundreds of other volunteers. They were asked to go to nearby department stores Marshall Fields and Carson Pirie Scott that opened up their stores to provide blankets and sheets to provide comfort and warmth to the survivors, and to cover up the deceased.

Several nearby buildings and warehouses were commandeered to serve as temporary morgues for the hundreds of bodies being recovered. One warehouse, which later became the site of Oprah Winfrey's Harpo Studios and is now where the McDonald's Corporation Headquarters is located, became one of the larger temporary morgues. Nearly 400 bodies were lined up in rows of 80, and friends and family were allowed in 20 at a time to try to locate and identify their loved ones. Funerals, which at the time were typically held in the family residence, were plentiful for the coming weeks, especially in the town of Cicero where a vast majority of the victims and their families had lived due to its close proximity to the Western Electric Hawthorne Works.[94]

Within three weeks of the disaster, every victim in the temporary morgues had been identified by their next of kin except one, a young presumably 7- or 8-year-old boy. The workers in the morgue referred to him as "Little Feller." One of the Catholic churches held a ceremonial wake in Cicero for the young victim, which was attended by all the children in the associated Catholic school. Shockingly, a few of the children in the second-grade class recognized Little Feller as they passed by his casket. He was 7-year-old Willie Novotny. Willie was not identified because his parents, Agnes and James, and his 9-year-old sister Mame, all perished in the Eastland Disaster as well, but they all had identifying information on their person. Because the parents were the only ones who knew Willie was with them, no one alive could identify him.[95]

In total, 844 people died in the Eastland Disaster. Just 10 weeks earlier, the Lusitania had been torpedoed and sunk in the Atlantic, with a death toll of 785 passengers. In 1912, 829 passengers had died aboard the Titanic (plus 694 crewmembers). Both of those disasters took place on the high seas.[96]

Ted Wachholz, president of the Eastland Disaster Historical Society, expressed his theory on why the *Eastland* looms less large than the *Titanic* or the *Lusitania*: "Even though more passengers perished on the *Eastland*, there wasn't anyone rich or famous onboard…it was all hardworking, salt-of-the-earth immigrant families."[97]

"In the end, blame was pinned largely on Erickson, the chief engineer, for mismanaging the ballast tanks in the hold to right the *Eastland* before it capsized. Erickson, who initially was represented by Clarence Darrow, died as the legal proceedings dragged on. That made him – in the view of G.W. Hilton, the historian and author who meticulously analyzed thousands of pages of maritime and legal documents about the Eastland disaster – a convenient scapegoat."[98]

Civil lawsuits to resolve more than 800 wrongful-death claims dragged on for two decades. Maritime law limited liability to the value of the *Eastland*, set at $46,000. Claims filed by the salvage company hired to tow the vessel from the accident scene and the coal company that supplied fuel took precedence in any recoveries. In the end, victims and families received little or nothing. Although the overwhelming evidence strongly suggested that Captain Pedersen had been negligent, he was never found liable in any civil lawsuit, nor was he criminally prosecuted. Further, none of the officers of the steamship company were found guilty of any crime. All criminal charges were dropped, and the owners avoided any legal finding of civil negligence. "The blame, G.W. Hilton concluded, rested in a poorly designed boat that had been rendered top-heavy as a result of the post-*Titanic* safety measures."[99]

Mae and the Conlon children ran into Tim's arms as he walked through the door. The news had traveled fast about the *Eastland*, causing the Conlons paralyzing worry about Tim's well-being. They thanked God for sparing their lives and prayed hard for all the victims and their families. It really was too much for Tim and especially Mae to handle. It caused Tim to again reflect tirelessly upon his life, why this happened and why were they again spared. Every night for the next several months Tim would hear the horrific wailing of the drowning passengers as he first drifted into a deep sleep, causing him to wake up, yelling out and hyperventilating.

Mae was so upset she wanted to move away from Chicago. This caused Mae to occupy much of her time on where they should move.

Tim, of course, didn't want to leave. Chicago was the only town he knew. Although he may have had an inside track into working for another sister Bell Company wherever they ended up, Tim loved his position as Toll Chief at Illinois Bell, which had taken a lifetime of hard work to land.

Chapter 21
CALIFORNIA HERE WE COME (1916)

The compromise reached between Tim and Mae was for Mae to travel with her mother Cecilia, who had been living with them, and their four children to Los Angeles to visit Cecilia's brother Charles for an extended vacation. Cecilia had a large steamer trunk containing all of her belongings. She would move into one of her children's homes for three to six months. Then, when Cecilia felt she was "overstaying her welcome," she would pack up the steamer trunk and move to another of her children's homes. Most of the time, Cecilia would give no notice and just show up at the front door with her steamer trunk.

Cecilia Kelty McEwen, Mae's mother, born in 1859.

Cecilia's brother Charles had moved to the southwest United States in his 20s, living in Arizona. In 1914, he retired and moved to Los Angeles. He always raved about the beauty of Southern California to his sister in his regular correspondence, wherein he encouraged Cecilia to come out for a visit. "You won't believe the beaches out here. The waves are constantly crashing and the weather is in the 70s and 80s all year round."

Tim, of course, could not take time off for the trip due to his responsibilities at work. In 1916, traveling by train from Chicago to Los Angeles took two to three full days, and changing trains along the way if required would add another day or two of travel. With only limited vacation time for the year, it would be impossible for Tim to travel somewhere that burned two to three days each way.

Mae booked one-way train tickets for herself, the four children, and Cecilia to leave for Los Angeles at the end of May 1916. This itinerary meant taking the older kids out of school for the last month of the school year. Depending on how much they enjoyed California, they tentatively planned to spend the month of June before returning home. Mae planned to investigate available housing and schools to determine if a permanent move out west was desirable.

One of the allures of California besides the mountains, beaches, and year-round gorgeous weather that intrigued Mae was the growing silent movie industry. Charlie Chaplin's *The Tramp* and DW Griffith's *The Birth of a Nation* had just come out in theaters in 1915, and silent movies were becoming the rage across the United States. In 1916, Dorothy Conlon was an adorable ten-year-old girl who loved to sing and dance. Many of Mae's friends and relatives said Dorothy should be in the movies. Mae's sister, Loretta, who was a professional theater actress, agreed and offered to make connections for Mae and Dorothy in California.

"The art of motion pictures grew to full maturity in the 'silent era' from 1894 to 1923. The height of that era, from the early 1910s to the mid-1920s, was a particularly fruitful period for artistic innovation. The film movements of Classical Hollywood began during this period. Silent filmmakers pioneered the art form such that virtually every style and genre of filmmaking of the 20th and 21st centuries have their artistic roots in the Silent Era. The Silent Era was also a pioneering one from a technical point of view. Three-point lighting, the close-up, long shot, panning, and continuity editing all became prevalent long before silent films were replaced by "talking pictures" or "talkies" in the late 1920s. Some film scholars claim that the artistic quality of cinema actually decreased for several years during the early 1930s, until film directors, actors, and production staff adapted fully to the new "talkies" around the mid-1930s."[100]

Tim had originally voiced his objection at the idea, accusing Mae of "running away." "Everyone I know that has moved to California was running away from their problems as opposed to having the guts to stay and resolve them. All the talk of the beauty of the sun and the beaches is a facade. You won't meet anyone who is actually from California. They all moved there to escape something."

After much debate, it was settled – the extended trip to the West Coast was on. Mae, her four children, and her mother embarked on the long two-and-a-half-day train trip to California. Tim stayed home. He wished his family a bon voyage but was so upset knowing how much he would miss them.

As for Dorothy trying out for the movies, Tim thought it was a frivolous long shot. "Dorothy, do your best by being yourself. If they don't like you for who you are, I wouldn't want to have anything to do with them anyway."

After the first week of being alone once again, Tim missed his family terribly. This was the first time Tim and Mae had ever been separated for longer than a few days since they began dating. Tim again took to writing about his feelings with another poem, one that he sent to Mae in California:

California

I put your picture on my desk
Underneath the glass,
So, I could see the classic face
Of my charming little lass.

I put it in my pocketbook,
And took it out again.
Then I put it on the dresser.

Then I put it in a frame.

It looks so lonesome standing there,
So different from the rest,
That I picked it up to kiss it,
Now I kept it in my vest.

Now, every time I think of her,
I take it out and see,
The sweetest, dearest, little girl,
That's all the world to me.

Every time I meet a stranger,
Be he friend or be he foe,
I tell them she is different
From all the girls they know.

And when sometimes I get lonesome,
And feel a little sad,
I just take out your picture, Mae,
And it always makes me glad.

Tim - 1916

Tim stayed in touch with a few of his friends with whom he had hung out in his early twenties. They were his drinking buddies when Tim was a bachelor. His group of friends frequented most of the saloons in the near north section of town at one time or another. With Mae gone, and with Tim feeling very lonely and a wee bored, he thought it was high time to reach out to his former main wing man, Jimmy Gallagher. Jim was thrilled to hear from Tim. They decided to grab dinner downtown and then hit a few taverns and haunts from their single days.

Tim and Jimmy G., as he was known, had a wonderful time at dinner, catching up on the old days and reliving some funny stories from the past. After dinner, Tim and his mate strolled north down Clark Street. As they crossed the Clark Street Bridge, they both stopped, made a sign of the cross, and said a silent prayer for the victims and families of the *Eastland*, which had capsized on the river a year earlier just below where they were standing. Tim heard the echoes of the screams in his head and felt a chill run down his neck as he again saw the terror in the eyes of the ghosts thrashing in the water.

The first stop was Engels, where Tim, Jimmy G., and the rest of their crew were well-known back in the day. A younger Tim Conlon along with a dashing Jimmy Gallagher were usually greeted by the owner, and the bartender would have already poured their favorite drinks before they sat down at the bar. This time, the crowd was fairly sparse for a Friday night, and the owner Tommy Engel was nowhere in sight. The bartender was a younger man with a scowl who ignored the pair, paying more attention to the apparent regulars at the other end of the bar. Finally, he asked, "What do you fellas need?"

"We used to frequent here a bunch in 1903. We'd love to say hi to Tommy."

"That was a long time ago – haven't you heard? Mr. Engel passed away in 1910, I think. His son owns it now with a couple of guys from New York. Now, what can I get you?"

Tim and Jim sat by themselves drinking the new cocktail of the day, the Old Fashioned. The young pretty women walked by them without even a glance, with the younger, more rambunctious men getting most of the attention from other patrons and the bartender.

Tim and Jim took in two more stops before calling it a night. At each tavern they sat alone at the bar, not seeing a familiar face, which was a far cry from the days their gang ran the show. Jimmy G. looked sad, staring down at his drink, likely due in part to his growing whiskey buzz.

"Jimmy, my boy, don't let it get you down. We can't go back and expect things to remain the same. Thank God! The past is in the past. Anyone who tries to live there will be lost. Let's enjoy the present. I'm so happy to reconnect with you, and I look forward to having you and your wife over to our house when Mae returns from California."

Jim shrugged his shoulders, "As the Romans said, carpe diem, I guess."

The next morning, struggling from a slight hangover, Tim reflected on his trip down memory lane, now called Clark Street, and wrote a note to Jimmy G. with this poem:

> I like to walk down Clark Street, Jim,
> When I go out to lunch.
> It brings back nights of long ago,
> When you and I were young.
>
> Downtown was not so colorful,
> In general, not so gay.
> So, they crossed the bridge on Clark Street,
> To sing and dance and play.
>
> Some went on to Engels
> To sing with gay soubrettes,
> And some of them stopped at Barclays
> With crowds that were ringing wet.
>
> Some of them stopped at Murphy's
> On the corner of the Square,
> To hear the latest in politics
> And perhaps find Busse there.
>
> Jack Dalton's place was famous
> For the gay birds of the past.
> But time and good-looking women
> Are things that do not last.
>
> Mont Tennis had his Crystal Bar
> That brought the crowds to see,
> Just what Monty looked like,
> But never in sight was he.
>
> Thomas Mackin had the Revere House,
> Where he had cockfights on the roof.
> And many a poor old rooster,
> Never return to his coop.

The Lakeshore crowd was not so shy,
And of course, they were graceful and gay,
So, they helped to make things lighter,
And danced 'til break of day.

Now let us think of Frowley's
With Alec, Tom, and Mike.
And listen to the warbling
That came from the boys on the pike.

McVickers was easily the classic,
And Charlie Rigg sure was the clown,
King's Black Derby Hat was in fashion.
While Duffy favored the brown.

But it mattered not much to Duffy
If the color was blue, gray, or brown,
It was just another disaster,
When the blondes or brunettes came around.

I was up to the old scene yesterday,
And walked around the place,
But no one came to greet me,
Not one smiling face.

So, I guess we'll have to change the act,
And put on another show.
For there's nothing left for you and me
At the scenes of long ago.

And I could keep on writing
And dream of the golden pass,
But there's one thing I remember, Jim,
It's your smile in the mirrored glass.

Tim corresponded with Mae and their children throughout Mae's extended West Coast trip. Long distance phone calls to and from Los Angeles were fairly expensive. Tim's routine was to sit down in the parlor at his desk after dinner and write a detailed letter to Mae about the day's events, sometimes including a poem. Tim discussed his nightly dinners at Aunt Annie's house. Annie McEwen was Mae's sister, who lived several blocks away, and who graciously invited Tim to dinner every night during the trip. Tim went to Annie's most nights but regretted it every time he sat down and laid his eyes on Annie's husband, Claude. Tim described Claude in one of his letters as "a very opinionated oaf with disgusting personal hygiene. I really don't know how poor Annie stands it. Last night he treated me to a demonstration of how to clean your fingernails with a fork right before dinner was served."

Tim, however, loved Annie's company very much. She was educated and an instructor at the Chicago Art Institute. Annie's interesting and charming stories were such a juxtaposition to her loudmouth husband's dull, misinformed bromides. It was all Tim could do to not resort to punching Claude in the nose when he would belittle or insult lovely Annie, which Claude tended to do after his nightly glass of whiskey. One night, when Annie announced her promotion along with a bump in pay at the Art Institute, Tim applauded. "Way to go, Annie! I'm so proud of you and how hard you have been working to achieve your raise. Tell me all about it…" But Claude instead, out of perverse jealousy, stormed out of the dining room and left the house for a walk. Tim completely ignored Claude's tantrum and continued to ask question after question of Annie about her new position.

As Tim left to say goodnight, he kissed his sister-in-law on the cheek. "Annie, I've learned that no matter how hard we try, we cannot control how small-minded people act or feel, so it's best to focus on the things you can control, like your good self. And one more thing, Annie, as the Romans used to say, 'Don't let the bastards get you down.'"

Mostly, though, Tim expressed in his nightly handwritten letters how much he missed his sweet Mae and their children. Tim was at first surprised how much he missed them, and secretly was disappointed in himself for becoming such a sentimental sap. He had gone through a good majority of his life on his own, proving to himself that he did not need anything from anyone to survive. Over the years, Tim built up such a formidable fortress around his heart and soul to protect him from further mental and physical pain. Mae melted most of his barriers with her beautiful face and sweet demeanor. Tim questioned himself as he lay in bed about why he had become so melancholy. His heart ached to see again Mae's smile, Dorothy dancing and singing after dinner, Dick coming home just in time for dinner with his baseball cap on sideways and his shirt covered in dirt and grass stains, Dorothy teasing Dick about being sweet on the girl next door, and even Bob crying for a bottle at night. These are not the complaining emotions of a helpless weakling, they were the feelings of a dedicated husband and father who worked hard every day to support, comfort, provide guidance, and teach his family life's lessons.

"My wife and children are my purpose. This is what I worked for so hard and for so long to achieve. My family is my dream. Without Mae's love, I would be lost. I would quickly become again that hardened, tough, angry, sad, and lonely man I was before we met. I have evolved as a person. I only pray and vow to continue to be the best man, husband, father, friend, and employee I can be." Tim closed his eyes and quickly fell asleep, knowing that missing his family was not weakness, but strength.

Of course, Mae missed Tim too, but taking care of her four children ranging in age from one to nine years old was a full-time job. Still, Mae took time every night before retiring to write a letter to Tim. At first her correspondence was filled with details of what each child and her mother had done that day – headed to the beach to play in the sand and swim, hiked the trails of the nearby mountains, read, visited her cousins in the area. One day brought especially exciting news,

Mae's sister Loretta, as she promised to try to do, had at last lined up Dorothy to meet with a Hollywood silent movie agent. Mae hoped this could lead to a possible audition for Dorothy, who had such a sparkling personality and who enjoyed acting in plays at school in Chicago. "Dorothy's meeting with the movie agent is tomorrow. Our dear is so excited! I am taking her, and Mother Cecilia will watch the little ones." This was a thrilling time for Mae and her brood. It finally took her troubled mind off of the *Eastland*. Mae wrote to Tim that she had really come to love the West Coast life, again encouraging Tim to consider transplanting to LA.

Mae woke up early to fix Dorothy's long blonde hair and get her dressed for the big day. Uncle Charles drove them to downtown Hollywood in his new Model T Ford. After Charlie dropped Mae and Dorothy off, they arrived in the agent's crowded reception area fifteen minutes early. A snooty receptionist announced that the agent, Mr. Silverstein, was with another client and that several people were in line ahead of them. After sitting nervously but patiently for several hours, Dorothy Conlon was at last called into the agent's office. As Mae walked in, Shecky Silverstein, a portly, balding man with thick glasses and a bushy mustache, greeted them. "So, this is Loretta's little niece. And you must be her sister Mae. I heard so many wonderful things about you both. But I must say, Mae, Loretta didn't mention what a stunningly beautiful woman you are."

After asking Mae multiple inappropriate questions about her personal life, Silverstein finally turned his attention to Dorothy and invited her to perform a mini-audition, asking her to tap dance, do the Charleston and ballet, all of which she performed well. Then he asked her to show various emotions while reading a part from *Oliver Twist*, which the director was casting in the next few weeks. Dorothy tried expressing anger, surprise, fear, happiness, and sadness. Shecky gave her a few tips on the fly and told her to try it again, and again.

After an hour, Silverstein remarked, "Well, Mae, little Dorothy certainly has her good looks and can dance just fine. Not so sure yet about the acting. The director is pretty tough on the young ones to really sell the emotions on the silent screen. That's the life blood of silent actors. That being said, Dorothy, keep practicing what I told you, and Mae, work her hard for the next week. They are casting for *Oliver Twist* next Thursday over at the Paramount Studios, in Hollywood, and I think I can arrange an audition."

"As for you Mae, with your classic beauty, have you ever considered acting? Maybe we could meet for dinner after work to discuss?"

While Mae was partially flattered, she didn't just fall off the turnip truck and recognized a cad when she met one. She, however, did not want to insult old Shecky with the audition hanging in the balance.

The chess game was afoot.

"Thank you so much, Mr. Silverstein. Dorothy and I will work tirelessly this week on acting. I can assure you that Dorothy will be fully prepared for the audition, and I'm sure she will do her level best. As for me, I appreciate all the compliments, but acting has never crossed my mind. Also, that was so generous of you to offer your guidance over dinner tonight, but I must take care of my elderly mother. Nevertheless, I will give some serious thought about maybe pursuing acting. Could I come back to you, after we focus on Dorothy's audition?"

Check.

"Yes, of course, but I'm not sure when I will be able to schedule the audition – I said next week, it actually could be several weeks down the road. Let's get a dinner in the books and that way I will be able to confirm with you the timing of the audition for little Dorothy."

Escape.

"It is so hard to arrange someone to look after Mother when I'm away. Let's get through Dorothy's audition first, then we all can get together for a celebratory lunch after Dorothy gets the part."

Check.

Silverstein chomped down on his cigar tightly and nodded. "Okay, Mae, let's get the audition and the part, then you and I can plan a meeting to discuss your giving acting a shot."

"Sounds great, Mr. Silverstein, we look forward to it. Now is there any paperwork you would like us to sign?"

Checkmate!

Time moved slowly for Tim while Mae and the kids were away. Periodically, he would momentarily forget the loneliness while busy at work, but Tim's heart would fill back up with the fluid of sadness when he took a pause. His family would occasionally pay Tim a visit in dreams at night, but the reality of once again being alone slapped him in the face when he opened his eyes to the morning light.

Tim resigned himself to the fact that Mae's extended stay in California might certainly be something more than a passing fancy. He still really didn't want to leave. Chicago had been good to Tim. The City of Big Shoulders had provided a comforting, nurturing start with a loving, caring family and a wonderful, fulsome education. Chicago had taken him back in, providing shelter and refuge from the Mad Monk, with kindness from the least likely of us – saloon keepers and prostitutes. Chicago had given Tim great guidance by being his only educator and coach after the age of eight, with so many life-altering moments that presented forks in the road. The city had taken Tim's hand and led him safely and morally forward. Chicago had demonstrated tremendous strength and fortitude when disaster struck with its resilience, comfort, courage, and humility following the Chicago Fire, the Iroquois Theatre Fire, and the Eastland Disaster.

Tim had experienced so many soul-crushing blows with the death of loved ones and of fellow Chicagoans that violently and randomly perished. Although Tim had been emotionally ruined and fragile to the point of breaking beyond repair following these personal losses and epic tragedies, he saw how the city and its amazing citizens rallied around one another, refusing to let the horrible pain and sadness ruin their life's trajectories. Each time, Chicago had tirelessly rebuilt itself and become better and stronger. Instead of throwing in the towel like the bare knuckler with swollen eyes and a bloodied mouth at Mush Mouth's, Chicago, though exhausted and in excruciating pain, somehow chose to rise to its feet, raise its scarred fists, and snarl at fate, "Is that all you got!"

Tragedies come in monumental and wee sizes, but even the ones relatively less impactful to the masses, like the death of a parent, are devastating to a child. Yes, friends and colleagues show up at the wakes, truly feel bad, and attempt to utter comforting words and prayers. Just their being present goes a long way to support a mourning friend and demonstrate that he or she is not alone. After the funeral, however, friends and colleagues rightfully move on with their lives and quickly forget. The mourning individual, however, never forgets. As time passes, maybe the widow or child is fortunate to be able to reflect on their loved one with a warm smile as opposed to tears welling up in their eyes.

Tim at long last deciphered that the only way to emulate the city's tenacity following tragedy after tragedy, large and small, is by having love in your heart for the deceased and for your fellow man. But that's not all; you need love for those remaining in your life and provide comfort to them by helping them navigate their own lives' paths.

Tim's limitless love for Mae and his children was what he was searching for his entire life. His life's journey presented many forks in the road, with some panning out perfectly and others resulting in complete failure. The love in Tim's heart caused much pain but was the engine that drove him forward and enabled him to arise with his fists clenched to "fight another day."

"How could I ever leave Chicago? If Mae wants to, is the answer."

The possibility of Mae and the family staying out in California for a long time was becoming a reality. Tim wrote to Mae in July 1916,

> I wonder what she's doing,
> That old sweetheart of mine.
> I wonder if she's lonesome,
> Out near the ocean brine.
>
> I wonder how her hair is done,
> Those long soft waves of brown.
> I wonder if she's thinking,
> Of her old hometown.
>
> I wonder if she loves me,
> In her same sweet quiet way.
> I wonder how she'll greet me,
> When she comes home next May!

For her part, Mae began to notice that even though the people she met in California were very nice and seemed to smile constantly, she could never get past "Hello, my name is, what is yours, I'm from Chicago, how about you…" As Tim forewarned her, back in 1916 no one was actually from California. Whatever reason brought them to the far reaches of California in 1916 was typically guarded and kept safely to themselves. Mae grew up with hundreds of neighbors living on top of each other, with rows of homes situated five feet on either side of her home. In Mae's neighborhood growing up, and in her current neighborhood, everyone knew everyone else, knew in what parish they were born, their kids' names, where they worked, their health, their parents' health, what car they drove, what trip they just took, whether Aunt Sally's gout was flaring up, Cousin Sue and Kathy were coming for a visit, Colleen's upcoming wedding, and that Dick and Toughy Griffith went on another bender and got banned from Barefoot Jack O'Keefe's.

On one hand, it was liberating to get away from everyone knowing everyone's business and was precisely the thing from which Mae needed a break. On the other hand, she missed the community and knowing that if a neighbor saw one of her children in trouble they would drop everything and help them. The neighborhood gave everyone a sense that they were part of something larger than themselves. If they did something stupid, they would have guilt that all the neighbors would know about it and be disappointed. If they did something great or admirable, the neighbors would beam with pride.

The Irish ghettoes in America's larger cities, along with those of Italians, Germans, Polish, and so on, were rooted in people with similar backgrounds missing their homeland that they had left, usually under adverse circumstances, and desiring to be near folks that knew and understood their culture and traditions. The immigrants were mostly unwelcome as they arrived. Signs were posted in businesses throughout New York following the Great Famine Immigration, "NO IRISH NEED APPLY." The great American Melting Pot had dividers between the various neighborhoods.

"Give me your tired, your poor, your huddled masses yearning to breathe free, the wretched refuse of your teeming shore." Just don't live on my street.

Mae mentioned to a lady that lived next door to Uncle Charles that she used to read tea leaves for her friends and neighbors and how that was an Irish tradition. The lady reacted as if Mae was some sort of witch and subsequently avoided eye contact with Mae and walked to the other side of the street when she saw her coming. Once Mae inquired of another neighbor at which parish the woman attended Mass. "Oh, we don't regularly attend church service except at Christmas and Easter." Mae began to think she was living on Mars. The only person that invited Mae out to eat was that vile four flusher, Shecky Silverstein. And Mae knew full well what he had in mind for dessert.

It turns out that the sun is pretty hot on Mars in the summer. Mae learned that she and her children could not spend more than an hour outside before getting bright red cheeks, ears, and shoulders. Sunscreen was not invented until the 1940s, so beachgoers wore full length coverups and hats. Mae's and Cecilia's fair Irish skin was no match for the cloudless skies of Southern California. The Conlons were outdoorsy folks, taking walks and playing outside most of the day even in the dead of winter. Now they were relegated to spending a good majority of the day stuck inside the modest unairconditioned home of Uncle Charles. The kids had each other but missed all of their friends in Chicago. Dorothy cried often, saying she didn't care about "the stupid audition! I want to go home."

Home is where the heart is, and it wasn't on Mars. Chicago was home, and that was where Mae ultimately concluded she wanted to be. Nevertheless, Mae and Dorothy had made a commitment to try out for the audition, and that day finally arrived one week after they met with "Silverslime," as Mae began to call him. So, off they went again to Paramount with Uncle Charles at the wheel. Cecilia stayed back to watch the other children. Poor Dorothy was so excited she barely slept a wink the night before. Mae was the costume designer, makeup artist, and hairdresser for the little starlet. Mae had been sewing nonstop to finish the dress just in time for the audition. They drove up to the studio's security guard house, and their names were on a list to pass through the large iron gate. Mae looked over at the nine-year-old Dorothy, who was wide-eyed. "Most people never make it this far, sweetie. Just try your best, and no matter what happens, we are all so proud of you."

Uncle Charles dropped the ladies off by the main office front door. They were greeted in the lobby by Silverstein, who was already halfway into his cigar. "Whoa, Mae, you look stunning, my dear. How's our darling little actress Dorothy doing?" He then moved in for a hug with Mae, who artfully stuck out her arm for a handshake instead. Frowning, Shecky grunted, "Follow me, girls."

They went down the hallway into a large waiting area, where there were more than 50 girls between the ages of 8 and 10, each one cuter than the next, along with their respective primping mothers who were constantly brushing their daughters' hair or straightening their little actresses' dresses. Silverstein gave Dorothy a few pages of the Oliver movie script that she would likely be asked to read.

"Remember, this is a silent movie and no one will ever hear you talk. So, you need to sell it with emotion in your eyes and your face." Silverstein said he would see them inside for the audition in a couple hours. "You're number 38, I think."

They sat next to a little girl with a pout on her face, clad in fancy clothes, who looked over at Dorothy, checked out her dress, and uttered, "Did your mom make that?"

Mae quipped, "No, it was designed by Jeanne Paquin, the famous French designer." Dorothy added, "Yes, from Paris, ever heard of her?"

Growing up in Chicago, both women knew how to handle a snotty brat. While lying was taboo in the Conlon household, there were no holds barred when someone started something. The snob and her mom got up and moved to another seat, which evoked giggles from sweet Dorothy and Mae.

The three hours it took before they were called seemed like an eternity for Team Conlon. What made matters more tense was the parade of girls who had auditioned and were crying when they left, with their mothers patting their backs. To relieve the tension, after one of the girls who was really upset yelled out how "mean and stupid" the director was, Mae asked Dorothy, "So, ya think she got the part?"

Finally, they were summoned to the audition room, where three men in suits sat on high stools in a semicircle. Dorothy was asked to stand in the middle. A younger man who escorted her to the center yelled out, "Okay, this is Dorothy Conlon from Chicago." The distinguished-looking director was James Young, who stated, "We are in need of a few orphans, one with a few lines and closeups and three who will be extras. Do you know the story?"

"Yes sir, we checked out *Oliver Twist* by Charles Dickens from the library a couple of weeks ago, and I read it. Every page."

The men chuckled. Tully Marshall, who was to play the role of Fagin, stood up to reveal a tall and slender frame. He then changed character with a snarl and intimidating eyes, looked down at Dorothy, "Let us read lines from page two, my dear." Dorothy was shaking and looked over at Mae, who nodded and whispered, "Show them what you got."

In Fagin's voice, "Don't look at your mommy, she doesn't exist. We are now in London in 1836, and you, my dear, are an orphan picking pockets for me." Fagin then raised his voice, "What could you possibly know about being an orphan?"

Dorothy took a deep breath and stood up straight and looked Fagin right in the eye, scowled with as much emotion as she could muster and yelled "A lot! My father was an orphan who survived on the streets of Chicago as a little boy. And he would never steal for a mean man like you. He made his own way, my dear."

Tully jumped out of character and laughed hard. "Very good, Dorothy!" The director, smiling, took down some notes.

Tully and Dorothy spent the next several minutes running through some of the scripted lines. Director Young thanked Dorothy and said, "Good job, young lady, we'll let Mr. Silverstein know in a few days." Tully, in the voice of Fagin, said, "Toodle-oo, my dear."

Silverstein escorted the ladies out and said, "Nice chops, kid! Young tells you right away if he thinks you don't cut it. So, we are still in the game. I'll call you as soon as I hear." He then stared into Mae's eyes. "How about lunch before you go?"

"My poor uncle Charles has been waiting in the car for hours, and we must get back to my elderly mother. As we previously agreed, maybe we can have a celebratory lunch if our little actress gets the part."

Checkmate.

The following is the actual text from Tim's letter to Mae on July 10, 1916:

Chicago, Illinois
July 10, 1916

My Darling, Sweetheart, and Love,

You left a month ago yesterday; it seems like a year. I am expecting a letter from you either today or tomorrow. I am feeling fine and my neck is improving rapidly. I have been sleeping very soundly and feel rested every morning. Well, I would rather have you next to me, love, and wake up feeling bum every morning. The last sentence does not mean to indicate however, that you were the cause of me not getting my proper rest. See, Mae, it just came to me. I know what it was. It was dear little Bob, calling for his bottle about 3 a.m. and then again at 5 a.m., but who could blame a little love like him for doing any harm. Now that he is gone west, and I look back and think of him, his crying was music to my ears. I would just love to hear him now and have him hollering at me to get in my lap and help me eat my supper. Tell me all about him and when you get a chance have his picture taken and send it to me.

And how is little Lucille? I miss that expressive look from those deep, dark eyes, beautiful, even when they frown. Aside from the fact that Lucille and Dick were always at one another. I am thinking of one night you and Richard went to the show, and Lucille stayed home with me. After Bob was asleep, Lucille came over to where I was sitting and said, "I am so tired." I talked to her for a few minutes, and as she stood at my knees, and looked into my eyes, I began to realize how beautiful they were. I know she will enjoy it in California as she is such an outside bird.

I miss Richard for several reasons. I miss him sitting on the radiator in the front parlor every morning. I miss his hat and coat off the chair and couch. I miss him Sunday morning while I have to go after my own paper. I miss his soiled hands at the supper table. I miss his battles with Lucille. I miss his little questions that never hurt myself answering, and last of all I miss the real boy coming in from playing tonight, with his hat back on his head, his red cheeks, and that real expression of love and tenderness saying, "Hello daddy, are you home already?"

How is my oldest girl and sweetheart? I miss her for the same reasons that I miss Dick. Only Dorothy is a little older, and as they grow older, you love them in a different way. I miss her playing on the piano and her dancing. I miss those wonderful eyes that reminded me every time I looked at them of my sweetheart. I miss her little spats with Dick, and I miss her sweet smile.

And how is dear mother? I miss her more than she thinks. I miss her in the morning and I miss her every night. I miss her company for breakfast – and at night to lock the doors tight. I miss her at the sewing machine and in the dining room. And I miss that old familiar expression, "I wonder where I left my glasses. Loretta, did you see my glasses?" And I miss her little advice to Loretta. "Be careful now. Two people were held up last week. Don't stay too late, Watch yourself, can't be too careful, My goodness, my it's a bad night to be going out, for two dimes I wouldn't let her go. What good is the old club anyway." But I miss her for other reasons too – she has been a good mother to us all and me. All love her.

Well Mae I suppose you wonder if I miss you? And why I miss you? Well, darling, I miss you for the best reason in the world. I miss you because I love you with the love that is more than love. I miss you because I am continually thinking about you, because I am dying to kiss you. I want to hold your hand. I want to look at you. I want to see you smile. I want to watch you getting supper. I love to hear your walk. I love your soft brown hair. I miss your laugh, and I miss your smile. I miss your greeting at night, and I miss your goodbye kiss in the morning. I miss the kisses I steal when you were tired after a long night with Bob. If I could have only stayed home and let you sleep, those memories would be much sweeter, but sweeter memories of mine of you would be hard to find. I could continue on and on until you would become weary of reading, but my love for you makes life worth living. It makes me strong and content, and who wouldn't be happy to have you. I know I was lucky to get you. All the time I am writing, I can see you and know how good you always looked to me. I will think of you always, of the smartest girl in the world.

Tell me all about yourself. How do you like the West? You must go swimming while you are there. It will do the whole bunch good. I have made up my mind to make the trip with you if you decide to stay there, and if the place is what your mother claims. I don't believe you will want to come back in a hurry.

Loretta is feeling fine. She gets a five dollar increase next year, she told Claude and me this in the kitchen the other night, but Claude walked out of the room, it was too much for him. I praised her to the sky.

Last evening Claude came in the kitchen again to show me how to clean his fingernails. He is some guy, that joker. I don't know what it is, Mae, but I lose my appetite when I look at him. Annie is fine and does all she can to make it pleasant. Loretta has a good strong stomach as he doesn't seem to bother her. I am glad of that. Well, I only have one meal a day with him so it isn't so bad (please keep this under your hat).

I have plenty of work ahead so I won't have much time to get lonesome. I will miss you every minute, sweetheart. When I am home, you know, I always wanted to be with you. But a person rarely realizes what love really is until your loved one is away from you. Well, sweetheart, when I think of you, dear, I just want to hug and kiss you (I didn't intend to write this, but when I wrote, sweetheart, I couldn't help but express my feelings). I can't think of any more news at present. I will have to close with a final goodbye. If you could only kiss yourself for me, dear, that would be fine. Goodbye, love, and kiss your mother and all the love ones for me. Goodbye, goodbye, goodbye.

Love Tim

After a long week passed in always sunny Southern California, Mae received a call from Silverstink (another name Mae came up with). "Mae, bad news – good news. It was close, but Dorothy didn't get the lead. The good news is they want her as one of the orphans as an extra. This could be a really good break for her and an opportunity to be noticed for the next one."

Mae feigned excitement. "That's wonderful news! I'll tell her right away. What does that mean schedule and logistics wise?"

"They start shooting in a few weeks. Once they get rolling, you and Dorothy will have to be on set every day starting at 7:00 a.m. for makeup and costume, and they usually wrap around 7:00 or 8:00 at night. Oh, and they shoot seven days a week so they can get everything done by their deadline of the end of September. And I'm sure you are wondering, how much…after my cut, Dorothy gets a dollar a day."

Mae almost started crying, thinking, "How can I possibly spend three more months here simply so Dorothy can stand in the background? Dorothy worked so hard, and we did make a commitment. I can't teach the children to be quitters. I wish Tim was here…"

Mae called all the children and Cecilia into the front room of Charles's house. Mae announced that Dorothy landed a part as an extra. The kids clapped and were excited for Dorothy. Dorothy was conflicted about how to receive the news, disappointed she didn't get a main role but happy she beat out all those other girls, especially the snotty ones. Then, Mae conveyed the timetable laid out by Silverback (Mae's third nickname for him as she thought he looked like an ape). That news was not well received by the children, including Dorothy, in the least. A hyperbolic chorus of, "I'll die if I stay here for three more months," "I miss my home, and Daddy," and "I've had enough of this joint."

Mae seized the opportunity to turn this stressful situation into a teaching moment. "There, there children. Enough already, Uncle Charles will hear you – he has been such a gracious host and opened up his home to us. Now, this has been a wonderful experience living in California, swimming in the Pacific Ocean, auditioning for a Hollywood movie and landing a part, and meeting people from outside of our neighborhood. We got to spend more time with one another, and I loved every minute of that. It's a big world that exists beyond the West Side of Chicago. And we all had the chance to see and live in another small, beautiful part of it."

"Normally, your father and I would insist on you following through on any of our commitments. Conlons are not quitters in any sense. But Dorothy, you put your heart and soul into this role, and you earned it. We are all so proud of you. But, as Fagin would say, my dear, I think it would be too much on you and all of us to handle for the rest of the entire summer. Poor Uncle Charles may evict us by then. Your father misses us so much. The Bible teaches us…" Mae read,

> *"To everything there is a season, a time for every purpose under heaven: a time to be born, and a time to die; a time to plant, and a time to pluck what is planted; a time to kill, and a time to heal; a time to break down, and a time to build up; a time to weep, and a time to laugh; a time to mourn, and a time to dance; a time to cast away stones, and a time to gather stones; a time to embrace, and a time to refrain from embracing; a time to gain, and a time to lose; a time to keep, and a time to throw away; a time to tear, and a time to sew; a time to keep silent, and a time to speak; a time to love, and a time to hate; a time for war, and a time for peace."* Ecclesiastes 3:1-8

In 1916, the typical parenting style was to announce the parent's decision as opposed to asking the impacted child what they thought, what their views on the subject were, how they felt, or whether they were comfortable with the decision. Accordingly, Mae announced, "And there is a time to get the heck out of California and move back to Chicago. Children, we are heading home!"

The children all cheered.

Mae thanked Uncle Charles profusely and coaxed her mother to come back with them after they had their extensive "should I stay or should I go" debate. Mae blew in a breezy call to SilverStooge (his fourth and final nickname) to express her gratitude. Not wanting to burn a bridge, Mae suggested that she would continue to think about giving the movies a try herself one day.

Mae then penned a telegram to her husband, "Our time on the West Coast is at an end STOP We are heading back home tomorrow STOP Can hardly wait to hug you STOP I also have something important to discuss with you STOP."

Tim was so excited to hear the news that Mae, Cecilia, and the children were returning to Chicago that he couldn't get the smile off his face.

Mae and Tim typically avoided public displays of affection as being inappropriate. But at Union Station, when Mae walked off the train with little Bob in her arms, they made an exception and embraced for the longest time, with Dorothy, Dick, and Lucille, surrounding them for a group hug that lasted several minutes. For Tim, it would last a lifetime.

Lying in bed that first night back home, Mae whispered to Tim, "Don't you want to hear what I want to discuss with you?"

"Of course, but I almost was afraid to ask. So, let's have it."

Mae looked into Tim's eyes and smiled. "I want to have another baby."

Chapter 22
LET'S HAVE ONE MORE (1916 – 1925)

Mae and Tim tried and tried and tried. During the next seven years, from 1916 until 1923, Mae sadly had multiple miscarriages. This was due to her increased age and the lack of sophisticated obstetrics care. In the early 1900s, it was common to have childbirth at home, like Mae did every time, with the assistance of a doctor, a nurse, or an experienced relative coming to the house to assist with the delivery. Little was done beyond warm towels and massages to alleviate the pain of childbirth. Beyond the rhythm method and poorly manufactured prophylactics, contraceptives were undeveloped or not yet invented. Consequently, it was not uncommon for married women to constantly be in some state of pregnancy. With poor medical advances at the time, a high rate of miscarriages unfortunately occurred.

In early 1923, Mae had her final miscarriage and came to the sad conclusion that her wish to have another child was not going to come to fruition. "Tim, I had such hope of having another child. I guess it wasn't meant to be." They thanked God for the children with whom they were blessed, and the "let's have our fifth child project" officially came to an end.

Hope springs eternal. And just like that, in late summer 1924, maybe due to the absence of pressure and stress of trying to get pregnant, Mae, at the age of 43, surprised Tim, at the age of 48, after dinner with the news that she was miraculously, somehow, someway pregnant. Tim was shocked, and a little embarrassed, to say the least. On April 2, 1925, Mae had her fifth child, at home, a healthy baby boy.

Tim and Mae thought long and hard about the name, as there was a strong probability this was their final opportunity to honor someone important in their life by naming their last son after him. Tim sat on the front porch finishing off the last cigarette of his daily pack of filterless Camels, and thought back on the people in his life that were important to him, someone who helped Tim in difficult times and provided hope. In reverse chronological order, Tim thought of his current friends, relatives, and coworkers, coming up with a few names. Continuing, he reminisced about the friends he caroused with on Clark Street as a single man, but no one name seemed to do it for him. Tim recalled how much Old Mush Mouth took him in and effectively saved his life, but Mush Mouth Conlon didn't exactly roll off the tongue. Tim pondered his second-grade gang and friends from the orphanage.

One boy stood out as someone who had immediately supported Tim in his moment of crisis. Someone who genuinely liked Tim exclusively for who he was, at a time when all of Tim's worldly possessions fit in a small cardboard box, at a time when Tim was truly all alone, and at a time when the only thing that gave him the strength to get out of his small cot every morning was hope. Tim thought of how Billy McGregor was all of these things to Tim. Funny how the friends you meet when you are eight have no agenda, no angle. You become friends based on the person you are, not who your family is or how much money or possessions your family has.

Tim, as he had done so many times throughout his entire life, relived in his mind the day he and Billy escaped from Queen of Heaven, and how he had waved goodbye to his best and only friend in his life at the time as they parted company at the fork in the rail line. Even though Tim was afraid and gut-wrenchingly devastated at traveling down the tracks to Chicago completely alone, there was hope. Hope that he and Billy would successfully escape their pursuing captors, hope that they would find a new life with new friends and reconnect with family, and hope that he would see Billy again. Tim's eyes welled up on the porch as he wondered whatever had become of his first true, unequivocal friend.

Tim walked back into the house to announce his idea of a name for his new son. "Billy!" As Mae's father's name was William, it was an easy sell. Mae's face glowed with love. "Billy Conlon is a perfect name."

Just after Tim retired that night, he thought of Billy and smiled, whispering to himself, "Hopefully, my friend, we will meet again someday down the tracks. If not, I will see you in my dreams."

Chapter 23
THE BANSHEE (1927 – 1928)

Now a family of seven, with the occasional Cecilia unannounced crashing at their pad, the Conlons outgrew their home. In 1927, Tim and Mae purchased a six-flat at 227 North Mason, near the intersection with Lake Street, in the Austin neighborhood on the far West Side of Chicago. Each floor was a standalone three-bedroom apartment with a kitchen, sizable living room, and dining room with a grand crystal chandelier, and a grand piano in the Conlon front parlor. The Conlons lived on the first two floors, with various newlywed cousins, friends, and tenants serially occupying the upper floors. Due to Tim's ingenuity, it was also one of the first apartments in Chicago equipped with refrigerators in each unit.

As time marched on, neighbors, friends, family, and in-laws occupied the various flats at 227 North Mason. The adult Conlon children would stay there until they saved enough money to rent or purchase a place of their own. Relatives or friends who were between jobs or having a financial rough patch were always welcomed at the Conlons.

One summer evening, a year after moving to the Austin neighborhood, Mae had a vivid dream of a beautiful young woman with long raven black hair in a red dress, singing a nondescript melody and dancing down Mason Avenue. In Mae's dream, the mysterious woman suddenly stopped, and her smiling face transformed into a serious, concerned, furrowed brow with sadness in her eyes. The lady then pivoted and walked toward the Conlons' six-flat. Just as the woman in her dream was about to rap on the front door, Mae shot up in bed frightened and whispered, "Oh no, we are soon to have our door darkened by a banshee."

Over the years at family gatherings, following dinner, Mae's mother Cecilia would turn the lamps down and light only a couple of table candles to create a somber and somewhat eerie atmosphere. She would regale the children and young adults, who were hanging on her every word, of ghostlike fairy women or, as the Irish call them, banshees, visiting families in the middle of a dark night with ear-splitting shrieking or sometimes quiet singing just outside a bedroom window or door. A banshee is a supernatural being from Gaelic Celtic folklore that takes the form of a shrieking or singing woman. It is believed that banshees warn of the impending serious illness or death of someone in a household.

Barely audible, Cecilia would describe in a dramatic whisper how some banshees are very beautiful women – "women with long, luxuriant tresses, either of raven black, or burnished copper, or brilliant gold, and whose star-like eyes, full of tender pity, are either dark and tearful, or of the most exquisite blue or grey. Some, again, are haggish, wild, disheveled-looking creatures, whose appearance suggests the utmost squalor, foulness, and despair; whilst a few, fortunately, I think, only a few, take the form of something that is wholly diabolical, frightful, and terrifying in the extreme."[101]

Cecilia would continue, "[I]n different instances, the banshee's song may be inspired by opposite motives. When the banshee loves those on whom she calls, the song is a low, soft chant, giving notice, indeed, of the close proximity of the angel of death, but with a tenderness of tone that reassures the one destined to die and comforts the survivors; rather a welcome than a warning, and having in its tones a thrill of exultation, as though the messenger spirit were bringing glad tidings to him or her summoned to join the waiting throng of his ancestors."[102]

Mae recalled that her mother's ghost stories would terrify her and the other children when she was a young girl, oftentimes causing Mae to find it difficult to sleep that night for fear that she would be visited by a banshee. Mae had never dreamt of or had a vision of such a spirit since her frightened childhood imaginations so long ago. This recent dream seemed so real to Mae, not unlike how she felt when she had experienced the Eastland Disaster premonition. Due to the potential fear and anxiety that may be caused by conveying her banshee dream to Tim or another family member, Mae chose to keep this one to herself…until a beautiful woman in a flowing red dress paid the Conlons a visit at midnight one week later.

Tim and Mae had retired to their bedroom at their usual time of 10:30 p.m. They read in bed for a half hour or so, then briefly discussed tomorrow's plans before drifting off into slumber. That evening, Mae was dreaming of walking in a nearby park with her children on a gorgeous summer day. A squeaking noise from outside detected by Mae's ears was incorporated into her dream in the form of Lucille's tricycle wheel that squeaked with every turn. Her dream carried on, but Mae was growing more agitated with the squeaky wheel growing louder, until she was roused awake. Mae looked over to Tim, who was already sitting up in bed. "Mae, do you hear that? What in the devil is that noise?"

Mae too sat up, listening intently to discern the noise. The squeak was rhythmic and slow: squeak, pause, squeak, pause, squeak, pause. Grabbing tightly to the sheets below her neck, Mae whispered to Tim, "It's the front porch swing."

Tim expressed with an incredulous look, "You're right. It's the middle of the night – who in the heck is on our porch swing?'

Tim and Mae donned their robes and tiptoed down the hallway toward the parlor. As they made their way, they passed all of their children's wide-eyed faces peeking out of their respective bedroom doors, as they too were awoken by the loud, unusual noise coming from the porch. Mae made a shush sign to each child she passed with her finger to her lips. One by one, they followed in line behind Tim and Mae, making their way to the darkened front parlor. Tim motioned with his arm to the rest of his family to stay back behind him as he approached the large front bay window to peer out to the porch. Tim first focused on the swing on the unlit front porch. The nearly full moon provided just enough light to make out the swing, which was fully rocking back and forth, making the squeaking noise each time it passed the center line. Tim then saw the silhouette of the person on the swing, but was only able to see the back of whoever was on the swing from his vantage point from the window, just a few feet away from the person's head. With adrenaline kicking in, Tim's heart beat faster as he rubbed his eyes to assist his focus. He zeroed in and detected a woman with thick, long black hair that floated up each time the swing reached the top of the arc back and forth. Her flowing red dress also flared upward and outward with the movement of the swing. Tim noticed her right hand and forearm on the armrest were pure white, almost translucent like an opal. The end of her hand was adorned with long, sharp, ruby red fingernails.

Mae, and then the children, slowly made their way alongside Tim to take a peek, halfway hiding behind Tim and grabbing onto pieces of his pajamas for protection. They all were terrified of the intruder, but as they observed the woman swinging back and forth, with her tresses and frock floating gently with each swing, the Conlons were calmed. Mae looked up at Tim and shrugged her shoulders indicating a "what should we do?"

Just as Tim took in a deep breath in order to prepare for a loud and authoritative, "Can I help you, ma'am?" out the window, he was interrupted by the woman's melodic humming. Tim remained silent. The children and Mae looked at one another in wonderment. The woman's song grew louder and louder, with the swing keeping steady time. It was a pretty but melancholy tune that neither Tim nor Mae could place. Her voice reached a volume and pitch that created an echo on the porch, which resonated into the parlor. The Conlons' initial fear turned to wonderment, as they were almost hypnotized by the swinging and the flowing melody.

No one could put a finger on how long the song went on; later estimates from all of the Conlons varied from ten minutes to an hour. The woman's song abruptly ended, and the swing and its accompanied squeak simultaneously stopped. The porch was completely silent. She sat motionless with her back to the Conlons. The trancelike calm over the Conlons ended too, converting to outright terror. Now what?

The woman did not turn around as she stood up and slowly walked down the porch toward the front door. Although they could hear her heels make a deliberate thud on the wooden planks with each step, she seemed to glide motionless across the porch, with no noticeable movement of her head, arms, or legs. They saw her profile, with skin matching her white translucent forearm, a dainty nose, and high cheekbones. Tim later guessed she was in her twenties, but Mae and Lucille placed her decades older. The woman reached the end of the porch with the front door on her right and the steps to the street to her left. She paused momentarily, Mae put her hand over her mouth, and Bob began to cry. Tim clenched his fist, readying himself to confront the woman should she choose to approach the Conlon front door.

There was silence on the porch. Then, the woman let out a long audible breath that resonated throughout the porch and sent a chill down the backs of the Conlons. She ever so slowly spun to her left and descended the steps toward the street as she again began to resume humming her haunting melody. The banshee and her song progressively diminished as ultimately she vanished into the darkness as she strolled and floated down the street.

No one at 227 North Mason Avenue slept for a second the rest of the night. Mae tried to comfort the kids, "Not to worry about the lovely lady. She was on her way home, saw our porch swing, and could not resist giving it a try."

Privately, Mae revealed her dream about the lady in red from a week ago to Tim. "She was a banshee, Tim. But I cannot for the life of me understand her message." Mae needed an expert in the field to decipher the spectral midnight calling.

Cecilia was spending the night in one of the upstairs flats, having had a couple of sherries before retiring, and missed the entire episode. Over morning tea, Mae conveyed to her mother that they were visited by a banshee. Cecilia received the news as a matter of undisputed fact, as if Mae told her the newspaper was not delivered that morning. Cecilia was a devoted believer and considered herself well-versed in the field of Celtic folklore, myths, and banshees. She and Mae of course absolutely believed banshees actually existed, and as Tim would later say about a person's beliefs, "who am I to judge."

Cecilia was most interested in the banshee's appearance and seemed relieved that she was in the form of a beautiful woman, as opposed to a frightening hag. This indicated the banshee was a friendly messenger trying to warn, assist, and guide the mortals to whom she was paying a visit. Further, the banshee's hypnotic pleasant song was comforting and put the Conlons at ease, a stark contrast to the deafening shriek that accompanies a banshee warning of imminent death. The final factor that Cecilia focused on to interpret the message was whether the banshee ever turned toward the front door or looked at any of the Conlons through the front window, even if it was just a peek. "This is important, Mae, did you, Tim or any of the children ever catch the banshee's eye?"

Mae described in great detail each movement the banshee made before she disappeared down the street. Because a banshee can appear vastly different to each person that observes her visit, Cecilia interrogated Tim and each of the children. Mae and Cecilia both breathed a sigh of relief when all confirmed the banshee never turned toward the house or stared into anyone's eyes. Cecilia's final conclusion was that the banshee was indeed a friendly spirit visiting with good intentions, and that she was warning the Conlons that someone was in impending danger. Not that death was imminent, but that perhaps someone's health may soon be in jeopardy that could lead to death in the event the ailment was not taken care of with all deliberate speed.

Chapter 24
DR. MAYO (1928)

In 1928, Tim reached the age of 50 without ever going to the hospital. He was born at home and never saw a doctor his entire life. Tim smoked a pack of filterless Camels every day since he was a teenager, drank whiskey almost every night, never exercised, ate bacon and eggs for breakfast, and had plenty of red meat with generous dashes of salt on everything for breakfast, lunch, and dinner. He never was vaccinated, never prescribed any medicine, and never took any over-the-counter medications. Tim lived in squalor for years after escaping the orphanage and survived outbreaks in Chicago of smallpox, tuberculosis, and the Spanish Flu when masks and soap were not a luxury afforded to a street waif and hand sanitizers were not yet invented. Tim was blessed with an awesome immune system, was extraordinarily lucky, or both. That was, until shortly after the midnight visit by the Lady in Red.

About a week after the mysterious visitor jumped aboard the Conlon front porch swing, Tim woke up with labored breathing. Still lying in bed, he thought that the head cold going around the Illinois Bell office had finally caught up to him. Tim began to also feel some pressure on his throat, which he had mostly ignored the prior few days and chalked up to a stiff neck from sleeping on a new pillow. This sensation, though, seemed a bit different.

Nevertheless, Tim carried on as usual, ate his two eggs scrambled with several strips of crispy bacon, strong coffee, and juice while reading the paper to try to not overthink his symptoms. Then, with a kiss on Mae's cheek, off to work he went.

Tim noticed during his two-block walk from the El station to Illinois Bell's offices on Washington and Franklin that his breathing was growing more difficult, hearing himself now wheezing with every breath. "What the devil is going on with me? Hope this is not some sort of a precursor to what that blasted banshee was trying to warn us about." Tim chuckled to himself, "Banshee, yeah right…a lovely lady who had a couple too many at Barefoot Jack O'Keefe's and needed a wee bit of a rest on her way home is more like it."

For the next several days, Tim's labored breathing continued to be an issue, along with that nagging neck pressure that turned to downright pain. During a comfort break in the middle of the afternoon, Tim looked in the mirror and noticed a growth on the front part of his neck alongside his Adam's Apple. This got Tim's attention. "What in the world is going on?" Tim decided to pay his first-ever visit to the company nurse stationed at the Western Electric Hawthorne Works in Cicero. Nurse Kruse was a very serious and knowledgeable woman who spoke with a slight German accent. Kruse examined Tim's neck, listened to his chest, and took his temperature. "Mr. Conlon, I'm afraid you have a nodule growing in your throat. You need to see a doctor to confirm, but I believe it is near your thyroid gland."

"Will it subside over time?"

"If I am correct that it is on or near the gland, no. It will grow larger and could potentially cause blockage to your airways. You need immediate attention."

Tim left the office and headed directly to the Chicago Public Library, where he spent the balance of the afternoon researching medical journals about his condition. He was always calmed when he passed through the library doors, the one place that cured his loneliness as a boy. It was a place where he could escape to Treasure Island or travel back to Ireland. This time, though, Tim needed the library to help him find the right doctor.

Tim concluded that he had developed something doctors in the 1920s only recently referred to as a "goiter," an irregular growth of the thyroid gland. The thyroid is a butterfly-shaped gland located in men at the base of the neck just below the Adam's Apple. A goiter may be an overall enlargement of the thyroid, or it may be the result of irregular cell growth that forms one or more lumps (or nodules) in the thyroid. An obstructive goiter is one that may block the airway and larynx. Signs and symptoms may include difficulty swallowing and breathing, a persistent cough, and pain.[103]

Most of the glands that form part of the endocrine system like the thyroid were a relatively new discovery, being first identified in the 1890s. They were later grouped as ductless glands or those that secrete substances internally. Endocrine surgery was first performed in the early 1900s, with a frighteningly high mortality rate. And surgery in the neck area was very high-risk at the time and was to be avoided if at all possible. Treating goiters with medications was not yet developed.[104]

During his research at the library, Tim came across a doctor in Minnesota that only recently performed successful surgeries to remove large goiters. Dr. Charles Mayo had coined the term "hyperthyroidism" for the first time in medical journals two years earlier in 1926. Charles and his brother, Dr. William Mayo, had surgically removed a goiter on an emergency basis in 1890, which was the first procedure of its kind reported in the medical journals. They employed a "slash and grab" technique. Hemorrhaging was heavy, nearly killing the patient, but the bleeding was controlled by packing the neck cavity with bandages left in place for several days and later surgically removed. This experience set Charles Mayo on a path of researching the thyroid gland and working on improving thyroid and goiter surgeries for the balance of his career, later becoming the Chief Thyroid Surgeon at what became known as the Mayo Clinic.[105] Brother William, however, found that procedure way too "intense," vowing to never perform it again.

Mortality figures remained high through 1915. Nonetheless, Charles stayed undeterred, especially as he was only referred severe cases for surgery as a final option. By 1925, with better surgical techniques, Mayo's mortality rate fell, due in large part to treating patients with iodine injections into the goiter preoperatively using a staged surgery technique.[106]

Still, removal of an obstructive goiter in 1928 remained very high risk. Dr. Charles Mayo performed more thyroidectomies and recorded the lowest operative mortality throughout his career. Charles became known as the "Father of American Thyroid Surgery".[107]

"That's my guy!"

Mae was convinced the banshee's foreshadowing was Tim's mass on his thyroid blocking his airway. Tim hoped it wasn't but could not get past the eerie visit from the Lady in Red and his symptoms appearing just a week later. Both Tim and Mae took his condition very seriously and sought out the earliest available appointment with Dr. Charles Mayo. They traveled by train to Rochester, Minnesota, packing for several weeks in the event the doctor wanted to perform surgery right away.

Dr. Mayo exuded confidence and expertise as they met in his office. "Nurse Kruse was spot-on, Mr. Conlon. You have an obstructive goiter that will increase in size with time and has the potential to completely block airflow to your lungs. Consequently, we need to remove your thyroid and the mass as soon as possible. As you mentioned, I have performed more of these surgeries than anyone in the country, but the first one I did was only a decade ago. While we have learned a lot and the mortality rate has lowered, we still have much to perfect."

The pre-op procedure and surgery were scheduled for later that week. Tim was alarmed, but as he did throughout his life, he took the news in stride and put his faith in Dr. Mayo's experience and skill. Mae was terrified, but knew it was the right thing to do. Mae also commented to Tim, as an aside, "We have to heed the banshee's warning."

"Dr. Mayo, I would like to be in the operating room with Tim." Mae felt she needed to be there not only to support and comfort Tim, but also to protect him from another visit from the Lady in Red.

"That's not allowed, ma'am."

"I will scrub up and not say a word – I just want to be there and hold his hand."

"This is a first…what if you see something that makes you upset, or worse, you faint? Then I will have two patients I have to take care of."

"I promise to keep my eyes shut the entire time."

After a long pause, "Okay, but you truly need to keep your promise and remain silent for the entire three-hour surgery."

"You have my word, Doctor Mayo."

"Don't I get a vote, Doc?" Tim chimed in. "Mae, you really don't have to…"

Mae quickly interrupted, "I am sitting in and holding your hand Tim, and that is that."

Dr. Mayo chuckled, "I guess, Mr. Conlon, that is that."

The surgery was scheduled a day after the pre-op iodine treatment. As planned, Mae scrubbed up with the team of doctors and sat by Tim's side near the operating table. They looked into one another's eyes just before Tim was administered the anesthesia. No words needed to be spoken. Tim thought to himself, "How lucky am I to have Mae as my wife." At long last Tim did not have to take a treacherous journey alone. Tim smiled at Mae and drifted into induced sleep. Mae, too, closed her eyes as promised.

Mae initially felt a positive vibe. After what must have been an hour into the surgery, an image of the Lady in Red appeared in Mae's mind. Mae gasped as she again had a vision of the banshee walking down the street approaching their home. Her song was more of a bouncy, cheerful tune. Just then Mae's vision was interrupted by chatter between Dr. Mayo and his team. "We have a significant bleeder, pack it in immediately and hold it in there tight." Mayo's words were quick and direct with his orders, but still came across with confidence.

After a few more minutes, "Doctor, we still have a bleeder."

"How many packs so far?"

"Four."

"Let's do one more, and get the sutures ready."

Mae was praying to God to guide Mayo's hands. The Lady in Red returned to Mae's mind, stopping in the street in front of her house in total silence.

Just then the heart monitor blared out a warning signal that Tim had flat-lined.

"Nurse, sutures stat."

"More packs, right there. Suction now. More packs."

The doctor's and nurses' voices faded to an echoed murmur as Mae's mind focused back to the banshee. "Please not now, please not now." The Lady in Red turned toward the house; she paused with a cold stare. Her expression slowly morphed from a somber one of concern to a glowing smile.

Mae was interrupted by the heart monitor resuming its rhythmic beeping, and the loud terse instructions barked out by Dr. Mayo changed to his regular calm banter.

The banshee resumed her haunting pleasant lilt as she turned around and drifted back down the street. The banshee and her song progressively vanished into the night with each step.

Tim survived the surgery and had an uneventful recovery. Before they departed Rochester for Chicago, Mae and Tim had one last visit with Charles Mayo, who provided his final post-surgery discharge instructions and what to expect in the coming weeks as his body recuperated.

"Okay you two, any final questions?"

Mae inquired, "First, thank you so much, doctor, for everything. I do have one question about the surgery. What happened when the heart monitor went off and I heard dialogue about a 'bleeder'?"

"That, Mrs. Conlon, is what we call a fork in the road. One of Mr. Conlon's vessels leading to his carotid artery was nicked, which caused a lot of bleeding. We tried to stop it with compression bandages, but that didn't work, so I was just about to surgically close it off, which is very high risk – something we really want to avoid, if possible, for a whole host of reasons. His heart actually stopped for several seconds with all the blood loss. And then just before I was going in with sutures, the bleeding slowed. After two more packs it stopped altogether. I and the team all breathed a huge sigh of relief. My head nurse even started to hum a happy little tune."

Chapter 25
AUTUMN (1937 – 1943)

Time marched on for Tim and Mae. Days quickly passed, weeks ran by, months flew, years raced. Tim would tell his now-adult children that "the Fourth of July seemed like the day after Christmas." Tim was fascinated by the concept of how time is relative. An hour to a kindergartner waiting for the clock to turn 3:00 p.m. seems the equivalent of a day to a six-year-old. Every ten minutes sitting in a hospital room waiting for a loved one to get through a surgery seems to last an hour. Your informative first year as a trainee or intern at a job seems equal in time to the next five years at the same office. As Gordon Lightfoot noted in his song "The Wreck Of The Edmund Fitzgerald," "Does anyone know where the love of God goes when the waves turn the minutes to hours?," when describing what the men experienced during their last moments on Earth in the frigid stormy waters of Lake Superior following the shipwreck.

Tim was in the autumn of his life, and he was content. Everything slowed down and provided Tim an opportunity to observe the vivid colors surrounding him. In 1937, at the age of 60, Tim retired after 43 years at Illinois Bell. Tim enjoyed walks with Mae through the wonderful parks of Chicago and along the shores of Lake Michigan. He also finally had time to get to the books he had on his must-read list. In between novels, even though he had been through the volumes of *The Book Of Knowledge Encyclopedia* numerous times before, Tim once again started at Volume A, and meticulously went through each volume until he got through Z. Tim had purchased his set when they moved to the Austin neighborhood, and became excited each time the annual pocket updates arrived in the mail. Tim was thrilled that his ability to entirely escape into a book had returned to the level he experienced as a young boy. While he still read every day as an adult, the distractions of life were difficult to park to the side. With his children now adults and the stresses of his job in the rearview mirror, Tim again could hyper-focus on written words and lose himself in a story. His near-perfect photographic memory returned with great acuity.

Tim loved the fall because it presented a vibe to all that it was a time to catch one's breath from the active, exciting summertime and to reflect on where you presently are amidst your life's journey. Where you are heading becomes less of a concern. Tim thought to himself that maybe it was time to do a few of the things he had deferred due to other events occupying his time. Tim laughed when he couldn't recall a single thing that had made him so busy and had caused so much stress over the past four decades. Tim realized that the beauty was that now there was no pressure to do or not do whatever he wanted.

Tim also mentioned to Mae that he could care less about what people thought of him and felt it was so silly and such a waste of time to have worried about such petty issues over the years. Mae remarked, "Time to be who you are, Tim, and do what you want… or not." Tim reflected that with a little more time on his hands he needed to remember to stop regularly for a moment and notice all of the glorious colors of the leaves filling the trees before they detached and fell to the ground.

And in the blink of an eye, Tim woke up one day to drive his youngest son, Bill, to St. Benedict's College in Atchison, Kansas, in 1943. World War II was well underway, and Bill registered for the draft in April when he turned 18. Tim was 66 at the time and had been retired for six years. Although Tim made a decent salary during his work life and was a good provider for his family, paying for his children's education beyond high school was not in the cards nor within the retirement budget. Bob Conlon, who was ten years senior to Bill, was awarded a football scholarship and attended St. Benedict's College a decade earlier. Bob was very affable and charismatic and maintained a strong relationship with the college and the football coach after graduating. Bob introduced Bill to the coach, who was scouting prospects in Chicago and attended a Fenwick High School game, where Bill was the starting quarterback. Between Bill having a solid game that night and Bob's connections, Bill too received an athletic scholarship to St. Benedict's. He went right from high school to college and benefitted from a four-year college draft deferment as long as he remained in school.

Chapter 26
EMPTY NESTERS (1943)

Tim drove Bill in his 1940 four-door Ford Deluxe west to Kansas on a hot early August day, as the football players had to report to campus early. Bill very much appreciated that Bob joined them for the two-day trip to Atchison. As they reached the town, the Conlon men stopped at a local diner for lunch. Bob said he would show Bill around and check in with the provost and head coach. Tim decided to let the two lads take the tour without him, and he remained at the diner reading the paper and having coffee.

The adults from left to right are Tim, Mae, Bob and Bill (my dad) Conlon. The children are Tim and Mae's grandchildren, Sue and Tim Lawrence. The picture was taken around the time Bill was heading to college in 1943.

As Tim watched his two sons walk down the street as adults, he beamed with pride. First, Tim was thrilled that the two brothers were the best of friends. Tim always preached to his children "friends are great, but friends come and go – family is forever." Tim was relieved that when he and Mae passed on, Bill and Bob would always have one another, knowing that they both genuinely only had each other's best interests at heart.

Tim never bragged and detested those that did. This one time though, Tim afforded himself a private moment in Ma's Diner to feel a sense of accomplishment by guiding and providing for his youngest son to be in a position to make it to college. "That little rascal that was always playing jokes on his siblings and causing havoc with his hooligan friends is now a big university man."

All Tim wanted to do at that moment, however, was to head back to Chicago. He was dreading saying goodbye to his youngest son. "Why am I acting like this? I barely spoke to Bill or Bob the entire trip. It's a simple thing really – just pretend you are fine, give the boy a hug, and wish him well." Although Tim kept giving himself a pep talk for a gracious goodbye, his stomach churned and he felt lightheaded. Tim thought to himself, "What is it, Old Boy, why are you acting like this?"

Tim closed his eyes and took in a deep calming breath to relax his body and quiet his mind. He then remembered his goodbye to Billy on the train tracks nearly 60 years ago. This memory was followed by his last hug goodbye from his mother when she left for work the day she perished, never returning home. Tim shook his head, trying to erase those painful memories, only to be replaced by the memory of his final farewell to his first love Cora in Little Cheyenne. This dream morphed into his waving goodbye to his sister from the parish carriage as he departed for the orphanage and left his home forever. Tim's heart began to race again as he was overcome with such sad memories that he had blocked out for so many years.

Tim was at last able to put together the pieces of the puzzle of why he was avoiding bidding Bill adieu. Tim had said goodbye to so many loved ones who he would never see again and was seemingly left alone forever. Tim always felt he had to be strong and move on in order to survive. He always knew that if his emotions were allowed to overtake him, he would let his guard down and be vulnerable to all of the turmoil that surrounded him. "Keep a stiff upper lip, Tim" was his mantra. Tim had successfully remained tough during times of adversity and had managed to move on. Any time grief crept in, Tim had an uncanny ability to contain his feelings and lock them away in the deep recesses of his mind.

Tim realized that he was soon to be an empty nester with his youngest off to college, likely to never return to live at home. While Tim finally fully comprehended why he couldn't bring himself to engage Bill and see him off properly, he returned to putting his sadness into a vault and toughing it out, again. Even knowing this was not the appropriate way to conduct himself, it was still not possible for Tim to alter the pattern that literally had kept him alive since he was eight. Instead, he pivoted by concocting a plan to say goodbye in a fashion that he could justify to himself as the right thing to do.

Tim lit up another Camel and tried to come up with the right words to use for his farewell to Bill. Tim wondered, "What wisdom can I impart to the lad…I already gave everything I got as far as life's lessons to him for the past 18 years. Bill is a kind, moral young man. He works hard and does his best at everything he undertakes. Billy is a great son and brother." Tim justified to himself, "No, I have no advice to add or magical phrases to utter." Tim's mind was able to solve the dilemma with a solution that would avoid a painful goodbye while at the same time provided a noble reason why to himself and maybe to his two sons as well.

Tim's mind drifted back to when his own father left him suddenly so long ago. The memory evoked an emotion so intense that it felt like it happened yesterday. Tim furrowed his brow at how his brother callously had abandoned him and had supported his move to the orphanage. Tim regrettably had zero relationship with his brother. He wondered how much different his life would have been if he had a strong bond with Michael like his own sons had. Instead, Tim was instantly forced to struggle through life alone. "Tim, you too won't live forever." Tim concluded his inner debate about the big farewell speech with, "The best thing I can do for Bill is to leave the final goodbye in the hands of Bob, his brother."

When the campus tour was over, it was time to drive the car near the dormitory and drop Bill off before driving back to Chicago. Again, to Bill's disappointment, Tim remained in the car.

"Dad, don't you want to see my room and meet my roommate?"

Tim knew that Mae would have said "get off your duff and go up to the room with your boys." Nevertheless, Tim could not overcome his being so hardwired for too long to avoid such goodbyes. Tim thought to himself, "Damn it, I can't do it."

"No thanks, Billy. Good luck, you'll do fine. Remember to write your mother every week."

Bill had never been west of Fenwick High School in Oak Park, Illinois. He, of course, was understandably apprehensive about starting college and joining the football team. Bob, always the wonderful big brother, volunteered to escort Bill to his room. Bill carried his lone suitcase he had borrowed from Uncle Claude, with a broken zipper and tattered corners. When they arrived at the room, his roommate had not yet arrived and it was completely barren. Bill unpacked and Bob was shocked and upset to see the scant amount of clothes that Bill packed, a few shirts and tee shirts, two pairs of pants, half a dozen pairs of socks and underwear, an old sweater, a pair of gym shoes, sweatpants and sweatshirt, some toiletries, and one bath towel. And that was it. No pictures, no radio, no posters, no blankets, no photos.

"Bill, didn't they tell you that you need to wear a jacket, tie, and nice slacks and shoes for travel to away games and the pep rallies for the home games?"

"I guess they did, Bob, but I don't own any of that."

Bob, who had on a sport coat and dress slacks, as men travelling in the day would do, stripped down to his tee shirt, boxer shorts, and socks and handed Bill his jacket, slacks, and wingtips.

Bill was in tears as he thanked Bob for such a wonderful gesture. "You can't go in the street like that."

"Not the first time I ran out of this dorm in my underwear."

"Why is Dad being so distant and uninterested?"

"He doesn't know how to act in this situation. Dad never went to college, heck he never went past the second grade. And his father died when Dad was eight. He loves you, Bill, and very much wants you to succeed. We all do. But Dad missed out on how to conduct himself when we grew up and moved on. He feels he did his job, which he did, and now the rest is up to you. No, Dad's not the most affectionate father on the planet, but he grew up entirely on his own. Dad didn't grow up in a loving home after the age of eight. He missed out on all that and simply has no idea what to do. The same thing happened when I left for college. That's why I tagged along."

"Bob, thank you for everything." As the brothers hugged goodbye, Bob stuck $100 in Bill's back pocket.

Bill never forgot the kindness and support Bob showed him that day and throughout his life. Bob in some ways was more than a big brother to Bill; he often served in the role of surrogate father. Bill named his youngest son after Bob and always told the story of his first day at college and how Bob demonstrated such love and selflessness.

Tim drove home smiling to himself and feeling proud that three of his children were privileged to attend college. "Don't you worry, Bob; Bill is going to be just fine. He is blessed to have such a wonderful brother." Tim's smile turned to a frown as he said to himself, "Blasted, I should have hugged Bill goodbye."

III.
SPIRITUAL AFTERLIFE

Chapter 27
CELTIC KNOT - TRIQUETRA

Tim was intrigued by stories he had read throughout his life about the ancient Celts. Their influence on Ireland and throughout Northern Europe fascinated Tim. His favorite Celtic symbol, which appears in stone carvings dating back to 3200 B.C., is the Triquetra, or the Celtic Knot. The Triquetra came to be known as the Trinity Knot after St. Patrick spread Christianity throughout Ireland in the fifth century. The Triquetra design features three continuous interlaced ovals with pointed ends, with the central oval pointing skyward and the two base ovals pointing slightly toward the Earth and outward to the ends of the horizon. It has a continuous flowing line, which denotes eternity. Some such symbols also contained an overlying, interlocking circle to demonstrate how everything is connected.

The Celts believed that everything important came in threes. The Triquetra symbolizes every being's birth, life, and spiritual afterlife. Other interpretations are that it signifies the Maiden, representing innocence; the Mother, representing creation; and the Crone, representing wisdom. The Pagans believed the three points were the three domains of the world: land, sea, and sky. This later evolved to a belief that the Triquetra depicts the mind, body, and spirit, which bond together to create one's soul.[108]

Early Christians in Ireland believed the Triquetra represented the Father, the Son, and the Holy Spirit, and later referred to the symbol as the Trinity Knot. The Triquetra appears multiple times in the Book of Kells, from 800 A.D., which contains the four Gospels of the New Testament in Latin and is on display at Trinity College in Dublin.[109]

Tim, who was raised a Catholic, certainly believed in the Holy Trinity, but felt the correct interpretation of the Triquetra was by the Celts who used it to symbolize birth, life, and afterlife and how every being and creature on Earth for that matter experiences these three phases and has done so since time began and into the infinite future. And, importantly, Tim always believed everything and everyone is connected.

Tim loved to sit and watch the waves roll in on Lake Michigan. He analogized a wave to the meaning of the Celtic Knot. Before it is formed, the molecules of a wave are originally part of a larger body of water. The winds and current collect a random grouping of water molecules and send them roaring to the shore. As the forces of nature build, the water creates a wave that is entirely unique in size, duration, and drama. Some waves last a long time, reaching great heights with dramatic sound and white crests. Others are short-lived and gentle. Still others never form or are barely noticeable. No matter the type or nature of the wave, they all cease being a unique wave as they meet the shore and crash onto the beach. The water that made up the wave disperses and recedes back into the original body of water. The water that formed the wave hasn't ceased to exist. The exact water molecules remain and ultimately create new rolling waves, and the cycle continues, wave after wave, until the end of time. While the arc of the wave is finite, the water that made up and formed the wave will always exist.

Chapter 28
WINTER (1962 – 1973)

Tim knew he and his lovely bride had reached the winter of their lives. In 1962, Tim was 85 and Mae was 80, they were both content with their lives with little regret. Like the waves on Lake Michigan about to crash upon the sandy shore, their lives had already crested. They enjoyed a lifetime of pleasant memories and survived the bad ones, all of which made up their long, colorful, and fruitful life's journeys. Regardless of who would live longer, Tim knew the time was drawing near to when he would have to say goodbye to his soulmate, leaving him alone one final time. Tim and Mae never thought for a fleeting moment that death would come to three of their children first.

Tim and Mae were enjoying a quiet fall Sunday when the phone rang. Mae got a chill down her neck and said aloud, "That's Margaret calling – I'm afraid to answer." Tim picked up the phone and, sure enough, Mae was correct that it was Dick's wife, Margaret, who conveyed the horrific news that Dick had died in his sleep the night before. Dick had been suffering from cirrhosis of the liver for more than a decade due to excessive alcohol consumption during his entire adult life.

As a child, Dick was a shining light in Tim's eyes. Everyone loved being around Dick Conlon. He was handsome in a rugged sort of way and had a very quick-witted sense of humor. Dick was naturally good at just about everything he did. He was a gifted athlete and as a teenager was known as one of the best amateur shortstops in Chicago. Dick had an amazing singing voice, and at the age of ten was selected to be part of the prestigious Paulist Catholic Boys' Choir, which was the preeminent boys' choir in Chicago, recruiting only the top one or two boys from the various Catholic elementary schools.

The Paulist Choir performed before several presidents and popes over the years. Although Dick seldom practiced, much to Mae's chagrin, he was often the featured soloist. Unfortunately, as time went on Dick enjoyed having drinks with his buddies at Barefoot Jack O'Keefe's more and more and spent less and less time on work, sports, and family. Dick was married to the love of his life, Margaret, and they lived for a time in Tim and Mae's six-flat. They never had any children. As Dick reached his 30s, his large gang of friends dwindled as they married off one by one and focused on their jobs and family. Dick used to sing, "Those wedding bells are breaking up that old gang of mine…"

Dick's best friend was Tuffy Griffiths, who had fought World Champions Cinderella Man James Braddock and Max Baer. Everyone knew where Dick and Tuffy were drinking on any given night. Fans would flock to that bar for autographs or a picture with Tuffy, and some foolishly would try to provoke Tuffy to prove some neanderthal acceptance with friends. As drinks were poured into the wee hours, if forced Dick and Tuffy would take on all comers that were insane enough to challenge the former heavyweight contender. Dick, being a good athlete and one tough hombre, and Tuffy were a very formidable duo. This lifestyle, of course, was a strain on Dick's marriage, but Margaret was a very devoted wife and very much loved him. When word got out that Dick and Tuffy Griffiths were on their way to Tim and Mae's for a visit, Tim hurriedly would hide all the booze in the house. Dick's wave was a glorious whitecap and roared when it crested, but it traveled at a such a high rate of speed it was never able to reach its potential height even though all the elements to create a large and long riding wave were present. Dick passed away at the age of 50.

In 1966 sweet, beautiful Dorothy, who was 60, died from liver complications, presumably cancer. Dorothy began feeling ill at the beginning of the year and worsened in late spring. Mae and the family all pitched in to be at her side as caregivers until she perished in August. Lovely Dorothy passed away gently, which is how she presented her entire life – a gentle and loving, shining soul. Dorothy was married to Bill Bolger, and they had three children – Joan, Dick (named after her brother), and Bill – and ten grandchildren. Dorothy was so loved by her family, her siblings, and her parents. Her smile was infectious, and her heart chakra poured out a love energy that was palpable.

Bob Conlon suffered from multiple sclerosis, and he too became very ill in 1966, at a time when medicine had very little treatment for that horrible, debilitating disease. Bob was eventually confined to a wheelchair with limited ability to move his limbs, and talking became very labored. The doctors taking care of Bob speculated that Bob's MS was triggered by the stress from an extraordinary traumatic event. Bob served in the Air Force during World War II and was part of a crew on a Curtis Hawk P-36, which was a single engine fighter aircraft, that crash-landed due to engine failure somewhere in eastern Europe. While the pilot died in the crash, Bob survived, although he suffered temporary blindness for several months.

While Bob's body was weakened, he was always strong mentally and continued to be a mentor to his little brother Bill. Bill and his friend Norm Collins were offered an opportunity to open a Ford auto dealership in 1960, out in the then very rural Chicago northwest suburb of Crystal Lake. At the time, Bill and Norm were car salesmen together at Brigance Chevrolet in Oak Park, and they contemplated giving their own dealership a shot. As Bill used to say, "We didn't have two nickels to rub together at the time." Being extraordinarily anxious about quitting their jobs and taking on a tremendous amount of debt, they both paid a visit to Bob, who Bill and Norm greatly respected, for his sage advice.

Bob sat slumped in his wheelchair and listened to the two young men lay out the pluses and minuses of accepting/rejecting the opportunity, often times talking in circles. When they were finished laying everything out, Bob beckoned both of them to come closer so that they could hear his strained whispered voice. "Boys, the question is not whether you should do it. The question is how soon can you get the dealership up and running. Mark my words, you guys will be the top dealer around." Bill and Norm forever marked Bob's words. Shortly thereafter, they bought the dealership in 1960 due in large part to being inspired by Bob, who motivated them from a wheelchair, and they quickly became the top dealership in McHenry County. Bill named his youngest son, who was born later that year, after his hero, Bob Conlon. Bob passed away in 1966 at the age of 51, survived by his wife and daughter.

The stress and grief from Dorothy's and Dick's passing and Bob's illness took a toll on Mae's health. Mae was 84 and her huge heart began to tire. She ultimately was bedridden, with family, in-laws, and Tim tending to her. Tim too was devastated by the deaths of Dick and Dorothy, and Bob's decline. However, Mae's failing health was too much to bear. Mae's beautiful wave was rapidly reaching shore. Tim wrote the following poem that he read at her bedside:

> Forget about the future, Mae,
> Just think of the glorious past,
> Of the days I spent with you, dear,
> And the love that will always last.
>
> Look up at the sky in the evening, Mae,
> When the stars come out to play,
> The show begins at twilight,
> And ends with the dawn of day.
>
> The stars that shine the brightest
> Are the Barrymores and the Cohans,
> And the ones that shine the dimmest
> Belong to another zone.
>
> The passing clouds are the dancers
> And will dance to your delight.
> The howling winds are the song birds
> That make the world more bright.
>
> The blinking stars will bring a smile.

We must always have our clowns.
The thunder will furnish the music.
Then you will know there's a circus in town.

The lightning will light up the world, Mae,
The brightness of the age,
One million things to see dear,
On the world's most wonderful stage.

And when the show is over,
And you pass through the open door,
You'll sleep the sleep of the innocent
And dream of the days of yore.

Photo of Tim and Mae Conlon later in life – undated.

Mae passed away quietly at home surrounded by her family on September 21, 1966. Tim watched as she lovingly looked into his eyes for the last time. As Mae drew her last breath, her wave had at long last reached the shore. And with her final exhale, Mae's wave receded to whence she came. The family members present all heard a faint, nondescript melody being hummed by a woman in the hallway outside the room as Mae drifted peacefully to the other side.

Tim's breath too was taken away as he thought of the Triquetra and envisioned his own life coming to an end soon, believing, hoping all waves that have reached their terminus would rejoin the waters of the others that passed before. Tim had zero doubt that he and Mae would be together again. Until then, as with all of his previous painful goodbyes, Tim gritted his teeth and tried to move on. He didn't publicly shed a tear and seldom talked about Mae, electing to keep that grief buried deep inside and privately focused on seeing her again in eternity. Tim knew they would be rejoined in the spiritual afterlife, as do the molecules of water rejoin deeper in the lake after their waves crashed the shores. Everyone's three phases of life are connected for eternity. Until that happy day arrived, Tim was alone once again.

Tim was always so proud of his and Mae's big and fun family. Tim reminisced about how Sunday family dinners at their house were bustling with the adult children, in-laws, grandchildren, aunts, and uncles. Tim loved to quietly watch the chaos from his chair in the parlor, usually while enjoying a whiskey. After dinner, Cecilia or Mae would tell tales of leprechauns, fairies, ghosts, banshees, and other Irish lore. Tim would then start the after-dinner entertainment off with a rendition of "Galway Bay," which he had perfected at Mush Mouth's so long ago. Then Bob's wife, Sally, would perform the cute and comedic "I'm Nobody's Moo Cow Now." Dorothy's daughter and son-in-law, Joan and Jimmy Barret, would sing a duet of "Sweet Someone, Whoever You May Be" with Joan playing the piano, for which they won a Chicago-wide amateur talent contest. Jimmy Rodgers, Lucille's son-in-law married to her daughter, Sue, would play the banjo and sing, "Will The Bubblegum Lose Its Flavor On the Bedpost Over Night?," cracking everyone up. Dick would break out into an impressive and powerful Irish tenor version of a variety of Irish rebel ballads. The grandkids danced along and then would conspire to put on an impromptu Snow White and the Seven Dwarfs. The house was so alive with music, chatter, and laughter.

Now, the parlor was dark and silent.

Bill and his wife Marge and Lucille and her husband Duane would take turns checking in on their father. Tim never complained about being alone, sadly due to his vast experience of handling solitude. His eyes began to weaken so reading was challenging at times, but he certainly never gave up trying and turned to his old friends on the bookshelf in the parlor to help him temporarily escape his loneliness.

In 1970, at the age of 93, Tim's mind had slipped a tad, but he was still sharp and could converse with visitors about current events and his views about crooked politicians. Tim, when asked, would occasionally reminisce about the old days, although he preferred to not go there beyond a surface level. Trips down memory lane were locked away safely in the vault, protecting Tim from reliving the pain of loved ones departing to the other side.

Tim reached the point where he needed a walker and assistance with daily activities. Although not thrilled with the concept, his children convinced Tim to move into a retirement home. Again, once there, he accepted his lot and never complained. He still wore a jacket and tie to dinner every evening at the old folks' home. At first, visits by the family were frequent, but Tim admonished them to enjoy their own lives and insisted he was perfectly fine on his own.

In 1973, at the age of 95, Tim's health began to decline further with frequent shortness of breath and pain throughout his legs and back. He spent more time lying in bed and required regular assistance from the nurses.

A priest paid Tim a visit one afternoon, per Lucille's request. After some preliminary chit chat, the priest inquired, "Tim, would you like a Final Act of Contrition?"

"Not in particular, Father."

"May I ask why not?"

Tim, who was, of course, very skeptical of priests given his experience at the orphanage so long ago, answered, "Well Father, all I have to say is I sinned, you sinned, we all sinned."

The priest politely smiled, blessed Tim, and went on his way.

One early winter evening, Tim was preparing to retire to bed. He shuffled to the window and lifted the curtain to look outside. He smiled to witness the gentle snow falling and covering the lawn with a white blanket. The fresh snow muffled the outside noise, making everything peacefully quiet. As he watched the snowscape form, Tim was overcome by a sense of calm. He drew in a deep, slow breath and closed his eyes for a moment, wishing this moment would not be fleeting. Tim then thought how autumn passed so quickly this year. Yet instead of missing the excitement that summer brings and the relaxation and slowing down that accompanies the fall, Tim accepted it was now winter's reign. Time for the flora and fauna to rest. He was in awe of the beauty of the winter onsetting before his eyes. Tim appreciated and embraced that it was now time for him to lay his head down for a restful slumber.

Typically requiring two nurses to lift and position Tim into bed, this evening he managed to crawl under the covers by himself. Laying down, Tim smiled with tears in his eyes, thinking for a moment how beautiful his life had been for him. "Life is precious." He then began to drift into that wonderful dimension between awake and asleep. Tim was surprised at how his leg joints and back muscles were so comfortable, with his annoying arthritis disappearing as he continued his path to sleep.

Tim was one moment away from reaching a deep slumber when he heard someone talking in his room. He tried to rouse himself awake but was unable to shake himself into consciousness. The talking was muttered at first but became clearer. Tim finally was able to discern that the chatter was coming from a young boy's voice, one that was familiar to him, yet Tim could not determine the identity of the lad. Tim struggled to open his eyes but could only manage a sliver of a crack. He could see the outline of the boy who then reached out to Tim's arm and shook it. "Come on, Tim, I have something really keen I want to show you." The boy continued to tug on Tim's arm. "Let's go, old-timer, we don't have much time!"

Tim finally came to and opened his eyes. It was a warm, lazy summer day without a cloud in the sky. Tim was standing in the middle of a park that was familiar to him, although he could not precisely place the location. Tim turned his attention back to the young lad grabbing his sleeve. "My God, it's you, Billy!" Tim gave Billy the biggest hug. "I never stopped thinking about you ever since we split up on the tracks after we fled Queen of Heaven." Tim began to sob tears of joy. "I'm so happy to see you, Billy."

"Ah, come on, Timmy, don't get all mushy on me. I've been watching you for a long time, and I was pulling for you every step of the way. You did good, Tim. I told you we would meet again."

Billy looked exactly as Tim left him as they strategically parted ways and waved goodbye during the escape from the orphanage – same clothes, and even the dirt on his face. "I have something to show you, Timmy my boy – can't wait for you to see it." Billy led Tim by the hand across the park and over to the entrance of the Old Chicago Water Tower.

Billy nodded toward the door, "Go ahead, Tim, you can walk through the front door – it's wide open."

"But Billy, I can't make it up the stairs with my walker."

Billy grabbed Tim's walker out of his hands and tossed it aside. "You no longer need that stupid contraption. Now go – they are all waiting for you." Billy had an excited smile beaming back at Tim.

Tim was initially afraid to take a step without his walker but gave it a try. "Well, that was easy." After the first few test steps, Tim gained his confidence and began to amble slowly and deliberately, without any pain. "Billy, how are you doing this?"

"I ain't doing nothing. Now, go. I'll see you again real soon and we will catch up on everything."

Just as Tim reached for the front entrance knob, the Water Tower door ever so slowly creaked open on its own. Standing on the other side was his old friend from second grade, Big Patrick. "Patrick! How the devil are you?"

"Conlon, I finally figured it out. We can be the first to perform the death-defying leap off the top of the Water Tower. We will be famous. I found this strong umbrella that we have to try out. I think it will work this time. Let's go!" Patrick ran up the spiral staircase three stairs at a time. "See you at the top."

Tim shouted out to the dashing Patrick, "Are you out of your mind? It can't be done. And besides, I'm not sure I can make it up the stairs."

Patrick's voice began to dwindle in volume as he continued to race up the stairs. "You can do it, Tim – we have all been waiting for you…"

Tim hadn't climbed one stair by himself in nearly a decade. Deep breath. "I made it…that wasn't bad at all." Then another step and another. "How is this happening?" Tim neared the first-floor landing and felt his entire body tingle. Tim's heart beat faster as he felt love wrap around his heart like he hadn't felt since he embraced Mae for the last time. As he reached the first-floor landing, he came upon a beautiful young woman. It was Mae, exactly as she appeared the first time he laid eyes on her in the toll room.

"My God, it's you, Mae." Tim and Mae embraced and became one again. "Mae, I missed you so much. Not the grand events or trips or parties, but the simple things. I missed seeing you in the morning when I opened my eyes, hearing you laughing at the table with your mom, catching your glance from across the room while you were sipping tea and you returning a knowing smile, your misplacing your glasses for the fifth time in one day, rocking on the front porch swing after dinner. Yes, Mae, it is the simple everyday things that I missed the most. Yet I always knew we would be together again – that's what kept me going. I knew you were never far away."

"I was always with you, Tim. I never left your side."

"I could have been better – I should have done so much more."

"You were wonderful, my dear Tim. You always tried to do the right thing, and you were always there for me and the children."

"I never did anything special or great."

"Your entire life was special and being who you are was great enough. But now you must continue your journey up the stairs to the top. You have to make this climb by yourself, but please know, dear, as I have always been and will always be, I will be with you every step of the way."

Tim was beginning to understand. For the first time since Mae's death, he knew he wasn't alone even though he realized that he must continue his ascent up the Tower alone.

As Tim approached the second landing, he felt much lighter on his feet and had a burst of energy. As he passed a window, Tim saw the reflection of his forty-year-old self. He sensed there were a few people waiting for him at the top of the second flight of stairs. Tim instantly recognized who they were, dropped to his knees, and reached out for a group hug. Young Dorothy, Dick, and Bob ran into their father's arms as they did every night as he came home from work.

Sweet Dorothy through her tears, "We love you so much, Daddy. Thank you for everything that you did for us." Tim didn't want to let go.

"I should have spent more time with you all."

Dick chimed in, "Dad, you were there when we needed you." And Bob remarked, "You set such a wonderful example for us." Bob then whispered in his father's ear, "Dad, you have to carry on your journey up the stairs." Dick chimed in, "Yeah, Dad, keep on going – we will see you again soon."

As Tim reached the top of the next series of flights, he again passed by a window that seemed to be higher up than the others. Tim realized it was because he now took on the appearance of when he was ten years old. "I feel so much better – no aches or pain. I'm light as a feather without any care or worry." Tim lit up as he was greeted by Old Man Mush Mouth and Maisey, who were clapping their hands, giving him a round of applause as he arrived at the third landing. "Sir and Miss Maisey, you were so kind to me – you saved my life. I never got a chance to thank you both for your amazing kindness to an orphan who had lost everything."

"No need, kid. We watched your life from afar and were so proud of you," said Mush Mouth.

Maisey, with her charming smile, said, "Yes, my boy, seeing you growing up to be such a fine man was our reward."

Tim heard a murmur of noise at the fourth and final landing. "Maisey and Mushy, I could not have, would not have survived without you. I have never forgotten you…but I think I have to keep ascending."

The din grew louder as Tim climbed to the last landing at the top of the Water Tower. Several of Tim's second grade friends were excitedly discussing trying out Patrick's new umbrella and arguing about how to jump and what technique to use. They all stopped when the eight-year-old Tim reached the top. "There you are, Conlon. What took you so long…Just kidding, Timmy. Check out the umbrella, you're gonna love it."

Even though Tim was now in the form of his eight-year-old self, he still had the wisdom of a 95-year-old. "Are you sure it works, Patrick?"

"I swear on a stack of Bibles, it is stronger and will not invert. We tested it with a sack of rocks several times."

Patrick then became more somber and with a serious tone uttered, "Tim, your entire life has led to this moment. They are all waiting for you outside. I'm honored to be your guide for this moment. Embrace the ride." Patrick handed Tim the umbrella.

Tim then heard a pleasant, haunting melody being sung by a woman. He turned to see the Lady in Red standing by the open window at the top of the Water Tower. Her singing stopped, and she gazed into Tim's eyes. "Your time has come, Tim." The banshee bowed and raised her arm toward the window. As he passed by his spirit guide, she whispered to Tim, "Triquetra."

Tim knew what he had to do. As he had done before, he gritted his teeth, popped open the umbrella, and took a leap of faith out the window.

"Patrick was right, the umbrella did not invert." As Tim floated through the air, he looked down and saw thousands of people below cheering and clapping. Tim's vision was again as sharp as it was when he was eight, and he began to recognize individuals in the crowd. He saw his parents, his brother, his second grade school teacher, Cecilia, his coworkers, his drinking friends, Tuffy Griffith, Cora, the street waifs from Little Cheyenne, Dr. Mayo and Nurse Kruse, the young lady to whom he threw a life vest who was a passenger on the *Eastland*, his friends at the orphanage, the librarian who selected books for him at the public library, Claude, Mae's supervisor from the toll room, his sister Molly.

As he floated closer to the ground, Tim heard a loud guttural wail. Tim turned toward the noise and saw Brother DuValle standing across the street away from the crowd, dressed in his immaculate habit. As the wind suddenly kicked up, DuValle beckoned and Tim began to drift his way. The crowd cheered even louder, distracting Tim's fear. Tim was directly over DuValle and looked down upon him. "I've already shown that I don't fear you, you horrible wretch! Begone!"

DuValle's appearance quickly turned back into the decrepit beast he had become as he gasped his last breath in the filth of the streets of Little Cheyenne. The winds abruptly changed direction and blew Tim back on course to float directly above the middle of the roaring crowd.

Tim gently floated back above the sea of his friends and family. He began to recognize more and more people in the crowd. They cheered even louder as he was now only feet above their heads. Tim looked down upon them and noticed that the people below were all attached to one another, and appeared to be drifting back and forth as if they were all part of a massive body of water.

Tim smiled as his wave finally crashed to the shore and he once again joined all of his loved ones as he merged into the awaiting sea of souls. Tim at long last knew he would never be alone. He never was.

Triquetra

Tim and Mae - Triquetra

ACKNOWLEDGMENTS

Throughout my life I have said that I have been blessed with an amazing family and wonderful friends. They have always been there for me and provided encouragement to write Celtic Knot. There are several that I want to specifically acknowledge. I would first like to express a huge thank you to my wife, Pam (aka Lolly) for her tremendous support during the entire process, for her keen editing eye and for her terrific suggestions when I occasionally was stuck.

My former law partner and valued friend of 35 years, Bob Arnold, did an amazing job editing. Not only is Bob one of the best legal writers in the business, he has a clever mind and sharp wit. We have edited each other's work for more than three decades - I could not think of a better person to step into the editing role. Thanks Bob!

A special acknowledgment goes out to my friend and "brother" since second grade, Bruce Vierck, for enduring my regular yammering on about the book, and listening to me dramatically read multiple passages. Bruce provided excellent commentary, insight and ideas. And thanks to my sister Colleen Naughton, who also listened intently to various parts of the book and provided guidance and support.

To my dear cousins Sue Lawrence and Kathy Miller, who are the keepers of the Conlon family history, thanks so much for sharing your stories of our grandfather Tim, his poetry and wonderful family pictures. And a special thanks to my cousin Eileen Johnson, who is in the publishing world, for her words of wisdom.

To my amazing former administrative assistant, Linda Felau, who tirelessly worked on weekends and after hours typing, formatting and editing, and editing, and editing. You are the best Linda!

I appreciate and thank artist and author, Tony Fitzpatrick, for meeting with me and providing big brotherly advice about publishing, editing and coming up with an appropriate subtitle.

A huge shoutout to creative coach and author Brendan Sullivan for selflessly helping out a first time author with the business side of things, providing multiple creative suggestions and connecting me with Rick Kaempfer and Eckhartz Press. I'll never forget the time and valued advice you provided. Thank you Brendan! And thank you Cheryl Pernai for introducing me to Brendan.

To Rick Kaempfer and his wonderful team at Eckhartz Press (David Stern, Lauren Schultz, Jeff Waggoner), thanks for believing in Celtic Knot and getting it across the finish line.

Thank you to my wonderful children Erin Tierney, Packey Conlon and Jack Conlon, and their spouses, Drew Tierney, Katie Conlon and Alyssa Conlon, for politely listening to my going on about my book and reading early drafts. They all have a little bit of their great grandfather in them, and respect our family history.

To my mother Margaret Riordan Conlon, who passed away recently, thank you for always being my biggest fan and cheerleader. I read to her many of the chapters and she added several insights and vignettes about her in-laws, Tim and Mae Conlon, who Marge loved dearly. Mom, I know you and Dad will be watching over us all.

And finally to all my courageous ancestors, the Conlon's, Gillen's, McEwan's and Kelty's, we are forever in your debt for leaving your homes and loved ones in their beloved Ireland to seek a better life for your families in the United States. None of us would be where we are today without your sacrifices, hard work and love of family. The sole reason I wrote Celtic Knot was so that we will never forget you.

ENDNOTES

1. Funchion, Michael F.; "The Irish of Chicago"; lib.niu.edu
2. ibid.
3. ibid.
4. ibid.
5. ibid.
6. ibid.
7. ibid.
8. History.Com Editors; "Chicago Fire of 1871"; History.Com; August 21, 2018.
9. ibid.
10. ibid.
11. Fliescher, C.; "The History of Police Communications" legacy.cityofirvine.org.
12. ibid.
13. Chicago Loop; en.wikipedia.org.
14. Digital Research Library of Illinois History Journal, "The History of Chicago's 'Red-Light' Vice Districts; January 2, 2017.
15. ibid.
16. World Fairs; en.worldfair.info; Electricity-Expo based in Chicago 1893.
17. "Chicago Public Library Records: Early CPL"; "Biographical/ Historical"; Chipublib.org.
18. ibid.
19. ibid.
20. ibid.
21. ibid.
22. T.A.H.; "1880's Chicago Union Stockyard"; American Heritage; Vol. 52; Issue 4; (June, 2001).
23. ibid.
24. ibid.
25. ibid.
26. ibid.
27. ibid.
28. ibid.
29. History of the U.S. Telegraph Industry; Tomas Nonnenmacher, Allegheny College; Economic History Association; eh.net.
30. Encyclopedia of Chicago, C. Thale, Encyclopedia.Chicagohistory.org.
31. ibid.
32. History of the U.S. Telegraph Industry; T. Nonnenmacher, Allegheny College: Economic History Association; eh.net.
33. The Life and Times of Florence Kelley; Spring-Summer 1894: Factory Inspections and a Smallpox Epidemic; Florencekelley.northwestern.edu.
34. Coen, Jeff; "Family Secrets"; Chicago Press Review; Page 47.
35. Ashley, J.; "When the Outfit Ran Chicago, Volume 1: The Big Jim Colosimo Era"; (2008).
36. Binder, John; "The Chicago Outfit"; Arcadia Publishing; p. 9.
37. ibid.

38. "Western Electric – A Brief History"; Western Electric History; Bell System (1876-1983); Memorial.BellSystems.com/doc/western-electric.doc.
39. ibid.
40. "Leaving Europe: A New Life In America-Exhibition"; "Departure and Arrival – Ocean Voyage"; Europeana.eu/en/exhibitions/leaving-europe; December 15, 2012.
41. ibid.
42. Preet, Edythe; "Slainte! Trees, Tea and ESP": Irish America Magazine; April/May 2011; IrishAmerica.com.
43. ibid.
44. *Encyclopedia of Occultism & Parapsychology, Fifth Edition, Vol. 2*, edited by J. Gordon Melton.
45. Brandt, Nat; "Chicago Death Trap – The Iroquois Theatre Fire of 1903"; (2008).
46. ibid. at pp. 7-13.
47. Hatch, Anthony P.; Tinder Box: The Iroquois Theatre Disaster 1903; (2003).
48. "A Tragedy Remembered", NPFA Journal (July/August); National Fire Protection Association, 1995.
49. Uenuma, F.; "The Iroquois Theatre Disaster Killed Hundreds And Changed Fire Safety Forever"; Smithsonian Magazine; June 12, 2018.
50. ibid.
51. ibid.
52. ibid.
53. ibid.
54. ibid.
55. ibid.
56. ibid.
57. Brandt, Nat (2008); Chicago Death Trap; The Iroquois Theatre Fire of 1903.
58. Everett, M.; "The Great Chicago Theatre Disaster"; 1904.
59. ibid.; Uenuma, F.; Smithsonian Magazine; ibid.
60. ibid.
61. ibid.
62. ibid.
63. "Cathedral Tour"; Holy Name Cathedral; July 7, 2021.
64. Eastland Disaster Historical Society; Eastlanddisaster.org; 2024.
65. ibid.
66. ibid.
67. Stranahan, Susan Q., "The Eastland Disaster Killed More Passengers Than The Titanic And The Lusitania. Why Had It Been Forgotten"; Smithsonian Magazine; October 27, 2014.
68. ibid.
69. ibid. Eastland Disaster Historical Society, Eastlanddisaster.org.
70. ibid.
71. ibid.
72. ibid.
73. ibid.
74. ibid.
75. ibid.

76 Eastland Disaster Historical Society, Eastlanddisaster.org; Stranahan, Susan Q.; Smithsonian Magazine.
77 ibid.; Stranahan, Susan Q., Smithsonian Magazine.
78 ibid.; Stranahan, Susan Q., Smithsonian Magazine.
79 Stranahan, Susan Q., Smithsonian Magazine.
80 Eastlanddisaster.org; Stranahan, Susan Q.; Smithsonian Magazine.
81 Stranahan, Susan Q.; Smithsonian Magazine.
82 ibid.
83 Eastland Historical Society, Eastlanddisaster.org; Stranahan, Susan Q.; Smithsonian Magazine.
84 Eastland Historical Society, Eastlanddisaster.org; Stranahan, Susan Q.; Smithsonian Magazine.
85 ibid.; H. Repa, "The Experience of a Hawthorne Nurse", Western Electric News, August 1915.
86 Stranahan, Susan Q.; Smithsonian Magazine.
87 ibid.
88 ibid.
89 Eastland Historical Society, Eastlanddisaster.org; Stranahan, Susan Q.; Smithsonian Magazine.
90 Eastland Historical Society, Eastlanddisaster.org; Stranahan, Susan Q.; Smithsonian Magazine.
91 ibid.
92 ibid.
93 Eastland Historical Society, Eastlanddisaster.org; Stranahan, Susan Q.; Smithsonian Magazine.
94 ibid.
95 ibid.; "Little Feller Now Has A Name", Chicago Daily Tribune, July 30, 1915.
96 Stranahan, Susan Q.; Smithsonian Magazine.
97 ibid.
98 Hilton, G.W., "Eastland: Legacy of the Titanic"; 1995; Stranahan, Susan Q., Smithsonian Magazine.
99 Stranahan, Susan Q.; Smithsonian Magazine; Hilton, G.W.
100 Dirks, Tim; "Film History of the 1920's, Part 1"; AMC' February 7, 2014.
101 O'Donnell, Elliott; The Banshee; London, Edinburg, Sands and Co.; 1920.
102 McAnally, D.R.; Irish Wonders; 1888.
103 Goiter; "Diseases and Conditions"; Mayo Clinic; Mayoclinic.org; 2014.
104 ibid.
105 Hannan, S. Alan; "The Magnificent Seven: "A History of Modern Thyroid Surgery"; Science Direct; Vol. 4, Issue 3; Sciencedirect.com; 2006; pp. 187-191.
106 ibid.
107 ibid.; Hannan, S. Alan; Small Ridge, M.D., Robert C. and Morris, M.D., John C.; "A Century of Hyperthyroidism at Mayo Clinic"; Mayo Clinic; Mayoclinicproceedings.org.
108 O'Hara, Keith; "Triquetra Meaning + History of Celtic Trinity Knot Symbol"; The Irish Road Trip; Theirishroadtrip.com; April 29, 2024.
109 ibid.